Frances Campbell Sparhawk

A Lazy Man's Work

A novel

Frances Campbell Sparhawk

A Lazy Man's Work
A novel

ISBN/EAN: 9783337000561

Printed in Europe, USA, Canada, Australia, Japan

Cover: Foto ©Andreas Hilbeck / pixelio.de

More available books at **www.hansebooks.com**

LEISURE HOUR SERIES.—No. 122

A LAZY MAN'S WORK

A NOVEL

BY

FRANCES CAMPBELL SPARHAWK

NEW YORK
HENRY HOLT AND COMPANY
1881

TO

JOHN GREENLEAF WHITTIER,

With Love.

F. C. S.

A LAZY MAN'S WORK.

CHAPTER I.

HELEN BELL opened the door of the waiting-room at the Cross Road Station, and found a lady and gentleman seated there. She had stood a few moments on the platform watching the train she had left, as it labored with difficulty through the fast-deepening snow. The December darkness had closed in hours ago, and it might be near midnight before she reached her destination, if indeed she were able to reach it at all while the storm was at its fury. For the wind that swept in from the roaring sea tossed about the snow in emulation of the waves it had left, piled it in deep drifts across the track, and rushed over the plain, hurling its white burden hither and thither, and making the great veil of flakes from sky to earth quiver and whirl as it fell.

Under these circumstances it was a relief to the young lady to find that she was not to be alone while waiting for the branch train.

She had asked the station-master, in her anxiety, as she heard the energetic snorts of the engine,

"Shall we get through to-night?"

"Oh, I guess so," said the man. "But mebbe 't'll be some time 'fore it gits along," and he jerked his thumb over his shoulder toward the other track which seemed an unbroken line of white. "You'll find it good 'n' warm in the Ladies' Room," he added; "I 'tended to that."

She was thinking, as a tremendous gust of wind blew the snow into her face and almost took her breath away, how suddenly the storm had come. Early in the afternoon a dance of white frost feathers through the air, had begun, a most exquisite shower. She had watched it with delight as she sat at home sketching. The flakes came down like great white feathers with a motion of languid enjoyment, and clung caressingly to everything they touched, until all the roofs, and fences, and trees were mantled in them. The grand old elms across the way showed the finest tracery, the twigs of the linden stood out like branching coral, no bush was too insignificant to be loaded with as much beauty as it could bear. The dull sky had a faint flush of warmth as the cold blue-white of the snow shone against it. The air was as still as in a summer noonday; and few summer noons could offer a scene more exquisitely beautiful.

Helen remembered, however, that half an hour later as she was preparing for her journey, her mother had told her of a change in the wind, and warned her that the storm was already increasing, and by night would be very severe.

What an excellent illustration of the folly of not minding one's mother was furnished by the girl's situation at this moment. She laughed as she thought of it; then her face softened with the recollection of how wise and tender an adviser this mother had always been to her.

She closed the door of the waiting-room lightly behind her, and walked toward the great coal stove, red-hot in places with zeal for the comfort of its patrons, and stood beside it a little while, stretching out first one hand then the other toward the grateful heat, perceiving thankfully without seeming to look at her unknown fellow-travelers that they were persons whose presence would be a satisfaction in this tedious waiting.

"Well, now, Jack," began the stranger lady, continuing a conversation interrupted by Helen's entrance, "tell me the honest truth. What do you think of the prospect?"

As she spoke she drew herself up and put her hands to her bonnet an instant, as a judge on the bench might adjust his wig to listen with dignity to important evidence.

"The last time I looked at it," came the answer, "it was very snowy."

"Shall we have to stay here all night?"

"Possibly."

"Oh, horrors! Here, in this dreadful little room? There isn't even a sofa. But you are only teasing me, Jack, making me stay here all night."

The gentleman's laugh had a very pleasant ring in it.

"I make you stay!" he said. "How long is it since you have invested me with the office of 'clerk of the weather'?"

"Oh, of course, of course, you know what I mean. But, really now, do you think so?"

"I don't."

"What did you say it for, then?"

"I did not. I said it was possible. Not everything possible happens."

The lady looked at her companion until her severe expression relaxed into a smile.

"You always were a saucy boy, Jack; and you don't seem to have outgrown it."

Her hearer laughed.

The lady's eyes started upon a tour of investigation around the room.

"I declare," she said, as they came back to her companion's face, "it's worse than I thought, there is not even one of those red-and-blue pictures of the routes here."

"There's a time-table behind you, telling that the train leaves for Lowton at half-past five."

"It ought to be ashamed of itself," said the lady. "It must be ten now, if it's anything."

"Oh, yes, it's something, but it is only nine."

"And, then, there's that dowdy bit of looking-glass," she went on, taking no notice of this correction. "It's so small I couldn't see even my bonnet in it."

"Couldn't you, really, Aunt Delia?" asked the gentleman, with a look of critical measurement from the despised mirror to the speaker's head-gear. "I supposed these little things were a notion just introduced to suit the present style of ladies' bonnets."

"Impertinence!"

And she tossed at him one of the gloves lying in her lap.

In dodging it he threw back his head suddenly, and caught sight of Helen's face turned upon him, sparkling with merriment.

In another moment she dropped it so low that its expression was hidden, and turned away to one of the settees.

There was a brief silence, then the lady began again.

"I know, of course, it's very nice to do nothing, but it's just horrid to have nothing to do. Confess, do you like it?"

"I am not in that predicament."

"Oh, to be sure; you have the train to look after. I wish you'd go and see if it's not coming."

"It is not."

"You haven't found out."

"Yes."

"How could you without going to see?"

"Occasionally a train can be heard when it is coming."

"To be sure. But, then, you see, the snow may deaden the noise. But everything is all ready if it should come upon us before we know it; and you won't forget my shawl-strap? It's not time yet, though. Oh, dear, no."

Then there came another short pause. Then the lady looked up wistfully.

"I must be a great bother to you, Jack. I suppose you hate traveling with me."

"You're entirely wrong, Aunt Delia. I enjoy it very much indeed."

Aunt Delia meditated profoundly a moment.

"Like to get fun out of your poor old aunt, do you? Well."

The mixture of chagrin and resignation in the sigh which accompanied the last word was inexpressibly droll.

Presently Helen caught the whispered question, "Who

do you suppose she is?" and the low answer, not whispered, "I don't know." Then, "I wonder where she is going?" To this no reply was vouchsafed.

The lady, saying she was tired of sitting so long, rose, and began to walk up and down the room.

Then she stood beside the stove for a time, evidently debating something with herself, and looking frequently and earnestly at the stranger. But there was a dignity about Helen which repelled familiarity, although, in the end, it was not proof against good-humored inquisitiveness.

The lady took a few more turns and then stopped beside her.

"My dear," she said, "you haven't had anybody to speak a word to for an hour." The compassion of her tone showed that she felt herself touching upon one of the deepest of human ills.

The momentary breadth of Helen's smile might be pardoned, for it was very genial.

"Thank you, madam, for ending my misfortune." And she invited the lady to sit down beside her.

"Waiting for the train?" asked the latter, accepting promptly.

"Yes."

"You are going to Lowton?"

"If I can get there."

"Perhaps you live in Lowton?"

"Oh, no."

"Going upon a visit!"

"Yes, for a visit."

"You have friends there, I presume?"

"Yes."

The lady suggested the possibility of meeting her while in town. Helen politely acceded to this, but she did not fall into the trap the other had set for her and give the name of her friends.

The inquirer drew a little morocco case from her pocket.

"I am sorry I cannot return your courtesy, Mrs. Barney," said Helen a moment afterward. "I have no card with me, but my name is 'Bell.'"

"It's always safe," returned Mrs. Barney, "to have your name about you in traveling. If the cars should run off the track and take fire, and you get burned up, nobody could find out who you were, to send you to your friends."

"Wouldn't the card be burned up, too?"

"Well, I suppose it would in that case. But there might be other accidents, you know; you might be taken ill suddenly with paralysis, or something, and couldn't speak. But, my dear Miss Bell, don't let me alarm you. You look in perfect health; and you are young. But if you live, perhaps you'll be an old lady some day, like me. Anyway, it's a good plan to be careful. I've traveled a great deal, and I always am, very."

Mrs. Barney soon begged leave to introduce her nephew, Mr. Holden; and the conversation took a wider range, although Aunt Delia's personality was of too soldierly a nature ever to be elsewhere than in the van.

Helen enjoyed her comments upon the European tour she had recently made; they were sometimes really pertinent, and sometimes irresistibly funny.

She evidently had no great admiration for the Eternal City; she praised it languidly, and scolded at it heartily. She warmed up at last, however, and laid her hand impressively on the girl's arm. As Helen waited for some rhapsody over St. Peter's, the Pantheon, or a wonderful painting, she said emphatically—

"I tell you what though, Miss Bell, if you ever go there, Rome's a good place to buy tapes in, cheap."

The time passed very pleasantly, and the train came before they realized how long they had been waiting for it.

Helen was glad to be in the company of her new acquaintances, when the three reached the deserted station of Lowton.

"We're going round to leave Miss Bell first, aren't we, Jack?" asked Mrs. Barney as they seated themselves in the solitary hack that had waited in the storm for the tardy train.

"Of course," he answered.

Helen thanked them gratefully.

"Don't speak of it," cried Mrs. Barney. "I couldn't think of leaving you till I saw you safely housed; and Jack—he's always obliging."

Mr. Holden rang Mrs. Edgerly's door-bell, and then Helen, who saw that there still were lights below, begged him not to keep Mrs. Barney waiting any longer. As steps were heard at the door, and a heavy bolt was drawn, he left her.

But entrance was not so easy as they had imagined, for at that moment a shrill voice cried out,

"Don't open the door; it's a tramp."

There came a pause, and a consultation in the hall, not so whispered but that Helen learned that the servants had all gone to bed, and Mr. Mason had been in his room the whole evening with a headache.

"Let me take a peep," said a new voice; and a somewhat heavy tread came nearer.

But Helen drew back, and the would-be observer could get no satisfaction.

At length, in spite of an imperative "hush!" from within, a voice called somewhat brokenly,

"Who's there?"

"I, mum; very tired, and cold."

"It's a woman," said the questioner.

"There may be a man with her," came the quick answer; "don't let her in." These were the shrill tones again.

"Are you hungry?" came through the door in the pitying accents of the broken voice.

"Yes, m'm, awfully hungry."

"Are you a tramp?" tremulously.

"I never have been, but if you don't let me in, I'm afraid I shall be."

"Poor thing! How well her voice sounds. I pity her. She must have seen better days."

"She has never seen worse," called Helen.

"I shall open the door on the chain, anyway," asserted the slightly quavering tones; and, in spite of opposition, this was done.

A well-gloved hand immediately thrust into the space, a delicate face, and a pair of laughing eyes visible through the opening, betrayed the new-comer.

"You inhospitable people!" she cried.

She was welcomed with laughter and shouts of "Helen, you poor child!" "You saucy girl!"

"Indeed, I have seen better days, and nights too," she repeated merrily.

"I thought the last train was in two hours ago; we

had entirely given you up," said Mrs. Mason helping her to take off her wrappings, "and none of us heard the carriage. The express came with your trunk this afternoon, so we knew you had meant well by us."

Mrs. Edgerly, mindful of Helen's declaration that she was "awfully hungry," disappeared, returning soon with a most tempting display of food. Her grand-daughter, Bertha Edgerly, from her easy chair watched the proceeding.

Helen went to bed warmed and comforted. She laughed over her experience as a tramp, and wondered whose was the shrill voice she had heard before she gained admittance; but it was long in revealing itself in the well-modulated tones about her.

She went to sleep in a pleasant reverie of mingled amusement at Mrs. Barney, and recollection of her nephew's thoughtfulness for their comfort.

CHAPTER II.

BERTHA EDGERLY looked across the breakfast-table, the next morning, to see what her cousin was like. The two had not met for a number of years, and she thought Helen very much improved.

Nobody had a pleasanter way of taking life than Bertha. She fancied herself the queen of a tournament, dispensing smiles and prizes wherever she believed they were merited. No thought that her prizes might be worthless and her smiles unheeded, ever came to her. She enjoyed her exercise of criticism and award in the perfect security of one whose judgment and position are of unquestioned consequence. Regarded in the light of discipline and progress, such mental attitude is a failure; but for even, up-and-down satisfaction there is nothing like it.

Helen was tall and graceful, animated, without being exuberant in spirits; but Bertha could not fully decide as to her face, for it never seemed for two minutes exactly the same. Some bright fancy, like sunshine, lighted it up, or serious thought made it grave. Bertha did not tell herself that when she had looked once at Helen she felt a desire to look again. She only did so.

Helen found Mrs. Mason pretty, much prettier than she had appeared· the evening before. She was over thirty, but she had the complexion of sixteen, delicately tinted, and made the more brilliant by her dark hair. Her light gray eyes, with a tinge of green in them, glanced about vivaciously taking note of everything, and their discoveries were invaluable to her quick wit. She had a reputation in Lowton for both beauty and cleverness. If her bright red lips were a trifle thin, they shaped themselves so readily to the utterance of arch or courteous phrases that they were only beautiful and bewitching, like everything else about her. Helen, whose work had used her to the study of effect, saw that Mrs. Mason understood it well in her own person. Kitty used to say, laughingly, though not in jest, that one might as well be out of the world as out of the fashion, yet, for the sake of fashion she never wore an inharmonious color, or dressed in an unbecoming style. Everybody agreed that she was a charming companion, not talking too deeply blue to be amusing, whatever she might know, a good deal of erudition was put down to her credit—and an object to delight the eye of poet or artist; altogether, an acquisition to Lowton society.

Bertha was short and inclined to stoutness. Her eyes and hair were dark, her features good, and a share of Kitty Mason's superabundant spirit would have made her handsome. But lack of expression in her face prevented Helen from seeing any beauty there.

The new-comer soon turned from these two, however, and from Mrs. Edgerly's pleasant smile of greeting, to look curiously at Andrew Mason, the fourth and last member of this family, with whom she had come to spend several weeks. Mrs. Edgerly was her grandfather's cousin. Mr. and Mrs. Mason she had never seen before. She studied Andrew with something more than passing curiosity. That face would go down in her note-book, the secret treasury to which not even her mother had access, and from which she drew so many inspirations; but in what character would it be? He was not handsome, he was quite bald, and the hair that was left him, once yellow-brown, was now dulled by a tinge of gray; his features were rather clumsily molded; he was barely medium height, and stout; his blue eyes were half closed, as if it were too much trouble to open them wide, and his expression was one of indolent good humor. And of something else. Of what? She could not be sure yet.

"Did you come up from the station all alone, last night?" asked Mrs. Edgerly.

"No, a lady and gentleman were in the carriage with me."

"How nice!" cried Bertha. "I wonder who they were."

"Oh, some strangers, very likely," answered Kitty before Helen had time to speak, and that young lady finding herself with nothing to say, wisely said nothing.

"I should like to know who they were, repeated Bertha. "Describe them, Helen."

Helen did so. But either ideas differed, or there was some other cause of bewilderment.

"You said the lady came from Westville?" questioned Kitty Mason, all adrift.

"So she told me."

Up and down the snow-encumbered streets of Lowton labored the baffled curiosity of the ladies.

Helen was buttering her roll, with the innocent unconcern of one who sees no way out of her neighbors' difficulties, when Mr. Mason, who had not taken part in the discussion, because, as she saw, he was devoting all his attention to breakfast, suddenly drawled out:

"You know who they are, Miss Bell, don't you?"

The three ladies turned first to him and then to her, expectantly.

"Yes," she answered. "They were Mrs. Barney, and Mr. Holden."

"Why didn't you tell us, then?" cried her hostess, half offended.

"I was only waiting to be asked," said the girl, and her joyous laugh,—so like her father's—won Mrs. Edgerly's forgiveness directly.

Bertha sat silent a moment. Then she exclaimed:

"Putting last night and this morning together, Helen, I do believe you're a tease."

Mrs. Mason said nothing. The flash in her eyes made them colorless, but she dropped them directly, and after an instant's fingering of her napkin-ring, went on with her breakfast.

"Holden," repeated Mr. Mason slowly, "he's an odd stick—good fellow, though, and made of money."

"If you like, Miss Bell," said Kitty soon after, "I will take you over the house this morning. It's a poor amusement, to be sure, but it will make you feel more at home, and I may be able to show you a few interesting things. At least, it's the best we can do to-day, for it is too drifted and blustering to think of going out."

"Thank you, I should like it very much."

Kitty was sure she should enjoy her office of cicerone. The girl was used to simplicity in her own home, and it would be pleasant to see her genuine admiration of this house, whose luxuries she was to share for a time. It was in the full consciousness that it was her own home she was about to exhibit, that, as at her summons Helen came up the stairs, Kitty stood in the hall with the light from a great window shining down upon her, and the folds of her rich dress sweeping out behind her.

It is of no use to try to banish trains entirely, for they supply a need in nature and will not be done away with. The people who cannot carry sufficient dignity in their heads ought to make up the deficiency by the sweep of rich robes behind them; for a train suggests pages, pages rank and prerogative, and so an intoxicating dream of position rises to the brain and fills it, entirely overpowering any latent consciousness of a need for humility. Trains are an invention to keep up the balance of power, and the many wear them for the sake of the few.

Kitty then stood in gracious state and waited for Helen's approach, noticing that the girl walked very finely.

The hostess moved about with an air of possession, explaining that four years ago Mrs. Edgerly, at the death of her only son, had invited Andrew, her nephew, to make his home here for the remainder of her life.

"It was hard to leave our own beautiful home," she continued, "but, of course, Aunt Bertha's wishes could not be disregarded, and she urged us so strongly to come."

Helen wondered if their "own beautiful home" had been equally luxurious, but she was ashamed of the thought.

Although the girl keenly enjoyed the very handsome rooms and the artistic treasures they held, she was not in the least impressed by the grandeur, and something was wanting to Kitty's pleasure in the promenade.

Mr. Jack Holden, rising earlier than usual that morning, found, when he went into his library, that the parlor-maid was still at work there. He sat down before the blazing wood fire and opened the newspaper, for he had not touched it the previous evening.

"Were there coals enough here to kindle with this morning?" he asked abruptly.

"Yes, sir, plenty," answered the house-maid, stopping in her dusting to stare at him.

"Shure, what should he care for?" she said later, repeating his question to the cook, "he wouldn't be after saving a few chips, would he, and he so many?"

"It's no matter," Holden explained hastily, seeing her surprise; "I was sitting here quite late last night, and I only wondered if the fire would keep."

"Yes, sir, it did."

A thrill passed through Holden, at which he smiled in scorn. He had wondered, as he went to bed, whether the fancies of that evening would die out before the morning, like the coals he buried in the ashes; and these had lived and glowed, and wanted but fresh fuel to flame up more hotly than ever.

"It's nothing," he repeated, "it's of no consequence." And the girl finished her dusting.

After breakfast he walked down town to get the mail and see what was going on there. He took the way through Cedar Street, although the business part of the town was better cleared. He wanted a boyish struggle with the snow-drifts, for it seemed to him, that morning, as if he must have something to conquer. This was just what he had been needing all his life.

Besides, Mrs. Edgerly lived in Cedar Street, and he might get a glimpse of her young guest, to whom his aunt had taken so great a fancy. It was odd that she too, had suggested his calling that morning. But he did not care to do it. The lady was a stranger, he recollected, and last night's impressions should wear away, at least somewhat if not altogether, before he met her again. He might get a glimpse of her at the window, though, as he passed the house, and delight Mrs. Barney with an account of how she was looking and what she was doing.

How would she look?

Not in the cold daylight as she had done in memory the evening before, when he sat for hours by his library fire thinking of her, recalling her tones, the strength of her face, its purity, its play of thought, its mirthfulness, its capabilities of feeling, although nothing had called for deep emotion in the time he had spent with her. He had imagined her moving about the room with simple dignity, sitting in the chair opposite his before the fire—he winced as he remembered that last night he had drawn it up nearer to fill out the fancy. He had pictured her presence everywhere about the house, and with the thought of her, here in his home and hers, the place grew full of a new fascination. Mrs. Barney had often told him he ought to marry, that his beautiful house needed a mistress. But it was not that, it was he himself, as he sat there alone with his life in the silent hours of introspection, who needed Helen Bell.

But Jack Holden was thirty-four, old enough to have learned a little prudence, he told himself, in the midst of these dreams, springing up with determination, and going to bed to sleep off his folly. He had covered it with the ashes of suspicion and caution, and left it to die a natural death. Had it died, or was it like the coals he had compared to it?

But he was not going to call anywhere this morning; prudence itself could not forbid a glimpse at a window.

Fate did, however, for Holden, like many a better

man, suffered from being in advance of his time. Helen
had not yet returned to the sitting-room from her tour
of inspection, and every window he glanced at in his
slow passing-by, met him blankly with indifference to
a curiosity too timorous to give itself a name.

Mrs. Barney did not find the first week of her visit
in Lowton very interesting. She would not have her
nephew know this for the world, so, with her usual re-
ticence, she managed to tell him. She said he seemed
dull, poor fellow, and decided that he did not have
enough society. It was of no use to assure her to the
contrary, she persisted that she knew better. She thought
of something she was sure would be good for him, but
he might not agree with her, and she must use skill in
carrying out her plans.

Mrs. Barney prided herself on her tactics. She pre-
mised that all men must be managed, even Jack, obliging as he was; for if he once refused any request
she made, he was "a very Mede and Persian," she
told him.

She felt herself all the greater diplomat that she believed Jack considered her a model of simplicity; and
so he did.

Once he made her a present of some very handsome
ostrich plumes with the assurance that they exactly suited
her. She wore them with complacent pride, and never

a suspicion that they nodded assent to the saucy nephew's comparison of her concealment of secrets with that wise fowl's way of hiding himself.

The second week, however, promised better things. Holden came into the library one morning with an eager face.

"You've got an idea in your head, Jack!" she exclaimed.

"My dear aunt, I'm sure I hope so," he laughed. "But you announce it as if the thing were as rare as the advent of a new star. Not complimentary."

"But I haven't seen you look so young nor so handsome for a long time. Do tell me what it is."

Jack had no time now, he promised to tell her before long, and sped off in his light sleigh as soon as his man drove up to the door.

A few minutes later, Bertha came into Helen's room as she sat writing.

"Only think," she began, "how nice! Mr. Holden is down-stairs, and has been inviting us to go on a sleighing party to-night, if we have no engagement, because the moon fulls, and it is splendid weather. But he told Cousin Andrew he would put it off rather than have us fail him. I never knew he was so kind, or thought so much of Andrew—or any of us."

Standing before the glass she put up her hands and

rearranged the soft waves of her hair upon her fore-head as she spoke, and smiled back at her reflection there.

"Why don't you say you're glad, Helen?" she cried. "It's so nice to have it happen while you're here. And, oh, you must stop your scribbling, and come down-stairs with me; Mr. Holden asked for you."

"Asked for me?" said the other, not changing her attitude, but holding her pen suspended over the paper.

"Yes; he said, 'The young lady that came in the storm;' he hoped that she had not taken cold, and that she was still here to be of the party. Wasn't it good in him, when he'd only seen you once?"

"Very."

"But aren't you coming down?" as Helen went on with her writing. "Grandma sent me to ask you."

"Yes, I will, as soon as I have finished this letter. I have only a few more lines to write."

Mr. Holden caught sight of Helen's expression the moment she appeared in the doorway. He saw that her half-smiling preoccupation came from the train of thought called up by the letter that Bertha had said she was fin-ishing. She must have been very deeply interested in her correspondent. He came forward, holding out his hand with the air of a friend of the family.

"I hope Miss Bell has not so far forgotten her fellow-traveler as to need his introduction to her a second time," he said cordially, as Andrew uttered his name.

"I hope Miss Bell is not so ungrateful as to have forgotten either of two kind people who would insist upon seeing her safe through the snow-drifts to a hospitable door," said Helen. "How is Mrs. Barney?"

When he had answered, Bertha said she should call upon the lady very soon, with her friend.

Jack was sure his aunt would be delighted, and her anticipated pleasure was reflected in his face.

"Shall we see her to-night?" asked Helen as they spoke of the sleighing party.

He turned to the questioner at once.

"I am afraid not. She never gets into a sleigh when she can help it."

"Then she was all the more kind to me," answered Helen.

Did her listener's eyes have a very little reproach in them as he looked at her? He said nothing.

The evening was as fine as it had promised to be, and four people were filled with pleasant anticipations as Holden's double sleigh drew up at Mrs. Edgerly's door. Mrs. Mason was not of the party, being out of town for a few days.

"Be sure to keep Andrew laughing, so he'll forget Kitty's away," said Bertha to Helen, as the three stood on the doorsteps, while Holden was throwing back the sleigh robes.

But it was Bertha herself who needed the admonition, for when he turned and held out his hand it was to place Helen on the front seat, as he asked in a low tone:

"You will sit here?"

Bertha need not have walked about the hall the last quarter of an hour with all her heavy wraps on. She would have had the back seat just as surely if Mr. Holden had waited for her.

"I want your cousin to have the best possible view of the country," he explained to Bertha as they drove off.

"Ye-es, ye-es," said Andrew. "That's right. Glad you do. Miss Bell is an artist. She'll appreciate it."

Holden talked a good deal to his companion. He was trying to bring the same arch expression into her face that he had seen there the evening of the snow storm, when once, after Mrs. Barney had said a most amusing thing, her eyes had met his with irrepressible fun in them. She had, indeed, immediately recollected herself and looked away, coloring deeply. He wanted to see that bright look again, color and all.

The clear air was exhilarating. The fields along the roadside glistened in the brilliant moonlight, and the shadows of the leafless trees fell upon them in black lines. The sleigh sometimes glided past thinly wooded tracts where heavy masses of pine-trees stood out against the sky and threw their dense shadows on the snow.

"This is the world done in charcoal sketches," said Helen as they came out of one of these spaces into the clear moonlight again. "It is very fine, but it doesn't make one forget to be grateful for color."

She looked up to Mr. Holden for assent.

The swift motion, the companionship, and the gayety of greetings exchanged with some of the party they had passed on the road, had given her face a brightness which justified the gazer's comparison of it to that very ideal of life and color for which she was claiming admiration.

"No; far from it," he said in a low tone, and with a glance and manner that made her feel herself comprehended in the answer.

But before her surprise could change to embarrassment, he turned to Mason and was speaking to him about some incident of the day before.

The company which assembled that evening in a town a dozen miles away, was chosen from the best in Lowton. Holden was an admirable host, he moved here and there among his guests, with ready skill bringing together congenial people and introducing pleasant subjects of conversation. The supper left nothing to be desired, except a good digestion, if one had the misfortune to be without it.　The evening was a social success; no one's pleasure had been overlooked.

Yet, as Helen thought it all over in her room in the small hours, she had an intuition that it was her pleasure which had been especially considered.　But this had been done with such delicacy that she could offer no proof of it, even to herself.　She only felt it was so.

CHAPTER III.

THE day after the sleigh-ride Mrs. Barney sailed majestically into the breakfast-room, and, with a very dignified "good morning," seated herself at the table in ominous silence.

"Another beautiful day, Aunt Delia."

"Very."

A pause.

"Allow me to send you a little of this steak; it's unusually tender."

"No, I thank you."

"I'm sorry. Have some omelet, then."

"Not any, thank you."

"Why, what will you take?"

"I have all I need, thank you."

And Mrs. Barney, refusing toast and rolls, helped herself with a martyr-like air to a slice of cold bread.

Jack shot a half-amused, half-provoked glance at his house-keeper, who smiled comprehendingly, and then begged Mrs. Barney to tell her if there was not something she would like.

But Mrs. Barney would "cause trouble to no one." She went on with her meager breakfast in a silence broken only when a direct question assailed her.

Jack understood it all.

After his usual sally down town he came into the library, where his aunt was seated before the open fire with her fancy knitting. "If 'twere done, 'twere well 'twere done quickly."

"No letters for you this morning," he began.

"No, I suppose not," plaintively. "I've got to be an old lady. When people go they don't want me, and when I go they don't remember me."

"Six epistles yesterday, Aunt Delia."

A flash of triumph in the brown eyes, instantly subdued to sadness again.

"They only all happened to come together," she answered. "But you'll find how it is; you'll be one, too, some of these days."

"An old lady, you mean?"

The irrepressible ripple that threatened to draw out Mrs. Barney's lips into a smile immediately dissappeared, followed by a gentle sigh.

"Yes, you'll be old to," she persisted, "and, then, perhaps you'll be laughed at for not being elegant enough. Of course, you didn't care to show me to your friends."

"But, my dear aunt," began Jack. In spite of his general comprehension of her, he was sometimes puzzled to know if her feelings were really hurt, or she were feigning remarkably well. Mrs. Barney herself was occasionally a little puzzled as to the same point, for her acting, being only exaggerated nature, now and then went somewhat beyond her control. But at such times she gave her feelings the benefit of the doubt. This morning she went on:

"Yes, it's 'my dear aunt' here, alone; but you take care not to need to say it anywhere else."

"How can you be so absurd? I should be only too glad to take you anywhere, and show you to any of my friends."

The lady shook her head with melancholy emphasis.

"Try me," cried Holden afraid he had really offended her. "I'll do anything to make your visit pleasant."

She had him at last. Her eyes shone. She reached up as he stood beside her, and laid a hand on his coat sleeve.

"Then, Jack, we'll give a grand party."

"Thunder! Why, that won't do. I've given one last night. I shall lose my reputation for originality. Think of something better."

"I can't think of anything half so good. And you know you promised."

Mrs. Barney had killed two birds with one stone, gratified an old longing, and punished her nephew for getting up a sleigh-ride, an amusement in which he knew she could not join.

But the ride had compensated a thousand times for any infliction; and when he came to think of it, the party just at this time was not a bad plan.

"John Rathston Holden, what do you suppose you must do when you are going to give a grand party?"

This was a few days before the event. Mrs. Barney and her nephew were standing in the upstairs sitting-room which Jack called his snuggery.

"I have done everything a poor mortal could, already."

"Give a grand party," repeated this inexorable general-in-chief, "and not refurnish this room? Impossible. Why, I want it for a ladies' dressing-room. Of course you must."

"Let me see," she added going back to her interrupted studies of effect, "which would do better for the carpet and window-hangings, wood-color or scarlet? The walls will go with either, they look quite well, though you have smoked them up thoroughly. Wood-color is very genteel; but then red lights up superbly, and cardinal is all the rage now."

" I will tell you."

Mrs. Barney looked at her nephew, deliberating whether his taste were good enough to allow him a voice in his own house.

"Well, which?" she asked.

"Neither."

"You can't do better, Jack. What color would you like, then?"

"The color we have now."

The lady stared at him in such a manner that, had he not been stout-hearted, he must have quailed.

"The same over again?" she asked faintly, struggling against an overmastering suspicion.

"No, the same, without being over again. I have let you rearrange every other room in the house, Aunt Delia, and almost refurnish a number of them. It seems to me that not a place from attic to cellar has a home look but this room; and here I take my stand. If you don't like its appearance, shut it up, and use the others that you have been, as you say, remodeling."

" That will never do; this must be thrown open. If you want your friends to see you shabby in your own. house, leave it, of course. That elegant Miss Bell, too. What will she think of that carpet? I wonder how you came to get such a staring thing, it doesn't seem an atom like you."

"Do you think the carpet ugly?"

Mrs. Barney's face lighted.

"Hideous," she exclaimed eagerly, "and it's been down a long time."

"No, to the first assertion, though I have seen handsomer."

"What made you choose it?"

"I did not exactly choose it. I got it at second-hand."

"Second-hand carpets! Jack Holden, nobody but yourself would ever have made me believe you had come to that. Perhaps," scornfully, "the rest of the things here are second-hand, too?"

"Some of them. That's the reason I am not willing to change them, though I really don't like to say 'no' to you when you are so in earnest about it."

"Then you don't really mean to say 'no' to me?"

Her vivacity had suddenly returned.

"I do, though; because I shall not give them up until they're quite worn out. They used to belong to Ned Winters, poor fellow, in his prosperous days; but he had no head for business, and a few years ago he smashed up completely. You remember, perhaps, he went out West, and died there of consumption last fall. He had the prettiest little wife, and two children. I have had a good many pleasant times in his house with these very things about me. I took them when he moved."

"You bought them at auction, then?"

"Oh, no, they wouldn't have brought anything that way."

Holden stopped. He had not meant to give his reasons.

"I recollect," said Mrs. Barney, "hearing Will Warren say you paid two hundred dollars once for a secretary that wasn't worth fifty. I suppose this was the way of it, for I know you pride yourself on knowing the value of things."

"Warren was mistaken," said Jack, hastily. "It is worth to me quite all I gave. The arrangement of the compartments is the most convenient I have ever seen."

Mrs. Barney dropped into a chair, and let her eyes rove about the room thoughtfully a few moments.

"I remember, now, hearing how much you did for them all," she said. "You're a good fellow, Jack. What a pity you won't marry; you would make such a kind husband. And this nice house, too. I'm so sorry," she added as he answered nothing, "and so are your friends, indignant with that girl."

"What girl?"

Holden came and stood before her.

"Why, you know, that Miss—why, Jack, don't look

like that; I didn't mean to annoy you. I only mentioned what everybody knows."

"What is it everybody knows?"

"About that—how heart-broken you were when Rose Benton married, just after you went off to Europe; of course, we all thought it would be you, knowing you were so fond of her, and how long she had encouraged you. There, you're angry; but we have all pitied you so much, you ought not to be."

Jack burst out laughing; Mrs. Barney saw it was to cover his emotion.

"Rosie Benton! Why, I knew of her engagement before anybody in her own family did; I used to be postman between her and Fred until her father came round. She found people's suppositions about us very convenient, and she knew I didn't care. We used to laugh about them."

"Oh!" said Mrs. Barney with an odd mixture of satisfaction and disappointment in her tones.

Her nephew laughed again.

"Melancholy waste of sentiment, Aunt Delia. I'm sorry I couldn't have spared it to you."

"Then, Jack, if that's the case, surely you will, sometime—"

But with her nephew's eyes looking sternly into hers, it was not so easy to finish.

"I will go down town now," he said; "you have given me commissions enough to keep me until dinner-time."

But although Jack had chosen to look stern, his pulse-beats, long after he left his aunt, were quickened by her prediction.

On the night of the party, when Helen Bell came down-stairs she found Mr. Mason in his easy chair by the fire. The others were not ready.

He laid down his paper, and surveyed her with a smile of satisfaction. He had been so cordial in his manner to her from the first that she felt as if she had known him all her life.

"Turn round slowly, and let me see the effect," he said as she stood beside the table opening a club-book brought in since she had gone to dress. "Ye-es—you look very nice indeed, Miss Helen."

"Don't you like this?" she asked, coming up to him and holding out a black fan on which she had painted heads of wheat. Andrew praised its beauty.

"Sit down," he said after this, "and let us talk it over."

"Talk what over?"

"The party we're going to. If the others look as well as you do, I shall be a fortunate escort."

"Kitty is just lovely, she called me in as I went by. I'm glad you like my dress. It is Mrs. Edgerly's kindness; she would insist upon getting it for me. I couldn't have done all this myself. But I am afraid, Mr. Mason, I ought not to have allowed it. It was my vanity."

"I don't think so, and Aunt Bertha couldn't have done a more sensible thing. Miss Helen, 'take the goods the gods bestow;' and I think," he added with deliberation, "they have not come to the end of their gifts yet. They are only beginning to open their hands above you."

"Thank you for such a prophecy," cried Helen rising suddenly, as if the rich color that had come into her face would vanish with the movement like some reflection from a prism. But it lingered, being no reflection but the hue of joyful consciousness.

"I did not show you my bracelets," she added hastily, reaching out her arm to the light. "They are the only really fine things which have come down to me, 'all that is left, left of six hundred.'"

"Helen," called a plaintive voice from the stairs, "please come here."

As Helen reached the door, Kitty came in with a frown upon her fair face.

"That girl won't be ready to-night. Aunt Bertha wants you to see if you can do anything with her, Helen."

There was certainly some reason for Kitty's annoyance.

Bertha sat in a low rocking-chair, swaying herself back and forth with a slow monotony that was exasperating to one in haste. Kitty's sarcasms and Mrs. Edgerly's expostulations had been fruitless.

"O, Helen," she cried, "you'll help me now, you are an artist. They've been teasing me to death: 'hurry, hurry, hurry,' for the last hour."

"But it *is* time to start, Bertha."

"There! You are going to be just as bad as the others. How can I put on my dress until I know what I'm going to wear? And I can't decide whether my black lace or my white lace overdress would suit this color best. They have both told me first one and then the other, and I didn't like either. I've got confused, you see, and naturally I want to look as well as I can. You needn't be troubled," she added, "I'm awfully quick when I begin."

"How can you possibly tell, unless you put it on?" said Helen. "Stand up, please, and let me try."

As she spoke she took the dress from the bed, and before Bertha sufficiently recovered from her surprise to lay hold of any objection, the vexed question was already settled, for Helen, trying each with a touch, had declared, and arrayed her in the chosen one.

"There, that's the good of being an artist," said Bertha coming down-stairs in high good humor. "She knew what I wanted directly. This is the one I liked best myself, Helen; I should have decided upon it if you had not come up."

"When?" asked Kitty. "I never knew you ready to go anywhere yet."

"We have, once," said Andrew aside to Helen, who recalled the night of the sleigh-ride with a smile, and having begun to think of it, remembered so many things about it, and in some sort connected with it, that they were not quite all put away by the time she reached Mr. Holden's house.

The party was even a greater success than the sleigh-ride, since there were so many more to enjoy it. Mrs. Barney was an excellent hostess, and was in such a state of inward felicity that Jack, watching her with secret amusement, felt rewarded for his efforts. She showed Helen a great deal of attention. She had a feeling of satisfaction and of a certain right of possession in the girl, as if she had drawn her out of a snow-bank and presented her in Lowton.

"I had no idea," said Bertha on the homeward drive, that Mr. Holden could carry out this sort of thing so well. He has really taken pains to show us he knows how to do it."

"Us!" echoed Kitty under her breath with a flash of contempt at the complacent figure opposite. "*Us!*"

"You won 'golden opinions from all sorts of people,' Miss Helen," remarked Mason.

"He means because you wore old-gold color, Helen," explained Bertha; "Andrew is always saying cute little things."

Mrs. Mason made no comment then, although she had seen Helen's success that evening as plainly as Andrew. It was only in the stillness of the night, with her husband asleep beside her, that she vowed that the first violin in the orchestra of Lowton society should never sink into 'second fiddle' to give place to Helen Bell.

It was a week from this time that Holden, calling one morning at Mrs. Edgerly's, found Mrs. Mason alone with the sunshine. She was so sorry every one else happened to be away. Mrs. Edgerly was busied with her domestic matters, and Miss Bell and Bertha had gone to drive with her husband and a niece lately come, but she thought they would not be very long in returning.

As Holden sat talking and waiting, the shutting of a door, and the sound of footsteps made him more than once end a sentence abruptly to listen. But the footsteps passed. It was only one of the house-maids. Two days before, he had taken Helen, Bertha and Andrew Mason to see the sunset on Mansfield Hill, a height commanding a very fine view, but Kitty had scarcely seen him since the party. She began to talk about it now, praising all his arrangements, and going on to speak of the guests with a vivacity too amusing to let one remember that the comments were not always amiable.

"It was very fortunate for us, Mr. Holden," she said at last, "that you opened your house to your friends just at this time, for it gave Miss Bell a pleasant taste of gayety that comes to her but seldom, if at all, poor thing."

"That is a pity, for she seems to be fond of society."

"Yes, indeed! And how brilliant she looked the other evening. You must have seen her drinking in homage like a cordial that exhilarated her."

"No," interrupted Holden, "I did not. She seemed to me like a child having a thoroughly good time, only that she did nothing childish. There was the *abandon* of a true worker about her. It's one of the revenges fate brings upon us lazy people, I mean amateurs, that we don't enter into things with the zest of a person to whom amusement is a recreation. Your aunt says Miss Bell is one of the hardest workers she ever saw. She speaks of her artistic talent as being of a very high order."

"*Abandon?*" echoed Kitty. "I have heard this thing said about her before," she added, then broke off abruptly. "Her talents, you say! Yes," slowly, "she is a very talented girl, fairly brilliant, and she has abilities even more likely to be of service to her than painting pictures —social talents I mean," as Holden looked puzzled.

"Ah! yes."

"Give her the surroundings of wealth, and what a crowd of devotees would be always about her."

Holden was silent. He sat looking moodily into the fire, but he felt no warmth from it; a chill like ice had touched him.

"How very finely she carries her head," resumed Kitty, glancing up from the embroidery with which she had been too much occupied to notice her companion's silence, "and then she has a manner of looking sometimes as if she saw far-away things. I suppose they are great pictures she is painting in imagination. It is very effective. Altogether, she has a great deal of beauty. Don't you think so? I hope she will get this jewel well set; she ought."

The speaker took a few more stitches in lieu of any reply.

She stole a glance at her listener as she stooped and picked out another shade of worsted from the basket beside her. His face was very white, and his brows knit.

She slowly drew out her color, threaded her needle with it, and began to sew again. After a moment she held off the embroidery and studied it with an absorbed look.

"Don't you think that pansy is well shaded, Mr.

Holden? I really pride myself on my fancy-work; a mere touch of our Helen's artistic power."

Jack looked at it vacantly a moment, and answered, "Very."

Kitty rose, and taking the tongs laid the scattered brands together on the hearth, and replenished the fire. Then, after watching the eager flames dart up and enwrap the fresh fuel, she turned to her companion.

"You have not seen her sketches? I will make her show them to you; they are worth seeing, they are really very fine. How delightful it is to be able to do such things—for amusement. But it is drudgery to her, since she must work. Though the necessity will not be for very long; I can see she is resolved upon this, and who can blame her? It is so hard to be fettered, especially for ambition like hers."

" 'Fettered'?"

"Poverty fetters, Mr. Holden. An artist's life is generally a hard one, and Helen's is no exception. If her father and brother had lived, things would have been very different. Poverty is a constant penance to her artistic temperament that hungers and thirsts for luxury; and I see it is a penance she is determined to be rid of. Who has a right to blame her for that, poor child?"

"No, certainly not," said Holden rather inconsequently.

"I understand," he added after a pause—and his voice sounded strange to himself. "I see. That is why she works so very hard, she is determined to shorten the terrible years of probation, and win her place early. She has so much talent and courage and hope, she must succeed."

Kitty laughed.

"You are right, Mr. Holden. She has so much talent and courage and hope, and she *will* succeed."

She turned her eyes upon him as she spoke, and by a glance, made an accusation of her guest, an accusation of worldliness and unwomanly scheming that telegraphed itself on the heart of her listener. Why, he wondered, should he have trusted his instincts and believed in a stranger and—

"It is always so safe," continued Kitty, "to care most about things rather than people. Then, you see, one falls quite naturally into liking best just the people that will help forward the objects one has in view, like art and artistic culture; and one gets through life without suffering from sensitiveness. I sometimes feel as if I half envied Helen."

"I should not think you would."

His voice was low and hoarse with a bitterness in it Kitty had never heard there before.

"Yes," she said softly, "it must be a loss to one's self

to think of other people only for what they can do to further one's own purposes, and not to love them because you can't help it. But, Mr. Holden you mustn't speak of her in that tone. Helen is really good in a great many ways; I am fond of her; she is very charitable, and she has so little to be charitable with; she will make a most gracious Lady Bountiful, it's no wonder she plans to become one. She will do everything beautifully—if one does not ask intensity from her. I don't mean intensity in will power."

"You mean Miss Bell is cold-hearted?"

Kitty turned toward him in quick deprecation.

"She is very kind to everybody, and always ready to oblige and please people. I should not have allowed you to get any such impression."

"Is it true?"

There was an authority in the determined tone which she dared not ignore.

"Yes; that is my impression, or, more frankly, my knowledge."

She dropped her eyes, and sat idly pricking her needle into the spaces of her canvas, then looked into her companion's face with great seriousness.

"This was not what she seemed to me," said Holden.

"Nor to most people," was the answer. "But I ought not to have spoken at all. You are a gentleman,

Mr. Holden," she added earnestly; "nothing I have so imprudently said will ever go beyond you, I am sure. Helen is our guest; I admire her many fine qualities, her talents and energy, as much as any one. It was inexcusable to speak of a failing that concerned neither of us. I can't forgive myself."

She was silent a moment. But Holden did not speak.

"Yet, after all," she went on as if to console herself, "the very worst one can make of it is that Helen's temperament is artistic, rather than her soul. She toils not from love for her art, but for the rewards of work. In short, she is an excellent business woman. Of course she loves her friends, but they are always of the right kind, and her husband, when she marries—and she will marry brilliantly—will have no reason to complain, for she will be satisfied with her choice. She will not choose. imprudently, and throw away artistic possibilities like some women, because you see, her emotions will never get the better of her, they will always coincide with her judgment."

Life has its pay-days, when a man receives into his hand, at once, the result of months or years of character-building. Kitty well knew that she was playing upon a serious defect in Holden's nature, a defect perhaps largely due to circumstances, yet warping in him much that was good.

"Miss Bell's emotions, then, will always coincide with her judgment," he repeated with slow and scornful distinctness; "with her ambition, rather."

His face was white and set as he spoke, and scorn was not the only expression in it, though the most legible.

The door from the library to the room they were in opened so quietly that it must have been standing ajar, and Helen Bell, her pencil and sketch-block in her hand, came in.

She walked directly toward the door that opened into the hall, and at that point in the path nearest Kitty, stopped, and turned toward her.

"I staid at home, Mrs. Mason, on account of some work. A few moments ago I came into the library for the view from the east window. I have overheard the last sentences, for I did not know until my name was spoken whom you were talking of. I leave you free to finish up the subject, as you are so well able to do."

She had gone.

Kitty sat silent, trying with a trembling hand to take unconcernedly some stitches in her embroidery.

At last she looked up with a low laugh.

"The very cleverest thing I've known of her doing yet."

Holden made no answer. This must be true, he saw; but he was still quivering under the tumult of feeling

Helen's presence created. Her eyes hàd stabbed him with the memory of his instinctive trust in her. She had given him no recognition in the moment's pause she made, but he knew he should always feel the contempt of her one sweeping glance, after which, as her eyelids fell low, she had looked away as if he were forgotten. Was she not returning what she had received from him? he reasoned. Neither of them had anything to complain of; each understood the other—in season. He could not be sorry for this knowledge, though it cost him a heavy price.

He had gone to the house that morning feeling that his steps carried him there all too slowly; he came away confident he had escaped a snare.

Only a few hours before this conversation, Helen had yielded to Mrs. Edgerly's earnest entreaty that she would spend the entire winter in Lowton. She knew that this arrangement would please her mother, now staying with a dear friend who needed her in the sorrow of a bereavement.

Helen would not break her promise and mar the pleasure of several people on Mrs. Mason's account. She readily assigned to her a motive for her conduct; but it was not the real one, she never thought of this.

As to Mr. Holden, she remembered now hearing somebody say, laughingly, that he had a great dread of being married for his money, but she had forgotten it again.

She recalled with stings of pride that she had not repelled the look with which he sometimes turned to her, and had listened to him with no sign of disapproval when in speaking words of simple courtesy to her his tones had softened and deepened.

Her eyes were brighter the rest of the day, and her cheeks somewhat flushed, but her manner was unusually cool and self-possessed.

Kitty had bought her victory dearly; but Helen could not speak, and it was worth its price.

Two inmates of Mrs. Edgerly's house felt no surprise that the days went by without any sign of the neighbor who had become so frequent and welcome a visitor.

CHAPTER IV.

SOON after the Christmas holidays Mason came home one morning accompanied by Holden, saying that he had brought him here, in tow, to plead his own cause, and get a pardon, if he could, for having deserted them all.

"Mr. Holden has probably been more pleasantly employed," said Kitty with a smiling ease that surprised Jack. It was only a fortnight since that interrupted conversation of theirs in this very room, an event that three in the group assembled to-day could not have forgotten, and that one would certainly never forget.

He looked at her gravely, and did not remember to speak until he turned to shake hands with Mrs. Edgerly in the doorway.

"He doesn't say one word," cried Bertha, "so it's true."

"What is true, Miss Edgerly?"

"That you have been more pleasantly employed, than in coming here to see us."

"No," he answered, too gravely, he perceived, and added lightly, "but if I had been; would you have compelled me to say so?"

"Would you have said it?"

"It is not necessary to puzzle one's self about an impossible contingency," answered Jack with a forced laugh.

Helen was seated at the other end of the room, a young lady he did not know beside her. Andrew introduced him to his wife's niece, Miss Grierson, and he felt constrained to take a seat near the stranger for a time, wondering as he did it if Miss Bell would move away.

But after a simple "good morning" she took no notice of him whatever. When once he addressed a trifling remark to her, she was listening so attentively to something Mason was saying, leaning back in his easy chair, that she did not hear him at first, and brought herself only by an effort to answer. Holden could not say that her abstraction was put on for effect, because he found Andrew so interesting that both he and Miss Grierson by tacit consent stopped to listen.

"I saw your friend, Mr. Dewey, this morning, Bertha," Helen had heard him begin, and the extra drawl in the tone showed there were accessories to this fact.

"I hope he isn't coming here!" cried Bertha in affected dismay.

"Didn't seem to be thinking about it. He was in his very best style, in Mrs. Merton's front yard."

"What was he doing there?" questioned Kitty.

As Andrew cleared his throat, the laugh quivered in it, for Holden and he were looking at one another with the sympathy of a mutual recollection.

"What was he doing?" she repeated.

"I should say he was dancing."

"Dancing?"

"Ye-es, he and Mr. Vaughan's little black and tan. The dog was on the steps where he meant Dewey should not be, and Dewey was on the walk where he seemed to be meditating not staying a great while. He looked longingly at the door, and regretfully at the gate. I felt somewhat doubtful of the sequel. I watched him, as he stood thinking what a pity it was to have gotten himself up so for nobody but a 'dawg' who didn't seem to appreciate it, either. With this, he made a sudden push for the steps, and the dog made a sudden push for him. The dog's was a good deal more vigorous than Dewey's, and sent him back without much delay. 'Ha! poor fellow, good doggy,' he coaxed. 'Don't you know me? I'm not going to hurt you.'"

"It's a good thing for a man to know he is innocent of evil intent," drawled Andrew after the general laughter had subsided. "This didn't make any impression upon

the black and tan, though; he growled and snapped with
just the same spite as if Mr. Willie had asserted himself bent on plunder and foul play. Every time the
poor young man put his foot forward an inch, there came
a succession of barks. In vain Mr. Dewey looked up
at the windows for help. I wondered if Miss Fisher
were watching him. Miss Fisher, Bertha, is a dashing
young lady who has been in town the past few weeks visiting the Mertons. Your friend's toilet was made for her.
But however much he regretted this love's labor lost,
he became convinced at last there was nothing to do
but beat a retreat. And then, alas! it grew plain there
wasn't even that, for though the dog snapped, and
snarled, and threatened whenever he attempted a single
step forward, the creature seemed about to fly at him
and tear him to pieces if he could whenever he tried the
least retrograde movement. All his coaxing tones and
assurances had only an irritating effect. Oil is an excellent thing for raging water, but it doesn't put out
fire."

"Didn't anybody come?" asked Bertha.

"No; the house stood there blind and deaf, and
Dewey stood growing as motionless as if he were staring at the Gorgon."

"And what were you doing?"

"I? Oh, I was guardsman outside to see fair play,

and not let any other dogs in. But Holden here spoiled the whole. I'm going to report him to the 'Society for the Prevention of Cruelty to Animals.' Before I had even seen him, down he swooped on that valiant cur, and caught him by the ears, and held him fast. 'What! aren't you coming?' he called, for Mr. Dewey seemed inclined to be going. But at this he tipped up the steps—he progresses, Miss Helen, by balancing himself on one leg as if he were going to try a pirouette, and then experimenting in the same way with the other. He made a semi-circle round his assailant, generously leaving him as much of the field as possible. The dog burst into such a fury and made such lunges at Holden when he couldn't reach Dewey, that I was really afraid he'd bite him. But he had roused the castle at last, for the door opened, and Vaughan came out. 'What's this?' he cried to his dog, in a tone that took the creature's voice quite away, and left him with an humble air of apology for having under a mistake endeavored to guard his master. I could see Vaughan appreciated the protection. 'Your dog, sir?' asked Mr. Dewey in the tone of a censor. 'Quite a nuisance of a little animal, sir; and he hasn't a collar on either, ought to be shot.' Vaughan looked angry until he caught sight of Holden's face; for just then Mr. Dewey turned to his rescuer and thanked him nonchalantly: 'It was so difficult to keep off the little beast and ring the door-bell at the same time, he explained. Holden vanished suddenly, and outside the gate ran across me as I happened to be walking by."

"Mr. Holden behaved a great deal better than you did, Uncle Andrew," cried Jenny Grierson.

Andrew maintained that his friend had shown a deplorable want of appreciation of the fitness of things. For, if two boys were to be left to fight out their own battles, he said, he didn't see why two—

But Kitty abruptly asked him to replenish the fire, and he left his sentence unfinished.

"We had a splendid drive to Mordent yesterday,' said Bertha to Mr. Holden; "the sleighing is perfect.'

"Let us take advantage of it, then, to go round by the lake as we were talking of doing some day. What do you say, Mrs. Mason? Shall it be to-morrow?"

Kitty would like it very much, but she had an engagement, she said.

"The day following, then; or the next fair day?" he asked.

Bertha was delighted, Jenny Grierson smiled down at her knitting, and general satisfaction was expressed.

Helen took no part in it. Her hands lay in her lap clasped over a book she had been reading when the two gentlemen came in.

Jack looked across Miss Grierson toward her.

"I hope you will be here, Miss Bell, to go with the party."

"I shall probably be here for some time," she answered without taking her eyes from a child in the street she had been watching.

"Yes," Mrs. Edgerly chimed in, "Helen will be with us all winter, and we want to make it as pleasant as possible for her, and for Miss Grierson."

"She certainly knows how to smile as if she had feeling," thought Jack, as the girl's glance turned for a moment upon the speaker; but when she felt his eyes upon her, her face grew stern, without changing its position.

"You will go, then?" he asked as if to explain this gaze, but his manner was not perfectly cool with all his effort.

"If my friends go," she answered with deliberation. Then turning her head and meeting his eyes fully, she said,

"Why not?"

The blood rushed to Holden's face, and had not left it when Helen rose and seating herself beside Mrs. Edgerly, began talking to her. He had often felt imbittered because he thought too large a share of the deference he received was due to his wealth and position, but he had not realized how much a matter of course that deference had grown to him. Now, this girl, who had heard him speak slightingly of her, told him to his face that his opinion was not worth regarding.

Mrs. Mason had heard it, she was looking at him, and her half-smile expressed her admiration of Helen, but no surprise. He confessed the admiration, too, even in his defeat. For he saw she was not even angry, she found him fit only for contempt, ridicule, for there had been something like a smile hovering on her lips as she asked this question. The thought made him chafe.

Her expression to-day, proved the truth of Mrs. Mason's words. She had cared for his attentions through ambition only, she was really cold-hearted; he had not been able to take the matter so lightly.

"Yes, we are quits," he cried on his way home, repeating it to make sure it was true.

"Invite me to go in your sleigh, Mr. Mason," said Helen, softly, as they stood a little apart, waiting with the others, for Holden to come before they started on the proposed drive.

Andrew looked at her with curiosity.

"But my sleigh holds only two," he said in the same undertone, "and Kitty takes her invitation for granted."

"Arrange it in some way for me, please," she repeated.

Her face was deeply flushed, and she looked troubled.

"Just as you wish, Cousin Helen."

The tones were so kind she looked up in sudden gratitude. He saw the glistening water drops in her eyes for an instant. His look was so sympathetic, and so full of protection, that it seemed to bring her strength, and in this moment Andrew Mason learned a great deal about that real Helen Bell whom most people knew slightly.

When the party had all assembled on the steps of the *porte-cochère*, Helen stood a little withdrawn as Jack came up to help her into his sleigh, in which Miss Grierson was already seated, and Bertha was to follow. He had never seen her look so pale and haughty.

"That's not fair," cried Andrew, "you can't always have all the young ladies. Miss Helen, won't you accept a seat with us, there is plenty of room?"

"Thank you, with pleasure, if I shall not inconvenience Mrs. Mason."

If Mrs. Mason hesitated ever so slightly, Helen resolved to stay at home.

"Not in the least," said Kitty. "I should be delighted to go with Mr. Holden," she added, "if he will allow me; only too glad of a chance to desert this ancient gentleman, and ride with the young people," and she nodded saucily at Andrew as she passed him. He repaid the gesture by pinching her arm as he tucked the sleigh-robe about her.

There was one person in the world whom Kitty Mason

loved with all her heart, and this was her husband. She believed it impossible for him intentionally to do anything wrong; and this uprightness was the greatest comfort to her. She never expected to be like him, and she did not think it worth while to attempt his *rôle*, since she should never play it with the perfection of reality, and hated to undertake anything in which she could not excel. In her husband's footsteps she would be only a laggard, while in a separate department each did admirably. She knew that his way was the best in the world, but it was much too hard; she must have room for her own peculiar genius to develop itself. Truth was superb, she realized, but *finesse* was dear to her soul.

Andrew had first met her when an overwhelming danger threatened her; he had seen and loved the best that was in her; he had been able to save her, and had married her when his own pity and her fascination blinded him to her faults. They did this in some degree to-day, for it is easy to forgive a great deal to one who loves us, and to believe that a nature holding this germ of the highest power, is capable of development in right directions. This is what Andrew felt that he had the highest authority for believing. Perhaps he overrated her power of loving, when he considered this fire intense enough to finally sublimate her nature and cast out its dross.

The whole drive was not less than fifteen miles,

and they all came back merrily at sunset, none gayer than Helen, who always enjoyed being with Mr. Mason; he seemed to understand what she meant, and entertained her so well.

Helen seldom staid at home when any amusement of this kind was on hand; but it always happened, simply enough, that she and Mr. Holden never drove or walked side by side, even if they were in the same group; and when he came to the house—he had a habit of dropping in on his way down town, and Mason took care to return his visits—Miss Bell was so often busy with her work that he seldom saw her.

He came one evening. She was in the drawing-room.

"I have caught you now," he thought.

But she had no appearance of having been caught, she greeted him as politely as if they had never met before, and soon after, when the evening mail was brought in, she slipped away from the roomful of people to read her letters.

"They must be very important, or very long and interesting," Holden thought, "to keep her away all the rest of the evening."

They were more important to Helen than any one knew. The first was from the secretary of an Art Committee, informing her that her picture was accepted, and would be advantageously hung. The girl's eyes shone as she read.

"Thank Heaven!" she cried. "How I have worked, how much we have gone without, and now, perhaps, my reward is coming; I will believe it is."

But when she finished her second letter the warmth died out of her face, and she sat thinking with head raised and mouth firmly set.

This epistle was from an old school friend, an artist, like herself. She was not so much poorer than Helen had been until the last few months, when regular work had opened to her, but she was very much less courageous, and not disposed to be silent upon the subject of her hardships. Besides this, Helen knew that, while her own mother encouraged her in dark days and bore every privation with a cheerfulness inspiring deeper love in the daughter and nerving her to fresh efforts, her friend's parents were openly dissatisfied with slow results; they were both more or less invalids, aimless—unless determination to get whatever one can from others be an aim—and carping. Helen's picture and this friend's had both been sent to the Hanging Committee. Helen's had won a place; and, wrote the other, there was no space left for hers. "If it had not been for yours," she said, "mine would have had a chance;" she learned this fact from a private and reliable source on the very day her painting was rejected. The artist did not say in so many words, "Withdraw your picture;" but she would have been more honest, and no more exacting, had she asked this sacrifice outright.

Helen sat quiet for some time. Then, going to her desk she wrote a very few lines hastily, signed, inclosed and sealed the note.

Bertha knocked at her door, to see if she were sick, or had heard bad news. She said she was quite well, only tired, and if they would excuse her, would not go down again.

"But we're having such a good time," pleaded the girl, "do come."

Helen answered that she was very glad they were having a pleasant evening, but she must say "good night."

Bertha could not hear the sigh that accompanied her words.

CHAPTER V.

THE next day Helen was in the morning-room after
breakfast, looking out of the window — in the
dreamy way she often had when she was accomplishing
most, for she never knew where the subjects for her im-
aginative sketches would come from — a child running
past might bring a suggestion, or the curious shape of a
tree hold a grotesque fancy in waiting for her. She
understood that people, and new faces, and the stimulus of society were necessities to her as an artist, and
that often when she seemed most at play she was doing
her best work. For, the salt of genius in the character
needs the stir of life before it can crystallize into forms
of beauty; perhaps the stir may come from the throwing
of some foreign object into the mind; what that object
will be, no human foresight, not even the seeker's, can
perceive. When it comes the thing is done, until it does
come the world to be created is without form and void.

When Helen had seated herself with her eyes upon the

street, all the family were in the room; but as she fell into reverie about the letters she had received the night before, three of them went away to real or imagined duties in other parts of the house. One person only was left there sitting in an easy chair, watching the girl's profile against the window, and thinking she was much too pale nowadays, and somewhat thinner than when she came to Lowton; seeing a little sad droop of the mouth that was by no means there· because she had been industrious as well as gay for the past two months, reviewing trifling incidents, and studying causes with a keenness that would have alarmed Helen greatly, had she dreamed of it.

Presently she asked,

"Who is this, Bertha?"

"Bertha is not here," said a voice.

She turned suddenly, and found no one but Andrew in the room.

"Where are they all?"

"I heard Kitty say she was going to get her basket of worsted, and Bertha is making cake."

Helen laughed at his tone.

"Is this last a confidential communication?"

Mason uttered a subdued chuckle.

"We are all expected to stand in awe of her culinary attainments," he explained.

"Is she a wonderful cook?"

"Very wonderful. You must learn her receipt for cake-making."

"Thank you. I'll ask her sometime."

"Better ask me. I'm afraid she would forget to mention the most important ingredient."

"Is it always the same?" asked Helen.

"Always."

"That's odd. What is it? Plenty of sugar?"

"No, not always sugary," he drawled. "She walks into the kitchen, says a few cabalistic words to the cook, gives a stir or two to something mixed in a pan, and walks out again with great access of importance. After a while a delicious compound appears upon the table. Try it some day, Miss Helen, but be sure not to forget the cook, *she* is the necessary ingredient. She went visiting once, and Bertha gave us some yellow sponge dipped in soapsuds for tea."

Helen laughed again.

"How severely you criticise," she said.

"Why can't she say she does the cooking by proxy?" asked Andrew. "What is the use of acting, when nobody is deceived?"

"Then you approve of it when somebody is deceived."

She said this merely as a retort, laughing as she spoke. But to her surprise Mason answered gravely:

"A great deal of the acting is self-deception, Miss

Helen. Remember that when you are tempted to be severe."

She was silent. Was this what he thought of his wife? Was he trying to shield Kitty from her judgment? It was not likely. But the possibility prevented her answering him.

"I will tell you one person," he went on, after a pause, "who has a real horror of little deceits of all kinds; and that is why I like him, though he has some decided faults."

She looked up expectantly.

"I mean Jack Holden. One can always rely upon him, and there is nothing he would not forgive, I believe, sooner than having been deceived."

Helen fixed her eyes on Mason steadily, and answered:

"I know Mr. Holden very slightly, but I never saw anything particularly just or admirable in him. You have a much better opportunity of judging, however—"

"Than you permit him to give you."

Helen rose. She was sure she had neither betrayed consciousness in her answer, nor waited too long before speaking, although the sense of time had gone from her, but now her face flushed with indignant pride.

"I am going to get my pencil," she said. "I ought to be at work this morning," and went away for her materials.

"Than I permit him," she thought on her way upstairs. "How little Mr. Mason guesses. I am so glad it looks like this to him; I should make it so, if that were necessary. But it is the farthest from it."

When she returned to the room Bertha had come in again, and a gentleman was there whom she had never seen before. He was above average height, with a brilliant, dark complexion, brown eyes and hair, a Roman nose in miniature, and a mouth whose upper corners he had a peculiar habit of elevating, giving him a cynical expression that, united with a dignified bearing, would have been supercilious. But his absence of dignity was very noticeable; he was fidgety and self-conscious, most anxious to be an object of admiration, most fearful he should in some way excite secret merriment, and much more successful in respect to his fears than his hopes.

Helen knew instinctively this must be Mr. Dewey.

He was effusively polite; paid Helen three compliments in as many minutes, conventional little speeches that, with Andrew's mysteriously serious face to glance into as she received them, she enjoyed exceedingly. Then, suddenly recollecting himself, he turned to Bertha with words which were evidently meant as an apology for his not having included her in his most flattering attentions that morning.

Mason suggested he had better make up for lost time at once.

Mr. Dewey stared at him with an expression between perplexity and defiance.

"You don't understand about young ladies as well as you used to when you were younger, Mason," he began in a sibilant half-whisper, putting both hands into his pockets, and standing over Andrew in a half-apologetic, half-hostile attitude; "they like such things. There is a natural difference between the masculine mind and the feminine mind, and each should have the food it prefers. Ladies enjoy sweets."

"Do you enjoy sweets, Miss Bell?" asked Andrew.

"Certainly; sugar-plums, huge ones."

Mr. Dewey smiled a satisfied assent, elevating the corners of his mouth still higher.

The door from the library opened half way, and Mrs. Edgerly's voice said,

"Haven't you gone *yet*, Bertha? I wish you would call at Mr. Snow's on your way, and send him up *at once*. I want those curtains hung, and he told me he'd be here yesterday. I beg your pardon, Mr. Dewey," as she came in. "I didn't see you. There is no hurry. Miss Bell and Bertha were going out for a walk in the course of the morning."

But Mr. Dewey would not stay, and begged to accompany them.

When the two girls returned Jack Holden was talking with Andrew. He explained his presence here again to-day, by saying he had been asking Mason's advice about some little matter of business, and must go when he had said "good morning" to them.

This, apparently, took some time to do, for he was still seated when Helen came back from taking off her wrappings.

Bertha had thrown herself into a rocking-chair, her cloak over the arm of it and her bonnet still on. She was listening to Mr. Holden with a smile upon her face.

"But you haven't told us how nicely you played *preux chevalier;* we found it quite amusing, did we not?" she added, turning to Helen as she came in.

"No," answered Helen.

Kitty glanced at her with quick curiosity, noticing the gravity of her tone.

But Helen seated herself without saying more, and Kitty was obliged to wait until she could learn from Bertha, later, what both question and answer meant.

Holden looked surprised, embarrassed for a moment, then directly began to speak of something else.

Helen, as she sat there taking small part in the conversation, remembered what she had said to Mason about Mr. Holden a few hours before. The morning's incident to which Bertha was referring was very trifling in itself; but as an indication of character it had its weight.

The walk which the two girls had taken with Mr. Dewey, had led them down a steep street running into another scarcely less so. There had been rain in the night, and the sidewalks were very icy. A few rods before them was a woman who seemed in imminent danger of slipping down, partly through her great fear of doing it, for she shuffled and twisted about so much to avoid the worst places, that in all probability she was destined soon to find one of them, and succumb to it. She was a woman apparently of about sixty, dressed in rusty black. She looked thinly clad for the winter weather. In her hand was swinging a black bag, like that of an agent of the poorer sort. The supposed contents of this were a great source of amusement to Bertha and Dewey, as they announced the different articles that would be scattered on the sidewalk if only these oscillations should become a little more violent. Before they came up with her, Bertha stopped at the door of a house to deliver some message, and, as it happened, the woman stopped, too, a little distance off, and addressed a gentleman passing by, evidently hoping to find in him a customer. The man said "yes," "yes," impatiently, as she told him of the different things she had to sell, yet he lingered and bought something of her, as Helen was near enough to see, while she waited on the sidewalk for Bertha.

"Did you hear that?" asked Dewey. "She recommends him to buy her chromo flowers because they will last, and are better than the real ones. Isn't that the funniest thing out?"

Helen said "yes" absently. She was noticing the piteous look in the woman's face, and the respectability that made itself felt through her shabby garments and her importunity.

At this moment Bertha called her up to the door of the house, and when the two turned away from it, the woman was far along the street, clinging to the fence as she went on.

"Don't walk so fast, Helen," cried Bertha. "You will be down in a moment if you do."

"Then I shall wait for you to pick me up," she called back.

Just after the woman had disappeared by turning the corner at the foot of the street, a sleigh dashed by. Helen recognized Mr. Holden's horse. As she reached the corner she saw this sleigh drawn up to the sidewalk and its owner helping the poor woman into it with the utmost care. He was off again directly; she was sure he had not perceived her.

It was, indeed, a very little thing to give a strange old woman a seat in his sleigh down an icy street, when, in passing, he noticed her fear of falling, yet Helen would not now have said that she had never seen anything just or admirable in Jack Holden.

Bertha and Mr. Dewey, their pace quickened by her rapid steps, had also reached the corner as the sleigh was driving off. They regretted having missed the first part of the performance, and Helen remembered that they had not caught sight of the woman's look of amazement and gratitude.

"Did you find Mr. Dewey as entertaining as you expected, Helen?" Kitty asked abruptly, perceiving that Bertha was making some mistake, and not quite clear whether the young lady herself saw this, or in her silence was only meditating a further attack upon the subject.

"I had no great expectations," she answered, "and those I had were justified."

"That's a pity," remarked Andrew, "for he is sure to have you down on his list by this time."

"His list?"

"Ye-es," he drawled. "Mr. Dewey appreciates his masculine prerogative to the utmost. He keeps a list of all the eligible young ladies about Lowton, which he adds to at discretion. I don't think he is of Mormon proclivities, but he feels he has all the world before him where to choose, and he is anxious to choose the best thing out; so, I can't say you will be the favored one, Miss Helen, but no doubt you'll have the honor of a place among the candidates."

"I shall be very proud of that," she laughed.

"Ye-es, ye-es. I don't know how long the list is now. He had thirty names at one time."

"It varies," explained Holden, "because every now and then one of these beauteous ladies, either unconscious or unmindful of her great privilege, bestows her heart and hand upon some undeserving suppliant, and Mr. Dewey has no way left him of showing his contempt but by black lining her name off his roll of honor."

"Once he was hoaxed into putting down the name of a married lady," said Mason, "and he kept it there a month before he found out. Wasn't he furious!"

"Was it you did it, Andrew?" asked Kitty.

"Um!" said Andrew meditatively. "Had too big a fire made up here, Kitty, it's hot."

"But you ought to hear him talk literature, and art, and science, Helen," cried Bertha; "he really does know a great deal, he reads everything, and is up in all the 'isms' of the day."

"Ye-es, ye-es, that's so," assented Mason; "he hasn't ballast enough to keep down."

Holden laughed.

"May I not show these to Mr. Holden?" asked

Mrs. Mason laying her hand upon a portfolio on the table, and looking at Helen who, finding Mr. Dewey in the room when she brought it down, had left it there unopened.

The girl flushed. She was unwilling to express concern enough to speak the _"no" that came to her lips.

The sketches were well worth looking at, as Kitty had said, and received at least something of the praise they deserved. Helen felt a sudden thrill of fear as she saw her, in turning them over, hand to Mr. Holden the one she had been at work upon that day in the library.

In the background was the figure of a lady walking through a grove. Her face, which was shaded by a summer hat, was turned away, so that only the outline of the cheek was visible, her figure and motion were full of grace and freedom. Behind her, unseen, unheard, with an expression of eager longing and devotion, walked her lover; his quiet, yet hasty, steps evidently gaining upon her and about to reach her side. Helen remembered that on that morning she had perceived with confusion Mr. Holden's face in that of the lover. But to-day, after an anxious glance at the two persons before her, she saw that she had really changed the face beyond all recognition.

"This is a very spirited sketch, Miss Bell," said Jack, studying it attentively; "the young man's expression is fine."

"The conventional thing, I suppose," she answered. "People will have that kind of amusement, and it pays to represent it for them."

She saw the sudden flash of contempt in his face, and smiled.

"You do it uncommonly well for an outsider, Miss Helen," said Mason.

"You can't draw if your hand shakes," she answered; "you must be able to see things in perspective if you want to succeed in your work."

Holden glanced at Kitty.

"And Miss Bell certainly wishes that."

"I intend it, Mr. Holden."

"It is a fine thing to have an aim before one if—if one have nerve to throw aside everything in the way of it."

"Religion requires a man if he has made a vow, to keep it; and do you think the world is any less exacting?" answered Helen.

"I have never felt it necessary to try it."

"No."

In a moment he saw she must have misunderstood him. But there was nothing he could add without condemning her still more.

She took up some fancy-work and amused herself with it, glancing at the sketches only when some one asked her a question, but this was many times, for they led to a good deal of conversation. At last, as Andrew closed the portfolio, he said,

"You seem in a brown study, Miss Helen. I am sorry, for we have missed you here. But you may have been silently preparing more sketches for us in future."

"Oh no, I have been as idle as that well-known 'painted ship upon a painted ocean.' I have not had an original idea. There has only been a queer old saying from the Sanskrit running in my head, just as things will do when people feel stupid, and as inapplicable as such snatches usually are:

> "'A wealthy man not drunk with pride,
> A youth who fickle folly flees,
> A ruler scorning careless ease, .
> Among the great enrolled abide.'"

"She did mistake me," thought Jack. "To believe I could mean on account of having money; how uncomfortable! But I understand her. That, after all, is the main thing. She defies me now that I know. If only she had not overheard what must have wounded her pride so much."

He went home feeling that he had never seen the face nor the work of an ambitious, cold-hearted woman so much like that of a true one. Yet he had heard her own words of self-seeking and of mocking defiance.

How real she had seemed to him at first, how happy at times, and what a sense of hidden resource and strength her quieter moods had given him! When, before Kitty had spoken, he had gathered from light words of her own that want of money cut her off from many pleasures, the blood ran leaping in his veins at the thought that, if she would, he could give them all to her. This sense of ability to serve her thrilled him with a new and exquisite delight. On this day when every feeling he had left for her was a certain intellectual interest and an admiration of her cool pride and power, he remembered all his former trust in her and his hopes.

CHAPTER VI.

IT was a very stormy evening in the middle of February,
recalling to Helen the night of her arrival in Lowton,
in that first severe storm of the season. The snow fell
furiously, and the wind drifted it across the street, across
the gate, against the house, into its angles, where the
eddies whirled and piled it high.

Kitty had been feeling all day that her cold was so
severe she ought to send for the doctor, but she hated
the idea of being sick, and delayed from hour to hour,
sure she should soon be better. At night the storm that
had been increasing since four o'clock, when Helen came
in hurriedly from some errand, was so violent she did
not like to send any one through it, and liked still less
to bring out her physician, who was not a young man,
and never lacked for this kind of work. If Mason had
been at home, the messenger would have been dispatched
in the morning, but he had gone out of town several days
before. So Kitty decided that all she wanted was to be
let alone. She refused everybody's remedies, and went to

bed early, sure she should get a good night's sleep which would make her all right.

But the sleep did not come. Instead of it was restlessness, and about midnight an incessant cough began.

As soon as this cough had fairly established itself, Helen came out of her room, which was next to Kitty's, and walking up to the bedside with a small phial in her hand, said,

"I was sure you would want this, Mrs. Mason, before the night was over, your cough is so like mine when I take a sudden cold. Mamma insisted upon my bringing this medicine with me, it helps me more than anything else."

"Thank you," said Kitty trying not to catch her breath as she spoke; "I remember you told me about it, but I thought I should do nicely."

"I know you did, but my own experience has taught me better."

Kitty watched her idly as Helen turned up the gas and, standing beside it, poured out the dose from the phial in her hand. Apparently, she had not been in bed, for she seemed only to have put on a sack in place of her dress. She had been brushing out her hair, which fell about her shoulders to her waist like a dark mantle. There was no look of sleep in the bright eyes, or the resolute face.

"Where did you get a teaspoon?" asked Kitty as she watched her. "I suppose you went into Aunt Bertha's room for it. You disturbed her, I am afraid. There was one here, if you had asked me."

"But I didn't disturb any one. I brought the spoon upstairs with me to-night, I was so sure you would need it. But don't talk. Take this, and I know you will go to sleep."

"What is it like? I perfectly hate unpalatable things. I never take them; the doctor always finds me something else."

"I have nothing else," said Helen; "this is not bad. Take it, please."

Kitty daintily sipped at the medicine preparatively to taking the whole spoonful.

But she instantly sprang up.

"I wouldn't swallow a drop of such vile stuff for the world," she cried. "I never tasted such bitterness. I would rather cough for a week. How could you give it to me?"

Helen's lip curled, and her eyes flashed.

"I did not understand you," she answered. "I should not suppose anybody would mind a trifle like that in comparison with a dangerous cough. Think of it, Mrs. Mason."

"No, thank you. Only try it yourself."

"I have, many a time. I don't call it bad; but if you don't want it, good night."

When Helen had gone, Kitty took a bonbon from her box to sweeten her mouth, and her temper, and tried to compose herself to sleep and prove the needlessness of the other's nostrum.

But instead of doing this, she lay tossing restlessly, excited by a startling thought and filled with feverish fancies.

Her cough, which was partly nervous, subsided at last, however, and she slept fitfully, awaking with a sense of weariness. But she insisted upon going down to the breakfast-table, and was really no worse. In a day or two, through sheer determination, it seemed, she was comparatively well again. Helen, who never had more to do with her than politeness required, was unusually cool.

Kitty came into her room on the third morning after the fit of coughing.

"Will you let me look at that delicious medicine of yours, that I offended you so the other night by not taking?" she asked with a short laugh.

"Certainly."

But Helen seemed in no haste to get it. She went on for a few moments with what she was doing; then going to her trunk, came back holding the phial up before the other.

"This is it."

"Thank you. May I take it a few moments? I want to see if it looks like something I have," and she held out her hand.

"No," said Helen, "not the phial. I will give you some of it, if you want to try it."

"Should you advise it?"

"I advise nothing. I will give it to you if you choose."

"Thank you. I will keep some by me, and then if I feel worse I can screw my courage to the sticking point, and not fail ignominiously as I did the other night. You brought this bottle from home with you?"

"Yes. Have you brought anything to put it in?"

"No, I expected you would lend me the bottle; but no matter, I can get something in my room."

Helen's only answer was an attitude of waiting.

"You look very pale," she said, scanning Kitty's face closely as she returned. "You had better be a little more careful of yourself."

"That is only because you—I am much better," said Kitty, "and I am very much obliged. Now, I will not interrupt you any longer."

But she turned back to say,

"Oh! by the way, have you the prescription for this, in case I should want more of it?"

"No, only the number. But it was put up at home, and I can get the prescription for you sometime, I think. Meanwhile, what I have here is at your service, if you need more."

Kitty looked back, and saw her at once replacing the phial.

"I should think you would be afraid to put that into a trunk," she said, "lest it should spill."

"Not in one of the compartments. I don't like a room lined with bottles like an apothecary's shop."

"Ah! yes, I see." And this time Kitty really left her.

That afternoon, to everybody's dismay, Mrs. Mason insisted upon going out. She had an errand that nobody could do for her, although there were plenty of volunteers. She did not think the clear air would do her any harm, if it was cold.

Two days later she went to Boston, and did a little shopping which she said had been waiting much too long. She declared herself almost strong again.

"If Andrew were here," said her aunt, "you know you could not stir one step."

Kitty laughed.

"I am very naughty, of course; you must tell him. Dear Andrew, how we all miss him! But he will be here by the end of the week."

On Andrew's return Mrs. Edgerly invited Mrs. Barney

to dinner, and, naturally, Mr. Holden also. Jack had not been to the house during Mason's absence, but it was not on account of this that he had staid away. He had wound up some severe cogitations by calling himself a fool, and determining not to be one any longer, and the use of the epithet had seemed to have some connection with his visits to Mrs. Edgerly's house.

But now he must go with his aunt, and he resigned himself to this duty with great cheerfulness.

A short time before their arrival, Bertha announced that she had encountered Mr. Dewey in her walk the day before, and had asked him to meet them, thinking it would be pleasant for everybody.

"I don't know what reason you had to think that," cried Kitty, thoroughly angry. "I wish you would not interfere."

"Interfere! Interfere, indeed! Grandmamma, haven't I as much right as Kitty Mason, or anybody, to invite people to this house?"

"Why, yes, my dear," answered the old lady. "Kitty doesn't mean that. But, you see, Mr. Dewey is peculiar. I'm afraid Mrs. Barney won't enjoy him, and I know Mr. Holden won't."

"Bertha will, and that's enough," said Kitty under her breath. But the next moment she remembered that the trial would have some alleviation. Bertha, as she told her, must look to it that Mr. Dewey was well entertained. That would furnish her with occupation enough, while Jenny Grierson, who.had that day returned from a short visit to a school friend near Lowton, would be able to give all her attention to the other guests. Kitty was never indifferent to Bertha's interests, but if the girl would make foolish moves in spite of her, it was comfortable to have a docile pupil at hand to fill up the deficiencies—to fill them permanently, if fate would be so generous.

Mrs. Barncy seized upon Helen in the few minutes before dinner.

"Miss Bell," she said, "come and sit here on the sofa beside me, I want to see how you look; I scarcely know, it is so long since we have met. My dear," she added half aside, "I thought, and I told Jack, that I should see a great deal of you this winter. But it hasn't turned out so. Why don't you come to see me?"

"I will come, Mrs. Barney."

Helen noticed that Kitty smiled as she caught her answer.

"Yes, I will come very soon," she reiterated audibly.

Mr. Dewey had here the tribute of a few flowery words to offer to Miss Bell.

At dinner Holden sat next Miss Grierson, who to-day looked more fresh and bright than ever. Her simplicity pleased him; yet there was a demureness in her eyes, and her attitude, that gave promise of a fair amount of fun. Helen was opposite, with Mrs. Barney on her right. She gave Mr. Dewey leisure .to devote a good share of his attention to Bertha on his other hand, yet she seemed to enjoy talking with him. She was unusually animated, and more than once by some keen retort demolished his arguments in a way which was far from according with his theories of the relative powers of masculine and feminine minds. But he perceived it was only about trifles, and that it was because he had not really considered her a foeman worthy of his steel; and so solacing himself, he "smiled superior down" upon her, or tried to do it.

Jenny Grierson's conversation was not so engrossing as to prevent Holden from taking in the situation of affairs opposite him, and once he found himself and Andrew glancing cautiously at one another, and smiling in a way that showed an amount of mutual understanding which, when he came to think of it, surprised him.

Mrs. Barney glanced about, here and there, pecked at the dainties on her plate, and, in her good humored way, at everybody's store of personalities, with an air of thorough enjoyment. She inquired if Kitty's maiden name was Grierson, and on learning that it was, remembered having once met people of that name in New Hampshire. She was spending the summer roaming about there, and in the course of her travels went to a village where she had planned to stay a month. It turned out that she had not done so, but she remembered the passing through it, and, among other places, recollected a little cottage where she was told she might perhaps find board.

"It was a mite of a place," said Mrs. Barney, "but as pretty as could be, and the people were very nice. I should have staid with them if I had stopped at all. I have just remembered, hearing yours, that their name was Grierson, too. I wonder if they were relatives of yours?"

"My aunt always imagines that people of the same name must be next of kin," interposed Jack quickly. "She is archæological about it."

"That is, you mean she thinks we've all just come out of the ark?" said Jenny.

"No, my dear," said the lady, "not the ark, the country, and a beautiful country, too. Then, you don't know these people?" she said to Kitty, who was obliged to turn at her direct address, although she had just become interested in Mr. Holden's explanation.

Everybody now was waiting for her to speak, for Mrs. Barney's reiterated question across the table had caught the attention of all. Andrew was smiling at her.

"I lived in New Hampshire, and in the country when a child," she said.

"Yes, and this was in Notham. Was it there you lived?"

"I did for a time."

"Why, then it must have been you. Oh, it was years, and years, and years ago."

"Not too many, please, Mrs. Barney," drawled Andrew.

The lady looked at him in surprise, until a new light dawned over her face.

"Oh, well, I don't mean that. I mean only the right number to match with her now. Yes, it must have been you, Mrs. Mason; such a lovely little girl of about eight or ten, barefooted, like the famous Maud Muller, with a little old-fashioned red calico dress, and an old shaker bonnet, not on your head, but tied by the strings and hanging on your neck behind. You had been picking blue-berries, and were going to carry your little pail round to the people. I bought them all of you, though, to help out our luncheon as we drove through the woods. Oh, I thought you were the very loveliest, dainty little creature I had ever seen in my life."

"I thought she was a fair specimen of a little country girl, Mrs. Barney, when I saw her," laughed Andrew, "and that was years afterward, 'years, and years,' as you say."

If Kitty had ever permitted herself the use of slang,

she would have inwardly affirmed she "owed Mrs. Barney one." As it was, the sentiment in all its force silently reigned in her heart.

Mrs. Barney had reminiscences with her hostess; for while visiting in Lowton, during the lifetime of her sister, Holden's mother, she had met Mrs. Edgerly. She had them also with Helen, although acquaintance with her dated only from the night of the storm. As to the others who were strangers, she seemed resolved to have, in future, reminiscences of them also. It was in vain her nephew attempted more than once to parry her direct though unimportant inquiries.

"Well, Jack," she cried once, "why in the world don't you let people answer for themselves? I know they would rather, everybody would. Mr. Dewey can't object to telling me if his mother is living."

Holden desisted. He heard Miss Bell talking to her at intervals in tones full of respectful kindness; there seemed no mockery in her voice then, but he could not listen to the words, for Mrs. Mason spoke to him frequently. Miss Grierson was doing her part well, and Andrew said more than usual.

After dinner Jenny gave them a Nocturne of Chopin's, and other pieces, rendered so sympathetically that conversation almost entirely ceased. Bertha followed. Her execution was fully equal to Jenny's, but her style was so unemotional that one needed only to recollect to murmur applause at the end of the brilliant performance.

"I suppose music is, after all, the first of the fine arts," said Mr. Dewey, standing near Helen's chair, with one hand nervously fingering the flowers in a vase upon the mantel.

"You said that to the wrong person, Mr. Dewey," cried Kitty. "Miss Bell doesn't play, she paints."

The young man looked so crestfallen that Helen laughed.

"I am as fond of music as any one," she said; "and the arts are not jealous, they are sisters; each gains from the other's advancement."

"I am very fond of painting," said Kitty, "but I think poetry is really the highest of the arts."

"I believe it is the poets who have exercised the greatest influence over men," said Holden. "See, for instance, what the Hebrew element did for Europe in the dark ages. Historians have hardly begun to acknowledge it, but the Jews were the beacon lights of that night, when the Eastern Empire was broken up; they carried the Promethean fire everywhere."

"They are great musicians," said Jenny.

"Yes, composers and performers both. But they are preëminent in poetry."

"Indeed!" sneered Mr. Dewey.

"Yes," answered Holden earnestly, "we have nothing to be compared with what their poets have given us."

"What poets?" asked Dewey.

"Isaiah, David, and Job. There is no race like the Hebrews for sustained power."

"And yet, Jack," cried Mrs. Barney, "how funny it is, we always think of the Jews as peddlers and old-clothes men."

"Undoubtedly they were masters of their art," said Mr. Dewey answering Holden with a certain gracious condescension.

Mrs. Edgerly laid down her knitting to look at the strange person who was calling these inspired men "masters of their art."

"Art!" she repeated, an accent of reproof mingling with the wonder in her tones. "If they seem to have art, it is because what they say is exactly true."

"Yes, you are right," said Holden after a short silence.

Helen's lips, which had parted for speech, closed at this answer, and Kitty, who had shrunk into herself awaiting some sign of public opinion, and dreading to share the obliquy of being considered old-fashioned, smiled encouragingly upon her aunt, while Mr. Dewey looked down at her with an expression he intended should imply pitying indulgence.

"Our present means of rapid communication, our

railroads, telegraphs, and telephones have done and are doing so much for us," he began, addressing himself to Andrew; "they are making the discoveries of science so wide-spread, that eventually all people must be freed from the servitude of tradition."

"What especial discoveries of science are you thinking of, Mr. Dewey, that seem to you able to undermine our faith?"

There was almost the ring of a challenge in Helen's voice. She respected the results of science as much as did Mr. Dewey, and was far better able to appreciate the devotion of the workers and the benefits derived from their labors. But she drew a line between facts established and speculations which, at best, are only the erratic efforts of men confessedly in a Cretan labyrinth; and she saw that this young man represented a class of minds of light caliber, who believe themselves exponents of advanced thought when they assert as dogmas the theories that their betters have put forth as questions.

"Ah! well," responded Mr. Dewey, "I don't know that I can state it for you precisely in vernacular."

"Don't try," said Andrew; "give it to us in scientific terms; it will be much more impressive."

Mr. Dewey went on, ignoring this interruption, and still speaking to Helen:

"The gist of the matter is," he said, "that the body is composed of chemical elements, and dissolves into them again, and there is the end of it. What we call 'mind' is merely the electric result of the peculiar combinations of these atoms, and those combinations once destroyed can never be combined with the same result again. Facts are hard logic. With ladies it is different, but learned men are always incredulous about the supernatural. It has been so in all ages."

"Ye-es," said Andrew, "that's just it. Take the fifteenth century. It had its great scientific lights. There they sat in their wisdom at Salamanca."

"At Salamanca," cried Kitty, "the very focus of culture!"

"Ye-es. And there these solid men of learning sat in judgment upon the visionary Columbus, and argued against him with scientific accuracy. He had never been to that other hemisphere; if he sailed to the edge of the world, he would drop off into space. They proved that his theory would make men walk on the earth like flies on a ceiling, and that his idea was an absurdity. And they sent him away to learn the laws of nature. They argued well enough, but they left gravitation out of the premises. So their supernatural turned out only a part of nature they didn't know. They theorized as we do when we leave out God to whom the universe gravitates."

"How beautiful the human countenance grows with the light of enthusiasm upon it," thought Holden, "and hers is beyond anything I ever saw. I wish Mason would talk on so forever. What strange inconsistencies in her character—admiration for what is high, and at the same time a determined pursuit of really sordid ends."

"You don't mean, surely," cried Mr. Dewey, "that what you call faith, and all these creeds floating about the world, have done any civilizing for us? Do you really advance that idea?"

"Creeds are narrow," said Holden, "like all 'isms,' not excepting the scientific and liberal. But the civilization that is leading the world, is the service of humanity. Science saves a man's muscles, makes life more comfortable to him, and widens his opportunities. It has been said that Christianity opposes science, but this is not so. The opposition comes from the spirit of ecclesiasticism. The speculations of science began with the ages; Christianity has made it a living power, to open up new lands and homes to peoples who were once too low for hope."

"Yes," said Helen softly, "for humanity became the garment of a king when Christ wrapped it about Himself. Many who deny His authority are following Him to-day, and believing on Him for His works' sake.'"

"And it has brought down the price of ermine astonishingly of late," remarked Andrew.

"I wonder why there never were any painters and sculptors among the Jews," said Kitty, who had been using her eyes during her silence, and was not sorry to turn the conversation to less inspiring themes.

"You remember they were not allowed to practice those arts in the service of their religion," explained Mr. Dewey, "and that is the beginning of the greater part of artistic efforts; it seems to have a stimulating effect upon budding genius," and he glanced at Helen with a patronizing smile.

"How strange they were forbidden," Kitty said.

"No," answered her husband. "The Jews were called to establish a spiritual worship. Their God must not be debased in their eyes to a level with idols. He was the inimitable Source of the ideal and the spiritual."

"At any rate I am glad we are allowed painting and sculpture," said Kitty; "we have never perverted it."

"Before you say that," replied Andrew, "go into the churches all over the Continent, and see people kneeling, and saying their prayers, at the shrines of pictured saints, and wax dolls dressed with gewgaws."

"Just hear, Jack; that's exactly it—'wax dolls,' 'gewgaws,' oh thousands of them ! Only, some have elegant jewelry on, Mr. Mason. They are 'gewgaws' though, sure enough, if you are going to worship them."

"But in spite of all the false uses to which they can be put, the arts are the resources of life," cried Kitty.

Jenny Grierson flushed, and puckered her lips a little, and Mason uttered a quiet laugh.

Holden went home that night carrying with him the recollection of Helen's face lit up with its enthusiasm. As if to make atonement, she had grown cold enough afterward when the discussion was over, but the enthusiasm had been there unmistakably. He still saw before him her eyes as they had shown large and dark with dilated pupils, and clear as if the light of the soul was shining through them. In his fancy he saw this look of hers, until sleep came to him; but he could not believe it—he argued that her beauty and his own imagination must have given something of the expression he had feasted his eyes upon, when she was too absorbed in listening to Mason to be conscious of his gaze.

But had she really been unconscious of it? Or was this only a part of the whole? He had seen expressions of most passionate emotion come over the faces of great actresses when the *rôle* they were playing demanded it. He scorned the suggestion. Yet, he did not drive it away; he knew enough of Helen to admit its possibility.

He interrupted his cogitations to tell himself angrily
that he was a fool, which was perfectly true, but he could
not quite determine whether it was through believing in
her, or not believing.

At last he resolved to keep on the safe side.

But which was that?

CHAPTER VII.

"KITTY," called a voice in the upper hall the next morning, "are you in your room?"

"Yes, come in."

Bertha, with her arm in Jenny Grierson's, stood in the doorway.

"There is a gentleman down-stairs to see you."

Kitty turned to her suddenly, the lace she was folding fluttering in her hands.

"Who is it?"

"I don't know. Here is his card, I took it from Nora, on the stairs. 'Rufus Knight!' I never heard of him."

"What sort of looking person is he? Did either of you see him?"

Kitty's hands were still a little nervous as she arranged one or two things in her room before going down.

"Yes, I did, Aunt Kitty. I confess to peeping over the banisters as he came into the hall. The doors on both sides were open, and I had a good view of him. He is young, and I should say he is rather handsome."

"Don't stay here picking up things, Kitty; run down and find out. Jenny and I are dying of curiosity."

"Do try to want us for something or other while he's there," laughed Jenny.

"Where is Helen, Bertha?"

"I'm sure I don't know. What matter? In her room, probably, sketching as usual. She generally spends the morning at it, and it seems to me she has been worse than ever for the past few days."

"You have noticed that?"

"Yes; I spoke of it to her, and she told me at last that something she had counted upon a great deal this winter had to be given up, and she was obliged to work harder. I suppose something of hers didn't sell, poor girl."

"'Poor girl!'" echoed Kitty indignantly, then added, with a sudden change of tone into contemptuous indifference, "She'll do well enough."

"Don't be a goose, Bertha," she said a moment afterward. "It was not selling any picture that she had so counted upon this winter. She has failed in an attempt much more important than that."

"O Aunt Kitty," cried Jenny, catching her meaning, "I can't think she tried that; it doesn't seem like her. I believe in Helen."

Kitty turned and came a step nearer Jenny with sudden fire and wildness in her eyes, as if the slightest opposition here roused a tumult of feeling that threatened to throw her mind off its balance.

Jenny drew back in silent wonder; and in an instant Kitty was her smiling self again.

Her niece thought this thing over secretly a good many times. But she hoped never to say anything to bring back that look; and, then, perhaps she did not consider it very necessary that Helen should succeed, did she really have any such scheme as Mrs. Mason insinuated.

At last Kitty went down-stairs. The stranger was looking over a book of engravings on the table. He bowed suavely to the lady, and handed her a folded paper which he informed her was a letter of introduction from her dear friends, the Delvilles. He smiled at her with amused scrutiny as he did so, and sinking into Andrew's favorite chair, sat slapping his right glove gently on his knee with a well-kept white hand, and waiting until Mrs. Mason should look up at him again.

She did not do it at once. Her face had flushed deeply on reading the paper; but now this color gave way to an excited pallor. She met his gaze, and said,

"This is all very satisfactory, Mr. Knight. I am happy to see you. I am sure you were wise to come."

"You can't dub a thing wisdom, Mrs. Mason, until it's grown up. Sometimes wise appearing children turn out fools, after all."

"Chance enough to prove this one," said Kitty with a shiver. "Meanwhile, we will try to make Lowton pleasant to you."

Not long afterward she called the young ladies, to present the stranger to them.

Jenny and Bertha came without delay; but Helen begged that Mrs. Mason would excuse her that morning, for she was very busy upon work that must be sent off the next day.

Kitty frowned, and glanced at her visitor.

"That is the young lady guest you mentioned just now as the artist?" he inquired. "I am sorry not to see her; but genius is erratic, and I have a presentiment we shall make acquaintance later. I am too well entertained to be unhappy over her non-appearance this morning."

His sweeping bow included all the ladies with a self-possession Mr. Dewey would have envied. Kitty saw his eyes rest upon Bertha with smiling curiosity, and then turn to Jenny.

Kitty was very cordial, and told him they should hope to see a great deal of him while he was in Lowton, asking how long he intended to remain here.

Mr. Knight could not tell, it would depend upon circumstances; and he took his leave.

"We must try to make it pleasant for this stranger," she said when he had gone, adding that he was introduced to her by people she should be sorry to displease.

"Who are they?" asked Bertha. "Friends of yours?"

"Yes," said Kitty after a slight hesitation.

"Who?"

"Nobody you know."

"How odd! I thought I knew who all your friends were, even if I didn't know them myself. What's the name of the people?"

"I declare, Bertha, I should think you were Mrs. Barney. 'What is their name?' 'Where do they live?' 'How old are they?' next. What are you making such a wonderment out of nothing for? I shall not tell you, there!—to teach you better. And there is his letter of introduction gone into the fire, to reward your curiosity.

Bertha sprang forward to snatch it off the blazing log, but Kitty and the flames were too quick for her; the one held back her hand an instant, and the other caught the paper and whisked it up the chimney in a flash and down upon the hearth in a roll of quivering ashes. Not a blackened scrap was left on which a word could be deciphered, and Kitty left the room with a laugh, and a reminder that she had invited Mr. Knight to look in upon them in the evening, when they would be all together and he might find others at the house whom he would enjoy meeting.

"It seems to me he could scarcely happen upon an evening when somebody wouldn't be here," said Jenny, "unless it's very bad weather."

Kitty looked beaming.

"We do make it pleasant for people."

"I suppose she thinks it is all her doing," muttered Bertha as her cousin walked out of hearing: "but we did have company once in a while before she came. I'll tell you what, Jenny, you may say it to her if you like, I am going to find out who introduced Mr. Knight. I don't care a farthing to know, but she shall not balk me. I will ask him himself, if I can't get at it any other way. But probably Andrew will know."

"Don't make any trouble, Bertha."

Bertha looked at her in surprise.

"Why, Jenny, you don't mean she won't tell him all about it? What is the matter? Kitty was so queer!"

"I think she was only annoyed because you would question her when she was out of sorts."

"What is she 'out of sorts' about?"

"Nothing, that I know of. But don't you remember the old saying, that a person gets out of bed in the morning wrong foot foremost, and goes about ill-suited all day."

"Kitty's done that a good many times lately, then. She's ill-natured enough when we're alone; she's as sweet as sugar candy to outsiders."

"Sometimes people are troubled and can't say anything about it, and it shows in this way. I thought you got on nicely together generally."

"Yes, we do. Kit is very good, of course, and people all like her ever so much. I was only provoked for the minute."

"Miss Piqued Curiosity?" laughed Jenny.

Bertha laughed, too, and the slight annoyance was over; but it served to make her remember that there was something odd in the way Mr. Knight had been introduced to them. It did not prejudice her against him, however, it only roused her interest.

He came that evening and found all the family. He seemed especially pleased with Mason, and talked with him for some time, until, seeing a place vacant beside Miss Bell, he crossed the room and played the agreeable to her; with good effect, it seemed, for Helen talked and laughed gayly; and once he caught one of her sunny smiles which impressed him a good deal.

In a short time Knight was quite at home in Mrs. Mason's family circle. He paid Helen marked attention; and, after the insinuation of the other morning, both Jenny and Bertha understood why Kitty appeared so well satisfied with this.

But there was something strange about her; she seemed thoroughly at rest very seldom, and was best pleased when Mr. Knight was talking with Helen, or gone walking or driving with the young ladies. She always contrived, if possible, to have Helen with him.

About this time she changed her place at table. When Bertha wonderingly demanded the reason, she explained that the glare from the opposite window was unpleasant.

"How strange you never minded that before," her aunt said.

Kitty laughed, and answered that she had just waked up to it, and the thing was forgotten.

Now she sat beside Helen.

A week after this she came down-stairs one morning and found Jenny seated at the piano, her hands fallen on the keys, her face upturned, with a smile and two charming little dimples, to some one beside her who had been picking out another piece of music and was placing it before her, bending down as he did so to look into the bright, blue eyes.

"Why, Jenny," she exclaimed, "I thought you had gone to drive with your uncle!"

"No; he took Helen instead, because there was a

view he wanted to show her while the sleighing was good enough to drive to the very top of the hill. I'm doing what you asked us all, Aunt Kitty—trying to make it pleasant to Mr. Knight. I told him you would be down very soon."

"Yes, I was finishing my mending."

"I know you never like to be disturbed until it's done," said Jenny. "Mr. Knight, will you sing one verse of that song over again? I want my aunt to hear your voice."

"With great pleasure, if Miss Grierson will help me through it."

Kitty watched her niece and the stranger, but she saw only a common interest in music, and an expression of politeness in each face. Mr. Knight was a very good-looking young man, somewhat under medium height, but with a slight, well-proportioned figure. He was full of keen observation, and, as Kitty heard that morning, he had a rich voice. When he was discussed, Bertha frankly declared him "elegant," and Jenny smiled in a demure silence that might mean endorsement or otherwise. Helen, when questioned, answered with cool indefiniteness, until, as he had left the house one evening, Kitty pressed her for her opinion.

"Yes, he is pleasant," she said in answer, "but he overdoes it a little. His manners are very fine, but he hasn't grown accustomed to them, and he and they don't quite harmonize. I shouldn't have said this, Mrs. Mason, if you had not insisted upon my speaking."

Kitty looked blank for a moment, and very pale.

Nobody agreed with Helen, however, unless Andrew's sleepy smile were to be so interpreted.

"You're altogether too fastidious, Miss Helen," he said. "You'll never get on well in the world by that means."

Kitty affirmed to the others that Helen had been rude because the gentleman was her friend.

"Nonsense, my dear," said Mrs. Edgerly; "Helen is not that kind of girl."

"You know a great deal about her, don't you, Aunt Bertha?"

"Yes, I do; I know the blood that runs in her veins; and, generally, that's as much information as you need about any body."

"Perhaps—generally."

"Kitty Mason, what do you mean?"

Kitty gave no other answer than a significant smile.

"I insist upon your telling me at once; the girl is under my roof, and I won't have her maligned. If you've anything to say that I don't see, and ought to be told, say it, by all means; but I won't have slurs and insinuations made behind people's backs. Don't you know the meanness of them? And almost always," continued the old lady growing angry, "it's because a person is afraid to be above board."

"I'm not afraid of anything," said Kitty, "but—"

"'But'—what is it? Have you anything to say against Helen? If you have, say it out. She is under my protection, and I say I won't have spiteful insinuations about her."

"Much good your protection will do her, you will see," muttered Kitty, as she swept out of the room.

The next time Mr. Knight called, Bertha forgot she had not sent word to Mrs. Mason of his being there, and Kitty found the two in most friendly colloquy over a set of illustrations of Shakespeare. It reassured her. She resolved not to misunderstand him in future, for she saw that she might trust him with perfect safety.

The winter was wearing away; it was March, and the weather was more mild than March weather usually is. Several entertainments, though on a smaller scale, had followed Holden's party, and Kitty and Bertha were now anxiously debating what they could offer which should be better than all that had preceded it, not only in brilliancy, but in originality of invention.

"Why not give a fancy dress ball?" suggested Mrs. Edgerly, as they sat talking around the breakfast-table one morning, arranging plans for the day, as is the custom when the weightier subject of viands has been discussed.

But Mrs. Mason demurred. There had been one in Lowton only last winter.

The flash of pleasure which had come into Helen's face at Mrs. Edgerly's words died out.

"No matter for that," said Andrew, "it is good enough to repeat. `There is one recommendation about a thing of this kind—it sets everybody's wits to work, and everybody does something to help on its success. The more practice one has, the better one does it. You provide the rooms and the supper, but the 'feast of reason, flow of soul,' and all that, the guests bring with them. It's the right way. People always like best the things they have to work hardest for," he added smiling mischievously, as he settled himself in the most comfortable attitude his chair permitted. "A fancy dress ball, by all means, Kitty. Aunt Bertha and I will put our veto on everything else."

Mrs. Mason was pleased to see her husband so much interested, and yielded the point with a good grace. Bertha had already been half inclined to accept the suggestion.

Helen's eager look had not been Mason's only reason for his decision. "Although on pleasure" he "was bent," he "had a frugal mind." He had not been satisfied with the aspect of affairs lately. He had a genuine liking for Helen Bell, and at one time had believed that her winter in Lowton would be the means of opening up a happy life to her. But there was a hitch somewhere.

He leisurely sipped his second cup of coffee this morning, and meditated upon the fact that one could never tell just when the shining hours of fate would come, and that it was best to be always prepared to take advantage of everything.

Afterward Kitty saw an excellent reason for approving of this plan. She talked the party over with Mr. Knight, who was, of course, to have an invitation.

But Bertha still maintained that something was the matter with Kitty, she was so queer, and had taken to gliding about in all sorts of places, shod with silence, and picking up all kinds of trash, and trying to make out what it was, when it was just nothing. More than once, too, she had seen her throw a look of mysterious meaning at Knight; what the meaning was she could not pretend to say, but there was something.

Andrew also thought there was something, but as yet it was beyond him, too.

Meanwhile, preparations for the party went on; everybody was by turns consulting everybody else in whispers, a state of things Mr. Knight seemed to enjoy immensely.

Kitty thought he appeared to choose Helen for his especial confidant; but Helen kept her own counsel with a persistence that made Kitty inwardly furious. Even she could not find out whom the girl was going to personate.

CHAPTER VIII.

ON the night of the ball, figures muffled in their wraps ran laughing up Mrs. Edgerly's broad stairs, and issuing from the dressing-rooms in small detachments, a brilliant assembly gradually filled the drawing-rooms.

Mrs. Edgerly, standing to receive her guests, opened her mild eyes in amazement at some of the grotesque magnificence that shone upon her.

"And what shall I call you?" she asked one elaborate personage when the announcement of several names together had bewildered her.

"Me, madam?" responded a high-pitched voice belonging to a tall, ancient looking figure plentifully bedizened with silver lace, while a cocked hat was held ostentatiously in his hand, and, to Mrs. Edgerly's great surprise, the voice broke into music, and sang:

"Stick close to your desks and never go to sea,
And you all may be rulers of the queen's navie."

"Not of mine," cried a stern voice, and as if to make the burlesque still more absurd, Queen Elizabeth came up at this moment, and confronted the Lord High Admiral with a mien of royal displeasure, while something too much like a snicker marred the dignity of her companion, the courtly Leicester.

"What a convention of anachronisms," laughed Maria Theresa to Andrew, as leaning on the arm of her arch-enemy, the great Frederick, she looked about her leisurely.

"Ye-es, ye-es," said Mason, "and everybody seems to be in the spirit of the part to-night," and he glanced an amused comment at the couple before him.

"The Seven Years' War has ended," returned Frederick; "we have just signed the Peace of Hubertsburg; this is perfectly in keeping."

"I suppose Mrs. Mason is in costume?" said the empress.

"Your Imperial Majesty is right."

"Give my 'Imperial Majesty' a hint as to whom she is to-night—one little hint."

But Andrew answered that so warlike a sovereign must know how imperative it was that a soldier should never disobey orders; and when she turned to Mrs. Edgerly, that lady assured her she had promised not to say one word.

"There are anachronisms here indeed, since my will has no power," sighed the empress, moving slowly away.

Miranda cordially welcomed Julius Cæsar, whom she declared to be not only a cotemporary, but also in the same set with herself.

Question and repartee, jest and laughter, were heard on all sides. Gradually, the company fell into groups and couples, and a fire of cross-questionings began, over which now and then rang a triumphant laugh, as through the disguise of some historical character, or one well known in the world of fiction, looked the eyes of an intimate friend, or perhaps of one's next door neighbor.

But a greater number of the disguises proved impenetrable until the unmasking came.

Urania was standing well out in the room, watching some excellent personation going on near her. She thought she recognized Julius Cæsar, and so she ought, having once had, no doubt, great interest in the consultations of the astrologers concerning his star.

She was dressed in blue silk covered with stars, over which was thrown a dress of black lace. She wore a gold globe suspended from one bracelet, and from the other a smaller globe of silver with circles and meridians on it to represent the earth, while a miniature transit telescope, a circle, and other astronomical instruments in gold hung at her side. Judging from appearances, she made an excellent muse. But some one passing said to her hastily, in a whisper,

"Don't talk much, or you'll betray yourself."

"Never fear," was the answer, as Urania went forward at once, and in a moment her voice was heard in the group she had been watching.

Uncle Sam stepped out of one of Nast's sketches, and walked across the room. He came up to Urania, and stood surveying her with approbation.

"So you're the Muse of Astronomy?" he asked, taking out a huge jack-knife and beginning upon a piece of willow twig with which he had provided himself. "What a mighty lot you must know!"

"Of course," said Urania.

"Nice big place, this o' mine, to study the stars in; more room 'n you had when you lived over 'n that speck of a Greece."

"I thought I lived on the top of Mount Oly— Parnassus."

"Ye-es. Mighty blowy kind of a spot, and not much of a height after you got up there, though it looks a tough climb enough when you're at the foot of it."

"And proves much too tough for most of us," remarked a gray domino standing near.

"Guess you're 'bout right there, stranger."

As the gray domino moved away, he released himself from the group about him and followed.

"How well he does it!" said Urania.

"Who is he? Give us some clew," asked a wood-nymph clad in brown, on which were sewed quantities of leaves and tiny sprays of green.

The Muse declared she could not, in a manner which implied knowledge that she chose not to reveal, the air she meant to assume.

Uncle Sam overtook and walked beside the gray domino.

He entered into conversation with its wearer, his eyes stealthily attentive to every gesture of his companion as he questioned in excellent vernacular, and busied himself polishing his whistle, deftly catching the minute shavings in his palm, and throwing them into the fire as he passed.

After a time he and the domino parted by mutual consent, and he found himself much interested in an Italian countess wearing a corn-colored dress richly trimmed with black.

As this lady turned from him, a voice in his ear said, with soft distinctness,

"Fish, art thou in thy duty?"

And Beatrice—the Beatrice that made Benedict an example, or a warning, to all succeeding bachelors—

stood before him. It was she who had advised Urania not to talk overmuch.

"Have you learned yet?" she asked.

"No, I can't be quite sure," he answered without his nasal tone.

"You must judge by the voice and, I suspect, by the color. But remember, I am not sure of the last."

"I wish you were."

"So do I. But never mind, you are safe any time now, and the sooner the better, I think."

"Trust to me, fair Beatrice," as Henry the Fourth accosted him.

Beatrice instantly began a running fire of raillery and repartee upon the new-comer, in which amusement both quite forgot the practical gentleman beside them, and wandered off together, looking back when at the end of the room, to find that Uncle Sam had disappeared among his many admirers.

Sir Walter Raleigh stood talking to Mason. On the white satin lining of the cloak he carried over his arm, was painted a distinct muddy splash.

"She has puzzled us all," said Andrew aside. "Kitty has been asking me, but I couldn't tell her. If you could catch sight of a gold bracelet with a large topaz pendent by a chain, you might be quite sure, for I remember that perfectly."

"So do I."

"But it is not likely you will find any such thing; it is too marked."

"We're a droll looking set, though," cried a voice to Mrs. Edgerly. "Do you know, I couldn't for my life make Jack tell me what he was going to be? Oh, dear, he was right to be sure, for I've betrayed myself already, and I dare say I should have betrayed him in no time. But don't say, my dear, who Dame Fortune is."

Sir Walter Raleigh, with a courtly bow, offered Dame Fortune his arm across the room. She accepted it, being utterly at a loss to find Jack. The stranger condoled with her, and told her to take her perplexities as part of the joke.

"I am greatly at a loss myself to find some one I want," he said.

"I'm so sorry. It's not the person you came with, is it?"

"Oh, no; I recognize her easily enough."

"I wonder," asked Dame Fortune, "if you know which is Miss Bell? I would like to meet her very much."

"I do not, but since success must always accompany you, you will surely find her."

The lady laughed and wished, under her breath, that Jack could hear that.

The stranger saw Madame Fortune comfortably settled, and sauntered away.

He moved about the rooms with an air of scrutiny which he did not lose even when talking with the distinguished personages that accosted him; and he studied with so special an attention the figures of the ladies whose robes shone with a golden gleam, that one might really have accused him of a preference for the hue of the precious metal. But he seemed satisfied with none, nor did a glimpse of any bracelet like the one Andrew had described to him reward his search.

Urania intercepted and detained him for some time.

As he left her he caught sight, in a corner, of a little lady sitting apart in pensive attitude, looking as if she were meditating a poem. When Sir Walter approached her with an air of polite deference, she turned her uplifted face to him, and said with a burst of irrepressible feeling,

"I have such a passion for the truth. I dote upon it so that I go away into solitude, lest some of the petty wickednesses about me should jar upon my refinement. Sit here, opposite me, before the firelight, and tell me, as I fall musing, how beautiful I am. Philip told me so, and I know he speaks the truth always—to Mercy Philbrick."

"How dare you!" cried Sir Walter, laughing heartily. "How dare you," he repeated, "venture to jest at that skillful presentation of sentimental womanhood with a strong graft of Boston culture?" And he seated himself beside Mercy.

"Take care," she cried, "your cloak is brushing my exquisite basket of flowers. They are my trump card, I can't have anything happen to them."

"Trump card, indeed! That's entirely out of keeping, Madam Mercy. It sounds not unlike Miss ——"

With a little cry of terror the figure darted away from him. He rose and sauntered on again.

The scene was really beautiful, the masquerading being mostly of the splendid rather than the grotesque character, and Sir Walter enjoyed it with that keen relish for beauty which always distinguished him. As he stood half in reverie, Julius Cæsar came up, walking beside the gray domino.

"Pretty fair," he pronounced, scanning the courtier's rich dress with a mild admiration well spiced with criticism; "but I doubt whether that is the exact cut of the Elizabethan boot."

"Julius Cæsar is naturally versed in antiquities," laughed the gray domino; "but if one might venture to criticise his costume, that toga—"

But this Cæsar evidently resembled his illustrious prototype in aversion to criticism. He turned hastily to Sir Walter, and asked in a sibilant undertone,

"Have you found out anybody here? Do you know what Miss Bell is to-night?"

"No," said Sir Walter in an indifferent manner. "I can tell scarcely any one," he added.

"You mean the lady visiting here this winter, the one who paints?" asked the gray domino. "When I feel inclined to hunt her up, I shall look for a figure in a dark-brown dress, seated in artistic pose before a red curtain. Look, yonder is the curtain, but the artist does not seem to have got there yet."

"Not a bad suggestion," said Julius; "I'll bear it in mind."

"Not a bad suggestion," echoed Sir Walter Raleigh's thoughts, but he took care not to speak them; "I'll bear it in mind, too. I thank you, my unconscious gray domino."

Cæsar moved away, doubtless intent upon his new laws for the administration of the world, and Sir Walter addressed the gray domino.

"Fair unknown," he said with the florid courtesy of his time, "it is probable that in the far-off country in which each sometimes condescends to enact a *rôle*, we are not utter strangers, and let us take advantage of to-night's mysterious environments to suppose ourselves friends."

"Take the benefit of the doubt," said the lady. "And when the unmasking comes?"

"Then, may we not be friends?" was the answer, in a tone and with a gesture worthy of Sir Walter Raleigh.

The gray domino laughed, but her merriment seemed to have some hidden source deeper than the other's excellent acting. She laid her hand on his arm, however, and the two moved slowly through the rooms. Queen Elizabeth gave a most gracious nod to Raleigh, and, as was her way, shot a keen glance at his companion. But, strangely enough, both he and the gray domino felt no solicitude as to what her royal judgment might be.

"Only look at this a moment," he said stopping before the portrait of a beautiful woman that hung in the hall; "how wonderfully that bright, high gaslight brings out the coloring! It is a fine face, too."

"Look at it more closely, and I think you will change your mind. I remember, when I was a child, visiting once a lady I thought very fine-looking, and even beautiful, the first day I saw her; but before I had been with her a week, the face had lost all its strength to me, and the beauty faded out with it. This face of the portrait, too, has a superficial likeness of strength, but look carefully at the mouth, weak in spite of its graceful lines and its ripeness; and the curves of the forehead are too contracted for nobleness of thought."

"You are skillful in reading character; but see the beauty of the countenance!"

The gray domino turned to Sir Walter.

"The utmost simplicity of a child is beautiful in its appealingness," she said. "A child-like face, even in a woman, has always a grace and charm of its own, although we may see its want of strength; but assumption never pleases. Don't you see that face is haughty, and shallow, as haughtiness usually is? I like this one better."

She moved on a few steps as she spoke, and then stood looking at the portrait of a girl who might have been twenty. She wore a riding habit of dark green, and a falcon was perched upon her wrist. There was a stern sadness in the eyes that caught the gazer's attention at once, and the features were rather too strongly marked for beauty; but the curving lips were full of tenderness, and the line of the well-closed mouth showed power both in action and endurance.

"It grows upon you," said the gray domino; "here is a girl younger, very likely, than she looks; yet a woman with a history. She has wealth enough, probably, but in some way circumstances are against her. Yet there is that in her soul stronger than circumstances; she may never be a happy, but she must always be a noble, woman, for loyalty is written on her face. She is the stuff heroines are made of. Now turn back and look at the other portrait again, and you will see."

"I do see."

But it was not merely the contrast between the two portraits that he perceived; he had suspected the gray domino, he now said to himself he was sure he recognized her, and he was thinking more of her words than of their object. He stealthily measured her height with his eyes, and noted every motion.

"Yes, after all, it is the expression which makes a face," he added, "although I suppose artists prize its coloring extremely."

"I think they ought. But let me tell you a secret, it may be possible you have not found it out. Expression has a coloring of its own, the wonderful shadow tints."

She stopped suddenly, as if studying what she had said, then added in explanation,

"I see there must be a great fascination to artists in color, but I should think shadows would have even more. If I were an artist, I would choose, if I could, the power of using shadows with some touch of nature's marvellous effects, rather than that of excelling Titian in coloring. Color is certainly very beautiful, but the lights and shadows in a face are the story of a life. The artist who seizes upon these things is dealing in tints subtler than flesh—he is painting a soul."

"Then, you think it is only want of ability to read

what is written on a face that makes us ever deceived? You believe a man's face cannot be a barrier for him to successfully hide his habitual thoughts behind.

"I don't think it can; for if every muscle were kept under perpetual control, as it would have to be to show no traces of its play when one had felt any strong emotion, even then there would not be perfect security. There are the eyes—evil dulls them, and holiness kindles their depths."

"Pain dulls them too, or even overuse. And as to brilliancy—how often we see that, where the light is anything but sunshine!"

The gray domino shook her head.

"That is a different dullness," she answered; "and a very different brightness. In a man or woman devoted to self-seeking, or any pettiness, I don't say *I* could find this in the face, but I do say it is to be found there."

"You believe in first impressions, then?"

"Yes, in spite of the lady I spoke of, and this portrait—though the last comes a good deal from certain shadows not being painted in the depth which the original must have had. It is almost always the case that our first look at a face catches something of its real meaning. Our eyes are widest open then, afterward we may be blinded by some agreeable quality, or an atmosphere of flattery; we come to weighing probabilities, and there is no balance in the world so unreliable. Trust your intuitions, Sir Walter. Your El Dorado has been more than realized in this new world."

Her listener stood motionless an instant, evidently impressed. He felt sure his own disguise was complete; he saw that the gray domino was equally sure of herself, for her words had the freedom of impersonality, as well as the force of truth.

"You must be right," he said. "I am sure you are."

"When I have gone away from my intuitions at any time," she answered, "I have been forced to come back to them again."

"But every one may not have intuitions."

"I should be sorry for the person who is without them," she answered; "they are a picket guard."

Sir Walter did not seem to care about talking, save as a means of drawing out his companion. Her voice had kept its lowness and disguised accents—except that its undertone of enthusiasm came to him like a remembrance—but she seemed to have flung off a disguise, instead of having put one on, and to be uttering her thoughts more in joy at her liberty to speak them than for the sake of her hearer. She was feeling herself the unknown, and had evidently forgotten that later she must unmask. He held his breath, lest his recollection of this should be in some way wafted to her.

She, too, spoke less as they walked on. When a subject was broached each seemed to understand with few words what the other wished to say, and as her hand lay lightly on his arm, Raleigh could not of his own accord spare an instant's thought from the delicious consciousness of life that thrilled through him.

Once an impatient inward sneer at his credulity jarred upon his peace; it told him he did not really know this lady, and he did know, if he chose to use his reason, that she must be quite another person from the one his fancy willed to have her.

But his mood and the gray domino together were too much for him. She held him by an irresistible attraction. Whether in this he were fickle, or, as he dared to believe, faithful to those first intuitions she had unconsciously turned him back upon, this unknown lady was in some way very near to him. He would find who she was; this discovery was inevitable, and then—and then— what?

"My kind Sir Walter, I've found you again," said a well-known, undisguisable voice.

It was for the merest instant, and very slightly, but he was sure the fingers upon his arm had tightened their hold at those tones.

"Pray introduce me to this lady," continued the new-comer.

"I beg you will do so without delay," cried the gray domino, "there's nothing I desire so much as an intimate acquaintance with gracious Dame Fortune."

"I'll give both of you anything you ask, to the utmost extent of my power, if you will only tell me some of these people. I never did like mysteries—only my own, Jack would put it, if he were here. I think he's been very provoking and unkind to his poor, old—Goodness! there it is again. I really am possessed to tell everything."

The gray domino laughed.

"That's a good part of the fun," she said, "to see people forget themselves."

"Yes, I dare say. But I can't find any body else that will do it but me, that's what provokes me so. If my nephew only had told me—well!"

She stopped in despair.

"You were speaking of your nephew," suggested Raleigh. "May I ask who he is?"

"Why, no, indeed!" with an indignant gasp. "How can you ask me to tell you who Jack is? unless," she added in a sudden after-thought, "we exchange confidences. 'A fair exchange is no robbery,' you know. Will you?"

Another ripple of soft laughter from the gray domino.

"It would not be a 'fair exchange,'" she said in a tone the lady was not fortunate enough to catch. But Raleigh heard the words with delight. This was certainly some one who recognized Fortune.

"Did you hear Uncle Sam's last?" cried Urania coming up to them with a laugh that could belong only to Bertha Edgerly.

"No, tell us, do—and I, Dame Fortune, will befriend you. There! the first rhyme I ever made."

"He was boasting that he had outdone all the wonders of the children's fairy books," said the Muse. "'What's the last thing out?' Andrew asked him. 'The seven-league boots,'" he shouted like a flash. He meant the bicycle. But he went on to say he would have nothing to do with putting that on the world. Somebody asked him why not, and he said he was a woman's rights advocate, and wouldn't help the men to get hold of anything the ladies couldn't have a 'hand in,' or a foot on. Then he threw back his head and laughed, and said he was going to retire into private life and study how to be up with the mother country. He is sitting down to rest somewhere, I believe; he must need it."

Half an hour before supper, just at the time she had planned, Helen Bell slipped quietly out of the rooms and up to her own chamber. As she opened the door, a sound of movement surprised her, and to her amazement Uncle Sam came forward, saying he had gone up into the dressing-room to rest a few moments, for he had talked himself hoarse, but he saw now that he must have mistaken the room.

"Yes," said Helen, "the gentlemen's dressing-room is the next door on the right."

He bowed an apology for his mistake, and went away.

Helen looked after him with a frown. She felt, without being able to give any reason for it, that he had not mistaken the door.

But she put away instantly the swift suspicion of some sinister design that swept through her. Perhaps, after all, he had really mistaken the room, as he said; or, at the worst, this curiosity which he had indulged so freely in his assumed character was a real trait. He could not often have so good an opportunity of gratifying it, and she could not tell how widely he had been exploring. Her uneasy sense of danger was ridiculous.

Yet she was uncomfortable; she could not be fully satisfied with this explanation. She had felt, with Bertha, for days, that something was really the matter, though it was not easy to see how she could be concerned in it. Surely, now, Kitty could have no anxiety on Mr. Holden's account.

Helen would be sure to notice at supper who Uncle Sam was.

Sir Walter Raleigh saw a figure he had not observed before among the guests—a tall figure, her dark hair knotted at the back, wearing a simple black dress that did not quite hide her graceful ankles. But the most marked features in her costume, was a vest and sleeves of some silver-threaded material. Its effect was that of light steel armor. She held a distaff with scornful indifference, but her hand lay lovingly upon the hilt of a sword at her side.

"'Joan of Arc, a light of ancient France,'" he quoted. "Joan of Arc in her prison, with the fatal armor on, in which she had made her life glorious."

Then he turned away, glancing incuriously at several other yet unnoticed costumes as they passed him. For he had lost the gray domino.

He could not imagine where she was. He thought she must be eluding him somewhere, and she could do it easily, for every time he started in search, resolved to make the whole circuit of the floor at once, and so be sure to find her, somebody stopped him, to ask a question, to request a favor, to retail some bright speech just heard. People were beginning to long for their lost identities, and he could easily have discovered a number of them, had he tried. But he wanted to discover only the gray domino, for he knew that she would not speak before the time came, and he must be beside her at the unmasking, or she might be hidden from him by the crowd of others, and slip away before he could identify her.

But though he must certainly do this, it was difficult to say how it could be accomplished, when his former companion was nowhere to be found.

He resolved to be escort to the self-styled Dame Fortune, longing to win a smile from the veritable lady herself.

The consequence was that when at the signal every mask was lifted, a shrill cry of,

"Jack! Jack! I might have known; he was just saucy enough for you," drew all eyes toward the illustrious Knight of the Cloak at Mrs. Barney's side.

Where was the gray domino?

Nowhere to be seen.

She was not the person he had thought her, for Helen Bell was looking out with grave eyes from the face above the corselet of Joan of Arc. She was watching to see who Uncle Sam would prove to be, nor was she the only inquirer for that amusing gentleman.

He had disappeared. Nobody bearing the least resemblance to him could be found at the table, or in any of the rooms. There was a murmur of general disappointment, for his cleverness had piqued everybody's curiosity.

"Where is he?" called one and another.

"Here is an extra black domino," declared a lady. "I'm sure I counted only five before."

But it was promptly decided by general assent, that one could not be sure of a thing like this, for dominos, gliding about in all directions, were impossible to count. They disappeared and reappeared like strands in a braid; and all doubt as to this matter was settled when the sixth black figure displayed the dignified countenance of Mr. Knight, and discoursed in the choicest language, for not a domino there could have acted the part of Uncle Sam.

Mrs. Mason, appealed to, at last explained that he had begged her to excuse him, for he had letters to write which must go by the foreign mail the next morning. When asked to tell who he was, she laughed as teasingly as Beatrice herself could have done, and reminded her guests that she was bound by the children's pledge—"honor bright."

When Mr. Holden, making his way to Helen, complimented her excellent conception of her part, she smiled as she thanked him, and spoke of how well he had brought out Sir Walter, even to his cloak.

"You saw me, then?" he asked.

"Oh, yes, several times."

"I did not see Joan of Arc until a very little while ago; I think it was strange."

"Did you expect to see everybody at once in an assembly where each person you looked at held you with the spell of an incognito?"

"Can you tell me anything of the gray domino?"

"The gray domino! Was there only one?"

"I saw only one. There is none now."

As he spoke Helen glanced about her.

"I see there is none," she answered. "It may have followed Uncle Sam's example."

As she said this she turned her head by a sudden impulse, and met the eyes of Mr. Knight, who was standing near. He had overheard the conversation.

When she again spoke to Holden, there was a flush of deepening embarrassment upon her face. Jack thought her proposal to move further down the table, was because she did not want him to talk with Knight, and he asked no more questions about the gray domino.

But possibly he no longer doubted who that mysterious lady was.

CHAPTER IX

"MY aunt will be in very soon," said Jenny Grierson, as she yielded her hand to Knight's firm clasp, and permitted him to hold it in his own while he led her to a chair.

"I hope *not* 'very soon,'" he said. "I am quite content to wait for her a long time; indeed I am happy, as you must know, Miss Grierson, whenever you are so good as to take her place."

Jenny made no answer; she blushed a little, and fingered her cuffs nervously.

"That is, I mean to come in her stead," he went on. "You have a place of your own, a first place."

Jenny's blush grew more pronounced.

"Have you seen the last number of 'Scribner'?" she said, taking it from the table, and busying herself with turning the leaves. "I think our best magazines will stand comparison with those of any nation."

"Uncle Sam should be here."

"Isn't he?" she asked, looking at him archly.

"No—that is—well—really, Miss Jenny, you must do me a favor. Don't mention that suspicion to any one."

"Why not, now it is all over? I should think you would like to have people know it was you who did so splendidly."

"Oh, no. That is, I'm diffident—in short, Miss Jenny, you have promised, I believe."

"No, Mr. Knight, I have not done any such thing."

"You will, then, certainly!"

"Promise not to tell what I only suspect! Suspicion is a gaseous sort of thing, it always escapes. But you were Uncle Sam?"

"What makes you even think so?"

"Because—" but Jenny came to a sudden halt; the question seemed all at once very difficult to answer. Her companion dropped his eyes from her face—"because," she finished hurriedly, "he said something that showed he knew me, and I thought it must be you."

Indiscreet Mr. Knight, to have let the temptation to say a tender word to this girl overcome his prudence. How he would be laughed at in certain quarters, if the thing were known, and reproved, too!

But he did not intend it should be known. He had not for his own undoing, surely, trusted himself to the tender mercies of the most honest and beautiful blue eyes he ever saw. Whatever happened, he could not deny last night's speech.

"If I should make your 'gaseous suspicion,' as you call it, Miss Jenny, into the solid of a fact, would you keep it secret for me? But, stop—don't answer that. I *was* Uncle Sam; now I have thrown myself upon your honor, so you can't tell."

"No, I cannot now," answered the girl well pleased.

Knight was still angry with himself. If Helen Bell should speak! But he had his answer ready. Yet he had forfeited his position of perfect security, and the thought would have disturbed him still more, if it had been a less charming little hand which pulled him down from it.

"I don't see why it is not right to tell," repeated Jenny, "though of course I won't."

Knight leaned forward in his chair and looked into the questioner's eyes as well as she would let him.

"Can't you trust me for even a little while? I wish you would—" he broke off suddenly. "Sometime I will tell you all," he said; "it may be very soon, but I cannot now. You will forgive me, and wait?"

"Certainly," said the girl. "I never beg anybody's confidence."

"Anybody's?"

"Oh, you're here, Jenny," cried Bertha pushing the

door open hastily. "I've been looking for you everywhere."

"Yes," said Miss Grierson, "and won't you help me to entertain Mr. Knight until Aunt Kitty comes home?"

"She has just driven up to the door. I hear her coming along the hall. I'll run, or she will want me to carry her wraps upstairs, not to keep Mr. Knight waiting."

"I will take them," said Jenny, rising that she might meet Mrs. Mason at the door. "Good morning, Mr. Knight, if I do not see you again."

So Jenny Grierson, too, became aware of a mystery; she had no idea of its being a very grave one, and she said nothing about it, regarding silence as part of her promise. But she did not any longer laugh at Bertha, and she began to take note of trifles not thought of before. She recollected that Kitty always sat beside Helen at table now, and she looked at this change by the light of her newly gained consciousness, to decide if it were a mere whim, or had any connection with the secret that she found as fascinating as secrets usually are. Whatever it was, Mrs. Mason knew it.

Jenny scorned to pry, but she did not see why she need shut her eyes. She opened them a little wider, therefore, and saw, or thought she saw, that her aunt watched Helen furtively a great deal. At table she was very attentive to her, always insisting, though quietly, that Helen should have a dish offered to her before she helped herself from it. It seemed to Jenny an unnecessary formality to make it so much a matter of etiquette; but there was no part of the mystery in this, her aunt was compelling herself to be very courteous to Helen for the simple reason that she was not fond of her.

Jenny found nothing to gratify her curiosity, which before long died a natural death, and all the sooner because her mind was full of another subject. Her thoughts were turned upon the solution of quite a different problem; and as the days went by, the openings and shuttings of the hall door were secretly exciting sounds to her. She never listened more eagerly than to learn who had come in.

One question grew all important; she saw that Mr. Knight was certainly very attentive to Helen, and Helen was so interesting. Could this really be only because he would not seem marked in his attentions to herself? Or, she wondered, did he look at Helen in the same way as at her, and say the same kind of things? The girl half laughed, and was half indignant, too, because as the thought crossed her mind, she answered involuntarily, "He would not dare to try it." She wondered how Helen in love would appear, but she did not care to see at present.

"I want to say something to you. Shall I shut the door?" asked Bertha, walking into Kitty's room after Mr. Knight had gone.

"Certainly. What is it? Has Mr. Dewey proposed?"

"Kit, how can you talk so? Such an idea.

"Oh, then he hasn't come to the point. Take my advice, Bertha, and say 'no' to him when he does."

"Never fear my being foolish, *when*—"

"Surely, I don't. It all depends on what you call folly. Opinions differ."

"You know there's nothing serious. But it does no harm to play him off a little."

"Against whom?"

There was a mixture of amusement and scorn in Kitty's tone that the other felt without quite comprehending. She hesitated, and flushed a little.

"Well," she said, "against—anybody. How queer you are, Kit; I thought you knew there were more interesting people than Willie Dewey about."

"I do."

"Mr. Knight, for instance," added Bertha.

Kitty gave her a quick glance of alarm.

"Mr. Knight is not fit for you, Bertha. I hope you will never waste a thought upon him."

"No, indeed, not when it's so plain what your intentions with regard to him are. The mystery has all come out at last, and you might just as well have said in the first place what you wanted him here for."

Mrs. Mason's eyes dilated, and her dry lips parted as she looked at the speaker.

"But that's exactly why I came to tell you," pursued Bertha. "I've seen through you so well, and I appreciate your motives to the utmost, dear Kit, ridiculous, no doubt, as they are—" she waited an instant to glance into the opposite mirror, and poise her head a little differently—"and, as I said, that's the reason I've come to tell you that if you want Mr. Knight for Helen, your niece Jenny is more likely to get him."

"Oh, you think that!" said Kitty, and smiled to see the girl's satisfaction at her own acumen. Her relief at the result of Bertha's investigations was so great that, combined with the knowledge she had, it made her undervalue the warning.

"It's of no use to try to keep things from you, Bertha," she confessed. "But your fancy, my dear, is too absurd. Jenny, you know, is rather fond of a little quiet flirtation, and I suppose Mr. Knight likes some entertainment when Helen is at work; but don't you notice how attentive he is to her whenever she is free?"

"The attentions are all on his side. I don't think she likes him very well, she only tries to be polite.

Now, you may believe it or not, but Jenny is polite without having to try."

Kitty smiled serenely.

"Jenny is a little witch," she answered. "But you can't be sure how Helen feels about anything, except that she dislikes me excessively. You can all see that."

"Why, I don't know; she doesn't do anything, and I never heard her say one word against you."

"Doesn't do anything!" but Kitty stopped. "There are hundreds of little ways one can't take hold of, Bertha," she finished. "No matter though, I am above caring for these trifles. As to Mr. Knight, he is very friendly with me; I really know a good deal of his affairs —he speaks to me in confidence," as the other was about to question.

"Oh!"

"So let us wait patiently, and see how matters will turn out."

"I'll wait, if you will," laughed Bertha as she went away. "I dare say," she muttered, "you will be well enough pleased; something satisfactory will come out of it, on whichever side the gentleman turns his eyes. As if I could not see the difference he makes between Jenny and me; but Kit shall not get hold of that reason. I don't care for him, but he ought to show me a little more politeness in my own home."

"Jenny," she said, as the two sat over the fire in Miss Grierson's room, "Kitty says she knows all about Mr. Knight, he confides his private affairs to her, and he is quite devoted to Helen, only amusing. himself with you in the interims, while she is cultivating her muse. 'What do you think of that for high?' If you can't talk slang in your own room in the dead of the night, when everybody has gone to bed, what good is it, anyhow?"

Jenny uttered a forced laugh.

"Your aunt is the wise woman, Miss Jenny; she knows everything."

"I am aware of that," laughed Jenny again, this time somewhat more naturally. She was at the rebound from her instant acceptance of the statement, and, with that inalienable prerogative of relationship, was assuring herself that her aunt's sagacity was by no means infallible.

She had nothing to offer in confutation of the assertion but the recollection of glances and of disconnected words. But she could easily read the glances, and she believed what the words were meant to convey to her. Bertha's speech, however, found lodgment in her mind, and bore its nettles. She assured herself that she did not doubt, yet she was not quite at rest. She, too, began to balance probabilities, and to watch. It seemed as if gradually all eyes were being turned upon Helen.

Helen meanwhile went on with her work as quietly and joined in the amusements as readily as if she never dreamed that any one bestowed more than an occasional kindly thought upon her. She certainly had no idea of the web being woven about her. But in spite of Mrs. Edgerly's unvarying goodness and Andrew's friendliness, the atmosphere was beginning to be oppressive to her. She was glad her visit was almost over.

One evening Helen's face wore a troubled expression, which she explained by saying she had lost an excellent order that day through a delay in the mails. A friend had wanted a small picture to send as a wedding present. She had only then decided what to give.

"The time was so short," said Helen, "she wrote that if she did not hear as early as last evening she should be obliged to take something else instead, and asked me to telegraph. I did so immediately on hearing this morning, but it was too late. From the date of her note I ought to have received it yesterday. By my not answering, she feared I might be away, and should not have time to do the work."

"And the strange thing about it," she added when her hearers had expressed their sympathy, "was that there were two other letters of mine late. It does not often happen that three come to you at once by roundabout ways."

When Helen had gone to her room that night Mrs. Edgerly came in, and told her that a young friend was to be married by and by, and that she should be very glad if Helen would fill an order for her, at her own time within six months.

"Oh," cried the girl, her face growing crimson, "how I wish I had not spoken of it! It was very stupid in me; but I forgot for the moment I was not at home; and you know Mrs. Edgerly—"

"My dear," interrupted the elder lady, "I have meant all along to give you this order, but I didn't want you to be any busier while you were here, and so I was waiting until you went home."

"But, you remember, you have given me several, already."

"Well, my dear, and doesn't that little gem of yours look very pretty in the drawing-room? Why shouldn't I ornament my house, if I like?"

Helen looked up at her through a mist, and smiled. Mrs. Edgerly smiled, too, and nodded.

"I mean just that, my dear," she said, "your pictures are ornaments to anybody's house; and be patient, by and by everybody will find it out and want them; everybody that can afford them, for then they'll be very expensive luxuries. You have been so brave, Helen, things will be sure to come all right at last."

"Will they?" asked the girl sadly. Then she added, "Everything would be very smooth, certainly, if people were all as kind as you."

The old lady came up to her, with a look in her face of having something important to say, and laid both hands upon the girl's shoulders. But then she hesitated.

"My dear," she said at length, "there are things in most people's lives that they never talk about. I am very fond of you for your own sake, and anything I can do is always a pleasure; you permit me very little. But, apart from this, there is another reason; your father once gave help to my son in a way that makes me owe an unending debt of gratitude to him and his. It is not necessary to bring up the old story, it grieves me too much."

"Oh, no, no."

"My Harry had a kind heart, but he was very wild, and your father once saved him from—yes, I suppose it would have been a criminal act. He gave me back my son. His wife and daughter, Helen, have been too proud with me. It is not easy to feel myself so much in debt, and be able to do nothing. You must remember that, and not be selfish with me. And now go to bed easy in your mind, for this has been coming to you for a long time."

She turned to leave her, but at the door stopped, and coming back, said,

"Nobody knows about this, my dear, not even my own family; I don't think anybody now living does, except your mother."

The entreaty in her face, the pain in her voice, which showed she was already suffering from even so slight a breaking in as this upon the reserve of years, touched Helen keenly. She put her arms gently about the speaker, and kissed her cheek with a tender reverence.

"Mamma has never alluded to it," she said, "nor will I."

Mrs. Edgerly was satisfied.

The next morning Andrew intercepted the coachman as he was driving out of the yard.

"Where are you going?" he asked.

The man told his several errands, and that on the way home he was to call at the post-office.

"Yes," said Mason, "that's right. You always get the mail yourself, James?"

"Yes, sir, I always bring it up, unless you get it yourself when you're out."

"I mean, do you always go to the delivery window and take the letters from the clerk, or does any body ever bring them out to you while you sit in the wagon?"

"No, sir, never. Nobody never touches your letters that could do anything to 'em. The other day, Hero —he's a skittish beast, sir, anyhow—got frightened as I was coming home from some errands, and cut up dreadful bad; when I tried to stop him at the office, he behaved so bad he got to making the horse before him uneasy, and I was just a-going to drive him home and walk back there, when that gentleman I've seen here so often, comes out to the door. He had his letters in his hand. 'Hullo!' he says to me, 'what's the trouble? I'll git your letters,' he says, when I told him I couldn't leave the horse. 'What's the number?' And he came back in a minute separating 'em all from his, and handed 'em to me. I told him I was ever so much obliged, and he laughed and said, 'that was nothing,' and went off. He's the only one that touched the letters but me, since I've been here these two years and more."

"Was it Mr. Holden?" asked Mason.

"No, sir; I can tell Mr. Holden well enough; nor it wasn't that other gentleman that lives in town; it was the little man with the light hair that bows so much and is so quick."

"Mr. Knight?"

"Yes, I believe that's his name. There he is going by now, bowing to you, sir; he always sees everything."

Andrew laughed, though James could not tell why.

"Yes, that was Mr. Knight. What day did he hand you out the letters?"

James considered. "It was the night before last, sir. I was coming home from the saw-mill when Hero began to cut up."

This was the evening on which Helen's mail ought to have come.

"I find no fault with you now, James, but another time, if any such thing happens, drive home and go back again. Don't commission any body, no matter who he is, to get the mail for you."

"No, sir; but I hope there's no harm done?"

"You have done nothing out of the way this time," repeated Andrew. "I only warn you in future not to ask any one, not even Mr. Knight."

"I didn't ask him, sir; he offered the minute he saw me."

"Ye-es, ye-es."

Andrew wondered whether there was any connection between Knight's handling of the mail and the delay of Helen's letters. It was not enough to prove this, that the two happened on the same night. But there was something about the young man he did not like; he had a hard face, though it was always beaming with smiles and he was closeted with Kitty too much. Andrew saw there was some secret understanding between them. He had not a thought of jealousy; he knew his wife's heart was his, and he had much too great faith in her to imagine for a moment she was capable of the vulgar wickedness jealousy on his part would impute to her. But he had seen better than Bertha that something was amiss with Kitty, and that it was in some way connected with Knight, whose influence over her was bad. Now the suggestion came to him that Helen's interests were involved.

Had he heard what passed in the drawing-room in the brief interview between his wife and this stranger on the morning Jenny left them together, he would not have been obliged to wonder whether these two facts were coincidence, or cause and effect.

"Kitty," he had said to his wife a few days before this, and he had put his arm about her as he spoke, "what is the matter with you, little one? Something is wrong; what is it 'a-working in your mind-like'?"

But Kitty had put him off, since it was of no use to deny that something was wrong. She told him other people's faults had troubled her, that she was not at liberty to speak of them at present, that sometime he would know; all her own affairs she brought to him without reserve. And Andrew was silenced, if not content, especially when she assured him Mr. Knight was one of the best people in the world, and a great comfort to her now. He had, indeed, ventured the single question, "Whose affair is it, then?" But even this he did not learn, and he was left to make his own discoveries, and draw his own conclusions.

A part of these conclusions, and his analysis of the characters about him were from time to time given to Holden.

Andrew had looked in to see him one morning, when Mrs. Barney, after minute inquiries as to the well-being of all his household, began to expatiate upon Knight.

"Such a nice young man that is I met at your house—that Mr. Knight—so affable, and so attentive! He came and sat down beside me while I was talking with Miss Bell, and made himself so agreeable."

"Ye-es," said the other, "he makes himself too much of everything. I wish he'd try the quiet dodge once in a while."

Jack laughed.

"He rather amused me," he said, "but I took a small dose."

"Ye-es; that was a very good thing—for you. I have an idea he's a pyrotechnic kind of fellow; when he has sent off all his squibs, he will go home for a new supply."

"Perhaps he will send," Holden suggested.

Andrew looked up in comic despair.

"The saints forefend!"

"What are you two talking about? Jack, what does

Mr. Mason mean by 'a pyrotechnic kind of fellow'? I thought those were fire-works."

"Ye-es, Mrs. Barney, that's what I mean; the young man is brilliant, and you can't tell where he's going to turn up, or what?"

"Well, of course I don't know him; he may be just as you say, though I can't quite get at the meaning of it; but one thing I can tell you, he has good taste enough to admire Miss Bell very much. That's plain to everybody."

"Ye-es," answered Andrew, very slowly, and paused; then added with quiet earnestness, "I don't see, Mrs. Barney, how any one can help admiring Miss Bell, and more, respecting and loving her. I am glad you do. She doesn't wear her heart on her sleeve, but there never was a truer one. I am sorry she is to leave us so soon."

"Oh! is she?" cried Mrs. Barney. "That's too bad!"

"I suppose from what you have said," began Holden, "that when Miss Bell goes, you will be relieved from Knight's presence?"

Andrew did not glance at the questioner, but turning toward the window on his other hand, fixed his eyes meditatively upon a fleecy, summer-like cloud sailing past. He waited, feeling the stillness that followed, and interpreting from this, rather than from his careless tones, the importance of the question to the asker.

"Ye-es, I shouldn't wonder if he did. It looks probable to me, upon the whole."

"Miss Bell is interested in him, then?"

This time Mason looked full at his friend, and said he hoped there was no possibility of such a thing; but how could he tell? "You know the old saying," he added: "Propinquity works wonders."

"O Mr. Mason," cried Aunt Delia, "Miss Bell is not at all the kind of person to like a young man just because he happens to be around. I had my own little cherished dream about her," she added with a sigh; "but no matter, it's no use thinking of anything I said to Jack. He is obdurate."

"I shall not let you say anything against Jack, Mrs. Barney; he is not the wisest man living, but he's a good fellow. Now step behind the door, Holden, and hear the other side."

"No, thank you."

"You don't want to improve, hey?"

Holden turned to his friend seriously, for he perceived the undertone of earnest in Andrew's manner.

"What is it you mean, Mason?"

But the coachman came to the door with a message; and after this, there were other interruptions, so that Jack never heard what Mason had in his mind to say; he only guessed it long afterward.

CHAPTER X.

IT was one of what Helen called her "dawdling days"
—days in which experience had taught her she could
do no work.   She had struggled a long time against this
conviction, calling her mood mere indolence which resolute will could overcome, and had set this resolute will
to the task, but always with the same result, her work
had never been worth keeping, and the fruitless endeavor
had injured the spontaneity of her fancy when the happy
mood returned.   With the goad of poverty behind, and
mountains of attainment in her pathway to be climbed,
it was hard ever to wait for moods.   Yet, at last, she
was learning that patience, which has in it the strength
of a reserve, and is sure to bring up the lagging relays
of force.

This morning there was no power in her.   She was
fit only for fancy-work; so after breakfast she remained
with the others, instead of retiring to her own room as
usual.

"Are you going to give us the pleasure of your society?" cried Jenny. "How nice!"

"You must be anxious to finish up your embroidery," remarked Kitty.

"Yes," said Helen coolly, as, with a nod and a smile at Jenny, she took up her basket, and seated herself near the window.

"I don't think Helen is much in love with fancy-work of any description," said Bertha; "it is more to have something in her hands that she works. She does it elegantly, but she never goes into raptures as we do over all sorts of lovely things."

"She is not of the rapturous kind, are you, Helen?" laughed Kitty.

"Not of that kind of rapture, certainly. But, Bertha, let me tell you, if you had ever had your own sewing to do, it would have made a great difference; you would have fallen out of love with stitches."

"Yé-es, she would find it odd," drawled Andrew taking in the indolent lines of Bertha's half reclining figure as she did her best to fill one of the large easy-chairs.

"That was too much for you, my dear," said Mrs. Edgerly.

"Oh, I have almost none of it to do now," cried the girl quickly.

"But I can't imagine how an artist can help admiring exquisite embroidery," said Kitty. "You can't deny that it's beautiful."

"I don't deny it. It *is* beautiful, of its kind, but you claim too much for it. I think it 'is' like what some one said about chess: not of importance enough for a study, and too laborious for an amusement."

Bertha shook her head, and Kitty answered,

"You will find a very general dissent from both those assertions."

"Yes, I am aware of that. The needle infatuation in America is one of the most striking anachronisms of this century. Here we are preaching the enfranchisement of women, and acting upon it too; yet we go wild with desire to reproduce the one special evidence of their restricted lives. The reason women embroidered so beautifully in the middle ages, was only because there was nothing else open to them. They were shut up in their castles and their convents, any knowledge of the outside world was forbidden, and if they gained it at all it was only by stealth; books were unknown, poetry and music were taught by the minstrels alone, and we should not probably admire their style. Women had only their needles, and they won a fame with these. It was a thing to be very proud of in the dark ages, but I can't see that it is to-day."

"Do you mean that domesticity is out of date?

asked Andrew, in answer to a look that swept over Kitty's face.

"No, Mr. Mason. Those poor ladies could never have turned amazons without brutalizing the world; they had to train the knights in their castles, or else the soul in chivalry would never have awaked. Women have the same task to-day; but life is more exacting, and a thorough knowledge of needlework is not enough to meet its demands."

"But remember," said Jenny, "this is only one of the modern accomplishments. We have 'ologies' and 'isms' by the dozen to be conquered besides."

"That's just the trouble. If you are going to make needlework an art, you must put your soul into it; and in this age the thing is next to impossible, and not worth doing, if it could be done. Why, think of those queenly dames of old, how they watched, through narrow castle windows, their knights go far away to battle, while they themselves were imprisoned in their own homes for months and years with their sorrows and their hopes. Think of them, with meager news, without a glimpse of the outside world, surrounded by their attendants. Stitches were their only resource. No wonder their tapestries are records of woman's love and woman's genius. She was not permitted to seek, and maybe save, her lover in time of illness; but she could depict his triumphs on the battle-field, his dangers, his imprisonment, perhaps, and death. So she stitched her heart history into her tapestry. Such a life is impossible now."

"We are aware of that," said Kitty; "but we still have a little time left for embroidery."

"Yes, 'a little time,' the odds and ends of our summer travels, and winter gayeties. When people combine attempts to imitate elaborate ancient needlework with an admiration of the broad style of painting, doesn't that show you what all the admiration amounts to? There is no genuine love for art in it."

"O Helen," cried Bertha, "you are very much mistaken!"

"No, I am not. Needlework is only a fashionable pastime to us; to the ladies of old it was a life-labor. And every art is a life-labor. If a work does not demand of you a consecration, don't miscall it 'art.' Needlework as 'art' is dead; it lives only as dilettanteism. We may give it a great deal of praise for its prettiness and daintiness, but it is not worth enthusiasm."

"I beg to differ with you," said Kitty haughtily. "I have seen exquisite landscapes wrought with a needle."

"A picture is of value," answered Helen, "not for what it represents so much as for the thoughts it suggests. You may say at first that still life cannot come under this head, but if you think of it, you will see it does. For instance, you are looking at a quiet lake, the shadows from the overhanging trees on its bank sleep upon it, the clouds as they float in a dream through the summer sky darken the transparent water. No man or beast is there to break the hush; it is 'still life,' but, nevertheless, it is life. For if a wind should come, how it would toss the branches of these trees, and whirl the clouds along! All the possible moods of nature may awake on this lake, its very stillness impresses you as a transient thing; you watch to see a quiver in the shadows, and as you look at them, they seem to shift. How much of all this do you get in needle pictures? You have no shadow, to begin with. I mean, nothing worth calling shadow."

"Oh, you're too sweeping in your judgments, Helen,' cried Bertha, rising and going to the closet for her basket of worsted. "Don't you think so, Andrew?"

"Perhaps so. Something of what she sees in a picture may have to be in the eyes of the gazer. You are a little sweeping, Miss Helen, for the rest of us; but there's a great deal to sweep—so perhaps, you might as well go ahead."

"I don't believe I agree with you, either," said Jenny. "Let me think it over, and I'll tell you."

"Do," laughed Helen, "while I go for the other

shade of purple which I must have left upstairs. I thought I had brought them all down. Remember, when I come back I shall count upon your support."

But she was gone so long that when she came back they had wandered far away from the subject of their discussion.

"Couldn't you find what you wanted?" asked Andrew, seeing a troubled expression in her face.

"Yes, after I had searched several drawers, and gone to the depths of the Saratoga; it had fallen out from the package, and slipped under some of the sheets of crayon paper in the bottom of my trunk. I can't imagine how it happened."

"You were very patient," said Bertha.

"I knew it must be somewhere, for I bought it a few weeks ago, and have not used a needleful."

"No wonder it annoyed you," Jenny said; "'the perversity of inanimate things' is dreadfully aggravating."

"I didn't know I looked annoyed; but if I did, it was not at that."

"What was it, then?"

"How sharply Aunt Kitty speaks sometimes," thought her niece. "I wonder if she is conscious of it herself?"

Helen paused. She had caught the shrill tones heard through the door on the night of her arrival

"It was nothing of much consequence, but I can't see

how it was possible to lose it, for it was in my trunk, and I always keep that locked, at Mrs. Edgerly's request."

"Yes, my dear, we hope to have honest servants, and we do generally, I know; but it's best to put valuables out of the way, and then nobody is tempted."

"But in spite of this precaution, you see Miss Helen has lost something," said Mason.

"It's not that the thing is of any value, it is only I wonder how it could possibly be gone."

"May I inquire what is this mysterious 'it'?" asked Mrs. Mason.

"Only that little phial of the cough mixture I brought here to Lowton with me. I care nothing about it, but it was certainly in my trunk, and I know I have not taken it out to use since the night you would not try it."

"I believe that," muttered Kitty, so low that her husband only who was nearest heard her words.

"Ask the chambermaid," said Mrs. Edgerly. "Please ring, Andrew."

The girl knew nothing of the phial, had not seen it.

"Certainly not," commented Kitty in her former tones, with only her former auditor. Then, when the girl had gone, she said aloud, "This loss does as well to get up a mystery about as anything else, for a little diversion this dull weather, when there seems to be a dearth of callers and every other kind of amusement; but you will find the phial when you look carefully enough, for I'm sure nobody would want to share that delectable stuff with you."

"Kitty!" said her husband.

Mrs. Mason glanced at him anxiously.

"Don't take me *au sérieux*, Helen, but I can't help laughing to think of its being that nasty little bottle you are troubled about. If it were mine, all I should be afraid of would be its turning up."

"I told you I did not care for the thing; I only wonder at its being gone."

"Kitty said nothing this time, but she looked at the speaker with a smile and nod of assent.

"When I lose anything," said Bertha, "I never mind, unless I want it that moment. I wait, and it turns up."

"I do sometimes," added Jenny, "when it's nothing of importance."

Helen said no more; but her unpleasant impression remained. She knew it must be only dislike which made her fancy in Kitty's smile a peculiar meaning besides her malice, always ready to enjoy everything annoying to one it followed with petty persecutions. But this loss, trivial in itself, tended to fix in her mind a sense of something being strange and wrong.

She remembered now an incident she had thought odd, but only so inasmuch as it was a liberty she would not have taken.   The evening before she had gone into her room and found Kitty there carefully looking over one of her boxes of paints and brushes.   Helen judged that they all might have received the same attention, for they stood on the table before her.   Bertha was watching her, and the two were talking.   Helen did not hear what they said.

Kitty turned at once and apologized.   She knew Helen would excuse her; there was nothing especially private about painting materials; they were not like one's letters.

She explained that part of a lily petal had been broken out from the inlaid work of the table in her room, and she wanted to cover the loss by a little white paint.   She was provoked with herself, because for the past two days she had forgotten to ask Helen for it.   She thought of it now while passing her door, and made bold to take it first, and get permission afterwards.

"Is this the right kind, and may I have some of it?" she added laughing.

There was nothing in this to seem more than somewhat strange in a lady of Kitty's standing, nothing in any one of the little things she remembered, when taken by itself, but when summed up, they had together an unpleasant look of surveillance.

Mrs. Edgerly was goodness itself to her, Mr. Mason was a friend, and Bertha—was Bertha, with strange ways sometimes, but, she was sure, not intending anything unkind toward her. Helen had had a gay winter, yet she was again glad her visit was almost over.

It seemed unlikely that any one would call that evening, for the dismal weather culminated in a persistent rain, which increased to a violent storm before midnight. But Mr. Dewey dropped in, and half an hour later Holden appeared.

Kitty was delighted; they were not to have a dull evening, after all. She liked Jack, and there was no longer any danger of Helen's influence. If the first warning had proved insufficient, she had a far graver one to give. She saw he still admired her, but he was afraid of her, and the girl was proud; there could be nothing feigned in that, unless, possibly, her withdrawal was to lead him on. She had not done this, however, and now she was going home. Kitty breathed freely at last, and welcomed Holden with a satisfaction that she had not always felt, however cordial her manner.

After the first words of greeting, and the few remarks of a commonplace nature that usually follow the entrance of a visitor, there seemed great danger of the evening turning out at least a very quiet one, in spite of Mrs. Mason's valiant efforts. Mr. Dewey was at the further end of the room talking to Bertha. From occasional phrases, they seemed to be discussing some question of conventionality; but whatever the topic, it was plain they were not anxious to make it general, and after two unsuccessful attempts by Kitty to bring them into the circle, they were left undisturbed. Andrew was very quiet; Helen said scarcely anything; Jenny was too much occupied with some subject of cogitation to be able to do her best; and Mr. Holden was, for him, stupid.

Kitty looked across at her aunt in despair.

Mrs. Edgerly was knitting. The click of her needles was very audible at times, then there would come a sudden cessation of the sound, her hands would fall by degrees into her lap, and she would gently bend her head as in profound meditation. At these times Kitty always asked her some question, and Mrs. Edgerly answered quite at length, turning upon her niece a pair of wide-open eyes with a slightly abashed expression in them. Kitty began to grow desperate, when it occurred to her that if she could not make anybody talk, she could find some excuse for their being so silent.

"Will you give us some music, Jenny?"

Miss Grierson rose reluctantly; if she were playing, she could not hear in case the door-bell should ring again, and she had been listening for it the last hour. But having begun to play she forgot everything in her music.

"Mendelssohn wrote those 'Songs without Words' for such interpreters as you, Miss Grierson," said Jack, as she left the piano with the echoes of the "Venetian Gondolier's Boat Song" still floating through the room.

Even the music failed to have any inspiriting effect upon the party, and Jack was about to go home, feeling he might as well not have come, when Andrew asked,

"What do you say to a game of whist, Holden? You are generally ready. Jenny, we count upon you; and, Miss Helen, I know from what you said this morning, you are not so devoted to that pretty piece of work that you can't lend us a hand."

Helen was going to refuse, but he looked so in earnest about it, she yielded. Jenny did not play, and Bertha volunteered to take her place. Kitty who had been intending to offer her services, leaned back again contentedly in her chair, and the game began.

But it could not be called a scientific one, for it requires at least as much concentration to play whist as to talk, and both feats cannot be successfully performed at once. Bertha paid no heed to this rule, she was constantly turning to say something to Mr. Dewey who had taken his place behind her, proposing to be a silent partner and amuse himself by looking on, but, instead, he dictated all her movements to the secret indignation of Holden, her partner, and when she demurred at any of his suggestions, argued so lengthily in his sibilant half-whisper that Andrew finally drawled out,

"This is what you mean by being a silent partner, Mr. Dewey?"

"Well, no," answered the young man with a laugh. "I have been quite active, I admit, and done good service, too; but I'll draw off now, upon honor."

Yet he did this for a time only, and the rill of conversation, that never quite ceased, grew gradually into a larger stream. Kitty was very quiet; she knew that her husband liked a good game, so she took up a book and watched the players between the turning of her leaves. But Jenny, at her uncle's hand, looked far wiser than wisdom ever does, and asked questions of him and of Mr. Dewey, until Holden in a safe moment glanced at Andrew with despairing annoyance.

Andrew answered by a slight shrug of the shoulders, so philosophical that Jack's equanimity was restored at once, and he felt even amused at his own discomfiture.

Helen's play was at first almost as vexatious as Bertha's, for, though she spoke very little, her thoughts were plainly not upon her cards, and she made a number of mistakes. But at last she roused herself, and by taking a clever advantage of Bertha's failures, atoned for her carelessness so well that she and Andrew came off victorious.

She nodded across the table with a triumphant smile at her partner as the result was declared. Holden saw it, as he had seen everything she had done that evening.

"I perceive," he said looking into her face and touching her cards lightly as they lay on the table before her, "you are one of those people who come out right in the long run."

"Am I?" she answered, straightening her pile as she spoke and turning her eyes upon Andrew, whose attention Dewey had claimed.

"But I understand it's not the winning you enjoy," Holden went on, "only the excitement of the game; and to please Mason, if he likes success," he added in a lower tone.

This time Helen looked at him steadily.

"You do not understand at all," she said, "if you think that. I care very much indeed for winning in every game I ever play, and so does everybody who comprehends what success means. Don't you care?"

"Not always. Probably," he continued, "because *I* do not understand what success means."

"If not," she answered him, "you are right; it is because you do not comprehend it."

Holden had not been fortunate in his choice of subject.

"Is she this to me only," he wondered, "or to every one?"

"Tell me, then, what you mean by success?" he said. "What is there in it more than a name? Is it not, after all, merely an empty husk?"

But Helen did not hear; she was listening to Mr. Dewey with an expression of dissent and suppressed excitement, that deepened as he went on. He had gone back to the subject of conventionalities, and was speaking of a lady friend of his, who had permitted her niece to call upon a young girl she had met somewhere and greatly liked.

"Mrs. Wetherbee gave her consent," explained Mr. Dewey apologetically, "because Julia was so bent upon it. But the worst of it was, that when the girl returned the visit, after a proper time, Julia wanted to go off and see her again directly."

"What, straight off?" laughed Mrs. Mason.

"Oh, no, but just as she would have done with any of her friends whom it would be desirable to cultivate; and it would never answer, because—" and the corners of his mouth elevated themselves still higher, while he twirled one way and the other, between his fingers, a rosebud he had taken from a vase on the table—"she isn't in our set, you see, so it would not do to pay her too much attention."

"Fortunate for her," muttered Andrew in an aside to Holden.

"Yes, 'it would not do to pay her too much attention;' those are the very words Mrs. Wetherbee said; they struck me as being so conclusive."

"Ye-es, they are, very," assented Andrew; "very conclusive indeed, I should say."

"Probably the girl was not in any respect such a friend as she would choose for her niece," Kitty suggested, "and she said this, not wishing to criticise her any more unkindly to Julia."

"No, no," protested Dewey, "that's not so at all, I assure you; she never minds what she says of people, only not to their faces. She told me she didn't know when she had seen a young girl with prettier manners, and, from what she had learned of her, a nicer young lady in herself, but it was out of the question she should pay her much attention."

Helen's eyes were fixed upon the speaker, and the flash of scorn that had passed over her face, still lighted it as she said with slow distinction,

"Mrs. Wetherbee must have a scant foothold in her set; it can't be her birthright."

"Oh, I assure you that is a mistake," cried Dewey; "there can be no doubt about her right to her position; but she goes into society a great deal, and knows how things would be considered. She is a thorough-going aristocrat, elegant and feminine, gracious, and, as one can easily see, blue-blooded; there is always a cool, high-bred languor about her. And as to her friends, she was telling me the other day she was not acquainted socially with a single person who worked for a living; she could not have meant gentlemen in business, but anything like class work. So you see, she certainly does know how her taking up this girl would be considered. It seems a pity, now and then, that such things must be; but, beyond question, they must." And Mr. Dewey ended with the satisfaction of one who has made opposition impossible.

There was a short pause. Helen looked at Mr. Mason. He would surely speak.

But Andrew sat silent, watching her with a smile that refused to give place to either indignation or sarcasm at such an assertion.

Unconsciously she turned to Holden with an involuntary faith in him. But neither had he any word to say. She did not know that both men were waiting for her to utter the protest written on her face, she wondered that there was nobody to defend a law higher than this shallow expedient. It was not Mr. Dewey alone whom she answered.

"Such things are a necessity to certain people," she said, "only because their dignity is too weak to come out from entrenchments. I never heard of Mrs. Wetherbee before, but she is not a genuine aristocrat. Social cowardice is a sign of insecurity of position."

"I'm not sure I quite understand you," sneered Mr. Dewey; "but it's of no consequence. May I be permitted to inquire what you call a 'genuine aristocrat'?"

"The narrowest definition you can give it," she answered, "must include birth and station that put their possessor above the fear of people he knows to be only equals, at best."

"That is the only definition there is, Miss Bell."

"Then you admit that the lady you were speaking of does not come under it?"

"I admit no such thing. I say she does. But people of this class are always exceedingly exclusive, not from necessity, but by choice. Look at the English aristocracy; they will have nothing to do with the common people."

"Their walls of caste seem to be of iron, but the general breaking down of ancient privileges threatens even these. I am glad you spoke of the English, for it is by the representatives of this haughty aristocracy that I can answer your question. You know there are some among them who give not only their influence and wealth, but themselves, with their abundant leisure, to bettering the condition of men and women that excessive ignorance and excessive labor are brutalizing. They don't enter into the work as a fashionable charity, but as a tardy justice to their fellow-men. Because they have all the gifts of fortune they feel themselves the more bound to work hardest in the best lines of labor the world offers. The Head of the Universe works, and work ranks idleness. It is not likely that their manners are languid, but they have no seamy side to fret the tender skin of poverty and suffering. You asked me what I called 'a genuine aristocrat,' I answer you—one of these."

"So far as I have capacity to understand you, Miss Bell, one must go down into the slums in order to get up on the heights. No doubt this is all evident enough to you."

"It is a law of nature, Mr. Dewey, that one must bend the knee to mount."

"Bending down to the slums would be too far for my taste. I confess I couldn't stand the odor."

"I suppose not. It takes my lord duke or my lady duchess to do that sort of thing well."

"They don't touch them with the tips of their fingers," retorted Dewey, an angry light in his eyes.

"They go down among these people who are ill in mind and body, and lay their hands upon them. They are building up that brotherhood which is to be an aristocracy of work, in which men will strive not to have most, but to do best."

"I'm afraid their ranks will fill up slowly," sneered Dewey.

"It will bring back the old meaning of the word in a higher sense, 'the power of the most worthy,' and that worth will be in character, and will admit members from all classes."

"I've heard young ladies sentimentalize a great many times," returned Dewey, "but I have never had the pleasure of hearing quite so much imagination at once before. It appears you are predicting an overturn of all well-founded social observances, and the establishment of some power of very mixed-up people that, as far as I can make out, would only be an army of hobby-riders riding to—I mean, a set of enthusiasts without any laws except their own sweet wills, or any leader. To say the least of it, it's very amusing."

"'No leader?'" repeated Helen. Her face grew pale, and her eyes filled with light. She was silenced a moment by her own intensity of feeling. Then she spoke her sudden insight like an inspiration.

"There was once a great ruler," she said—"you remember the story.—he called himself a king over kings, 'whom he would, he slew, and whom he would, he kept alive.' One night he had a vision. He saw a great image with a head of gold and a body of other metals. Then a stone, formed without hands, fell upon this image and ground it to powder, and the stone became a great mountain and filled the whole earth. The image represented the dynasties of himself and the succeeding kings; the stone cut out without hands a kingdom hereafter to be set up on the earth by other than human power. No wonder Nebuchadnezzar trembled as he dreamed of Christ; all unnatural authority, weighty or light, trembles before the brotherhood of man. The Mount on which the Sermon was spoken is filling the whole earth. It was intended that in its Speaker—our Divine Leader in all movements toward the freedom of righteousness—all classes should meet. He was born in a manger, a carpenter by trade, yet He was descended from a line of kings. But His throne was built upon deeper foundations; His nobles were to be not from Judea alone, but from every nation. Beauty of character, purity of thought, high purpose, and service from the highest to the humblest, are evidences that their possessors are children of the only Royalty that will endure, inheritors of the treasures of the ages, and heirs of the future. When God decrees, we—"

Suddenly some cruel reminder of the present brought back to Helen the remembrance of who were her auditors.

The look of exaltation faded from her countenance, and its glowing pallor was replaced by a flush that crimsoned the downcast face which the instant before had been uplifted in self-forgetful enthusiasm.

The silence that followed her words was sharp with agony to her; she endured it only for a moment. Was it Kitty's eyes fixed steadily upon her that had brought this overwhelming consciousness? She rose and moved toward the door.

When she reached it, Holden stood there to open it for her. She did not look at him as she passed out. His face was very pale, and his eyes followed her until she was out of sight.

"Why, what's that?" asked Mrs. Edgerly whom the closing of the door roused from a long and somewhat profound meditation. "Why has Helen gone away?" she added looking about her.

No one answered immediately at last Bertha said,

"She grew so excited talking, I suppose she said more than she meant, and so went to cool off. How excitable she is sometimes!"

"What she said was beautiful," cried Jenny. "I believe every word of it."

"Can you, indeed?" inquired Mr. Dewey.

Andrew smiled. He was amused to notice how differently the young man had spoken of Helen, and how little attention he had paid her since the day when, in the course of conversation, he had learned from himself that she was without wealth or brilliant prospects.

Kitty said nothing; her lips were closed like a vise, and her eyes had an expression Mason did not like.

"What was Helen talking about?" asked Mrs. Edgerly. "I must have gone off into a reverie. I do sometimes."

"Ye-es," remarked Andrew.

"When I am so lost," pursued the lady, "that I don't hear what any one about me is saying until my mind comes to the present again. What could Helen have got so earnest about?"

"A social problem," Kitty answered.

"Mr. Dewey had been telling us something a lady did, grandmamma, and she didn't like it at all."

"Mrs. Wetherbee, was it? I heard her name. I used to know her slightly when she was a school girl, but I have never seen her since her marriage. She married very well, I understood. She was a remarkably pretty girl, and had quite charming manners, though her father did make his money by selling rum."

The shout of laughter, from Jenny and Bertha, that followed this statement, bewildered Mrs. Edgerly. She heard, too, a low "Ha, ha!" from Andrew, and saw the amusement in his face.

"The blue blood is slightly diluted with alcohol, Mr. Dewey," he drawled, "and it is this which produces the undue elation in her that Miss Bell divined so readily."

"H'm!" said Kitty significantly. "I think," she added, after a pause, "we all of us have enough to do in removing the beams from our own eyes, instead of spying out our neighbors' motes."

"So do I, my dear," answered her husband.

They began to talk of other things.

"Mr. Holden," cried Bertha, at last, "you have not spoken one single word for the last half hour; not since Helen prevented our having a second game of cards. What can you be thinking of?"

"Perhaps he is in one of Mrs. Edgerly's reveries,' said Jenny in an undertone.

"I am thinking it is time for me to go home, Miss Edgerly," responded Jack with gravity.

Bertha was secretly of the same mind; if he could not be a little more entertaining.

But Jack Holden, as he went out into the night, had very little solicitude about Bertha Edgerly's opinion of him.

The storm that faced him, as he walked slowly home,

accorded with the arrows of his recollections, and the wind of self-reproach that went through him.

The next morning, at the earliest hour permissible for paying a visit, he rang the bell at Mrs. Edgerly's. The door was opened by Bertha, who had seen him on the pathway.

"Come in, Mr. Holden," she said with a conscious laugh that jarred through his nerves, "and make up for your last night's silence. I am sure it is good of you to be so prompt to condole with us on Helen's departure. You saw her drive away?"

"No. Where?"

"Why, home, of course. Where should she go, pray, after all this long time? Though her going this morning was a sudden notion. Yesterday she did not mean to leave for two or three days. I thought perhaps you had met the carriage, it has just gone to the train. But come in."

"No, thank you. I can only say good morning in passing. I am going up to town this morning. Any commissions for me? Speak directly, or 'forever after hold your peace,'" he added, laughingly, looking at his watch, however, with an impatience by no means feigned.

In a moment he had repented of his ill-judged offer. What if Bertha had any errands for him, and, as her way was, should keep him talking ten minutes, or even five? That would be enough to make him miss the train. He had asked only because he was actually here at the door, and he must bridge over the awkwardness of saying good morning, and good-by in the same breath.

But this time he fared better than he deserved, and was too grateful for Bertha's not being able at the moment to remember anything, to give time for a reverse of fortune. He bowed himself away directly, sure that this was a case in which no second thoughts could be so wise as the first.

Holden had always believed that Lowton abounded in hacks, but this morning he was not able to get hold of one, though he had the pleasure of seeing two or three whisk around distant corners while their drivers showed that indifference to pedestrians that might be supposed to come only from absolute independence of the wants of the public. But by great exertion he caught the train, and swung himself breathless upon the last car as it was moving out of the station.

After a moment's rest he passed through it with first a hasty survey of its occupants, as if a glance would enable him to single out the person he sought, and then, as he failed to do this, making a more careful examination.

How expressive people's backs were; he recognized his acquaintances as he came leisurely up behind them almost as well as if their faces had been toward him. Here was a respectable Lowton merchant who delighted to discuss the banking interests; there was a vacant place at his side, and Holden must walk by a little faster. Two seats down on the right was a young man like the princess in the fairy-tale of the distaff, that would talk with anybody about anything "from morn 'till dewy eve, a summer's day," and as to the young man, if the season happened to be winter, he was always ready to make up the time by candlelight. Jack must dodge him. But he had a spare seat too, and looking up at the wrong moment, called out,

"Why, I say, Holden!"

"Ah! good morning, Williams," answered Jack over his shoulder as he moved off.

The greeting, however, aroused the attention of two young ladies he was passing at the moment, who looked up and repeated his name with welcoming smiles, while one held out her hand with a pretty show of friendliness, and the other pointed to a seat before them. Jack thought it was a remarkable circumstance that everybody he preferred to avoid that morning should have a vacant seat to offer him; he hoped it would happen equally well when he should come to the one beside whom he wanted to remain. He took the little hand proffered, and promising to call upon its owner before long, refused the second offer with an apology for his haste, and was gone.

Helen Bell was not in this car, nor in the next one. He entered the third.

Here were several people with unoccupied seats beside them. The first lady he looked at among these was elderly, the second ordinary, the third wore heavy mourning. Holden wondered how many more cars he should be obliged to look through. But he had not gone far up the aisle when he saw before him Miss Bell's graceful shoulders and finely poised head; and saw, too, that his present vigorous attempt to pass a few hours in her company had been fruitless, for at her side sat Mr. Knight, talking to her in a strain which, judging from her attentive face and ready replies, she seemed to find agreeable.

Holden placed himself a few seats behind them. He remembered what Mason had said in regard to these two. There was nothing in Helen's look or manner to suggest any deeper feeling than the enjoyment of an amusing conversation with an acquaintance. But a public conveyance was the very last place a woman like Miss Bell would select for any expression of sentiment; and there was an alert self-satisfaction in Knight's manner that troubled and enraged Holden. He did not seem exactly lover-like, yet this might be his way of showing the security of possession. Jack did not approve of Knight's manner of doing anything, but every now and then he would check sarcastic inward comments on the man, by the remembrance of how humble he himself ought to be this morning. His feelings, however, did nobody any harm, unless, perhaps, himself. Knight kept his place at Miss Bell's side, and Holden, who had changed to a seat left vacant behind them after his entrance, had only a passing word from each. Helen colored, and half averted her face on first seeing him, then turned, and coldly bade him good morning. This was all that these miles of travel had given him, and this could scarcely be called satisfaction.

At the station he fared not much better; it was Knight who helped her from the train, and evidently intended to accompany her home. While he was giving directions about the baggage, Holden seized his opportunity. He expressed his sorrow at Miss Bell's leaving Lowton. She thanked him with a perfect understanding of his conventional regrets.

"But I shall see you again before long?" he answered eagerly.

Helen thought it very doubtful, she did not know when she should be in Lowton again. "But it may be," she added, "for people often meet unexpectedly. Yet, as this is very likely to be good-by, I will wish you health and happiness now, to make sure of it," she added with a smile that seemed half sad.

Knight had come up, and was standing so near that Jack could only say under his breath,

"This is not 'good-by.'"

Afterward he was afraid she had not heard him.

She turned abruptly as he released her hand, which in speaking he had firmly detained an instant, and moved away from him without further answer or look. Knight was still close beside her as the two passed from sight.

This was not like her coming into Lowton. That night had been the tide in his affairs; he had not taken it at the flood; and now, when he ought to have already become very much to her, she had not only neglected to ask him to visit her, but had refused his broad hint, almost request, for permission to do it.

Walking up and down the platform, waiting for the return train to Lowton, he felt no happier because he remembered that the present state of affairs was very much his own fault, notwithstanding Mrs. Mason. He ought to have comprehended both her and Helen better. He remembered the time when Helen Bell had been cordial. There was one day when, as her eyes turned to him, he had read in them a shy interest that filled him with delight. Afterward he had put the recollection from him, as his fancy merely, or else an interest in excellent accord with her judgment. Now, that the new faith in her, which had been dawning upon him for weeks, had burst at last into sunlit brightness, this recollection had come back with a tender hope. Helen Bell should be cordial to him again, when all that was best in him had been called into service to prove his reverence for her, and to show her how his happiness lay in her hands. He knew she was too noble not to forgive; and since, as he now believed, he had awakened the beginnings of interest, this, although it proved that she had so much more to forgive, gave him courage.

To-day nothing could be done; but—

"'To-morrow brings another day,'" he hummed, with a look of determination, as he steamed back to Lowton.

CHAPTER XI.

"THERE! Jack, you don't take one scrap of interest, but I have had quite an interesting day of it, though I am so tired; and I have something to tell that perhaps you would like to hear. You ought, if you wouldn't."

"What is it?"

But Mrs. Barney had by no means arrived at it yet.

"Oh, those great stores," she grumbled, "they are so crammed! The next day I run up to town, I shall go the night before—no, no, I mean the next time I have a day's shopping to do, I'll go there the evening before, to be on hand early in the morning before the rush begins."

"Well," returned her nephew meditatively, "this does interest me as connected with your movements; but there is nothing very exciting in the threat, especially as you have made it several times before, and have never yet carried it out. Is that what you had to tell?"

"Indeed!" returned the lady. "You don't care to hear, then? Your indifference will save me a great deal of trouble, certainly."

The toe of her little slipper silently caressed the bar of the fender, close to which her footstool had been placed, and she leaned her head against the cushioned back of her chair.

"In that case," she pursued, "as you are wandering about the room, and don't care to listen, I think I will take a nap. I am really very tired this evening. After all, it is I, not you, that are so much interested in Helen Bell."

Jack sat down at once.

"Your pardon, Aunt Delia. I am as restless as you are tired. But I was waiting to hear the account of your day in town."

"Yes," said Mrs. Barney, raising her head again with alacrity, for with her it was, as she put it, half the fun to be able to talk things over, "I dare say, my dear Jack; but you annoy me by interruptions, and by seeming not to care."

"I certainly do care; so please go on."

"Go on with what? Why, I haven't begun yet. You don't want the end until you've had the beginning."

Holden thought that depended upon what the beginning might be, and he knew it was so when his aunt added that she went first to the dry-goods stores. But he was discreetly silent.

"I'll tell you what, Jack," cried the lady already warming with her subject, and giving her head a small angle of inclination to look at him, as he sat further from the fire than she, "shopping is an art, and it takes a good deal of experience to learn it."

"That is why you experiment in it so much, I suppose."

"I? Why, I don't do anything at all 'in that line,' as the salesmen say. You should see what other people call shopping. Mrs. Windham, for instance; she has something new to be got at least five days out of the seven, I'm sure, and such extravagant purchases! But really, Jack, I only play at it."

"I have always thought so, but you seemed seriously hurt with me if I ventured to suggest such a thing."

"Oh, well, you don't understand; and then it seems quite different, too, don't you think, if you say a thing yourself?"

"Very different."

"In spite of my limited experience and my always strict economy—you needn't smile in that provoking way, I am a perfect model of economy."

"I thought so when the bills for refurnishing this house, at the time of the party, came in."

Mrs. Barney looked at the speaker with grave surprise.

"My dear boy, that was not for myself; it was for you. Do you imagine I think anything in the world within the bounds of possibility too good for you?"

Her surprise had deepened to a sense of injury.

"I did not mind, you understand, and it was all very handsome," Jack hastened to say.

"Yes, it certainly is very handsome indeed," she answered forgetting her grievance in her satisfaction. "But I was going to tell you what I have discovered about shopping. Two things especially. Always dress in your best. If you wear elegant things with a careless air, everybody that looks at you will see you have quantities more even better at home, while if you put on your old dress to get through the crowd with, they will be sure to imagine it's because you haven't any better, and they will push you about and neglect you accordingly, from the clerks down, or up, just as it happens. No, it don't answer to dress dowdily and speak to them as if they were gentlemen. Precious little trouble they'll take to do anything for you then; they'll look over your head and speak to somebody else, or begin to talk to each other. But put on an elegant silk, and sail into the stores as if nothing in them was quite worth your looking at; no matter if you're dying with admiration of the splendid stuffs lying all about, don't give them a glance more than out of the corners of your eyes. Sweep on up to the right counter, then drop down upon the seat in front of it with the air of being quite exhausted with the walk from your carriage up the length of the store. You see, Jack, by this time everybody will be ready to think you are somebody. You needn't smile. No less a person than Ralph Waldo Emerson says a lady or gentleman ought never to express too much admiration. Don't you suppose he knew what was proper?"

"And you are only giving an illustration of his theory in detail?"

"That's all, illustrating it as you say, just as Miss Bell might sketch it all out. Oh, I have something to say about her, haven't I?"

"Yes. Did you see her?"

"See her? As well find a needle in a haystack. But I've not come to her yet. You just wait, and I'll tell you. If 'order is Heaven's first law'—that's Milton, I believe—then we ought to be particular about telling things in detail. I wish you would not keep twisting your face about so, Jack; it's not becoming, if that's what you're doing it for.

"Well, though, to resume. Don't look at the clerk any more than if he were a machine, drop your eyelids and ask for what you want, and when they show it to you, ask if they have no better quality; no matter whether you like this or not, you should have a choice, and let it be seen you know there are better qualities."

"Is that shoddy style your way of doing things, Aunt Delia?"

"Why, I'm afraid I don't carry it out well. I always get interested in the people I am talking to. But I tell you, Jack, it takes amazingly. Everybody thinks your husband has been making an extra million or two the last year, and you've come to spend some of it for him, and they know that the later you've got your money, the more afraid you'll be of people thinking you still obliged to be economical. You'll get attention enough this way, and it's what you want when you go shopping. The fact is that in the Hub of Literature and Art they think as much of people's clothes as anywhere else."

"Very likely. And was shopping all you did in town?"

"No, indeed. Ah! yes, that reminds me. You are a little curious, too, Jack, I perceive. No, sir, shopping did not take all my time. I went to some of the picture stores. And what did I see there? Lovely things that if I had had my hand in your pocket-book, I should have ordered home."

"What paintings did you especially admire?"

Holden got up and walked to the window as he asked this question, then came again to the fire, and giving the backlog a vigorous push with the shovel, stood facing his aunt.

"I liked one or two of Hunt's very much, and there was a French artist very striking. No, I believe it was at the Art Museum I saw his pictures. But I liked Helen Bell's best of all."

"Of course," laughed Holden.

"No, Jack, not 'of course,' by any means. I have discrimination enough not to think a picture good because I happen to admire the artist."

"You are mistaken if you think I suppose Miss Bell's picture to be anything but fine," he answered. I wish I had seen it. What was the subject?"

"You remember Whittier's poem of 'Amy Wentworth,' don't you? The girl belonging to that proud old family. She was in love with the sailor. But she was as grand as any of them.

> "'strong of will and proud as they,
> She walks the gallery floor
> As if she trod her sailor's deck
> By stormy Labrador!'

Well, she was the subject of the painting, only she wasn't walking the gallery floor, she was on the beach. Oh Jack, you ought to have seen those waves! Why,

I seemed to be watching them tower up and curl over, and see the foam all breaking out green white; and there, in the sky, off in the distance, the sea gulls were flying, I suppose they were bearing messages to him, as the poem says. His ship is away, away off on the horizon, the sunshine strikes the sail and you can catch a glimpse of this. And the wind is blowing, not too hard, you know—a lady beside me, when I was looking at it, said it was all sunshine and free air."

"But you have not told me anything about Amy Wentworth."

"Mr. Impatience! I'm coming to that. I've always tried to teach you to save the best until the last. I've been enveloping you in her atmosphere."

"Oh, that's very fine," laughed Jack.

"Of course it is. Do you think I don't know how to describe a picture? As to Amy, she's walking close to the water's edge, as if she wanted the beautiful waves to touch her. The wind blows her cloak back, but she is holding the folds firmly with one hand, so gracefully. The wind touches her skirts, too, and they flutter a little. She walks like the goddess Virgil tells about."

"He tells about a good many."

"You understand me. I shall not condescend to explain. Her other hand is full of sea-mosses; she holds them out from her, and the long streamers are blowing

back against her cloak, and against her broad-brimmed
hat hanging on her arm. She is looking out to sea,
and she seems so full of the sunshine and the fresh
breeze herself. You ought to see her face ! It is so
glad, and so strong you get absorbed in the charm of
her expression and forget she is handsome besides. I
tell you what I think, Jack; Miss Bell could look just
that kind of way herself, if she were watching for a lover
she thought a great deal of. Why didn't you go to see
the picture the day you were in town ? "

There was no answer for a moment; then Holden said,

" I should, if I had known."

" You see, you shouldn't have gone just the day before I did, and never told me of it. And you staid such
a little while, too ! It wouldn't pay me to go anywhere
for two hours."

" It didn't pay me, for I could not do my errand."

" So you said; but you tried, and there is always a
great deal of satisfaction in that."

" Is there ? "

" Yes, indeed. But I've not told you all about the painting yet. It is quite large. As I was sitting there and talking with the picture-dealer—a very gentlemanly person—
about it, and telling him I was acquainted with Miss
Bell, who should walk in but Mrs. Winters. You remember her ? She knows everything, it seems to me,

about art and artists.   She admired the picture, too, and said it certainly ought to have been at the last exhibition. 'Why in the world didn't she offer it?' I asked.   'She did,' said Mrs. Winters.   'And the committee refused it?' I cried.   'Not they; but I'll tell you something about it that I learned from the best authority.'"

And Mrs. Barney gave a lengthy account, heard from Mrs. Winters, of Helen's withdrawal of her painting which made room for that of a friend.

Jack listened in silence, but his aunt could not complain of any want of attention.

When she had finished he made no comment.

"Should you have expected that of Helen, now, good as she seemed?" she asked him.

"Yes," he answered, and said nothing more, greatly to Aunt Delia's disappointment, who, as she told him, dearly liked a touch of enthusiasm.

A few mornings later Jack called at Mrs. Edgerly's. It was a week since the evening he had spent there, and if the intervals between his visits lengthened, he did not mean them to do so too markedly.   And, also, he did not remember exactly where Helen lived, though he had asked her something about her home, in one of the drives they took so long ago.

Mrs. Edgerly greeted him cordially, and said she was always glad to see him.

Mrs. Mason was at home, and the young ladies. Jenny, as it proved, unconsciously aided him in his errand by asking if he had not gone up to town with Helen the other morning.

"In the same train," he answered.

"Not in the same seat, Mr. Holden, when she was traveling alone?"

"But she was not. Mr. Knight entertained her all the way, and, as I suppose, saw her safely home, for they went out of the station together."

"Indeed!" said Bertha. "If he did, his politeness took him quite a distance."

Kitty smiled, but Jenny, to whom he had turned in answering her question, said nothing, only as he looked at her she seemed paler than usual.

Holden improved the opportunity to learn where Mr. Knight's politeness would take him, in case he accompanied Helen.

The conversation drifted off to other people and other subjects, and Knight remained an undercurrent in the thoughts of three persons, when Andrew, who had just come in, brought him suddenly to the surface again, by remarking to his wife, as he moved back from shaking hands with Holden,

"I met Knight down by the station, Kitty; he said he had just been to call upon you."

"Yes," said Mrs. Mason, "I told him he would be very likely to see you down town."

"Has he been here this morning?" cried Bertha. "Why didn't you tell us?"

"He was in haste and staid only about ten minutes. You and Jenny were occupied with your music, and he came into the east room."

"Didn't he ask for—us, Aunt Kitty?" said her niece, in a tone so low and quiet there was a suspicion of breathlessness in it which made Andrew glance at her. Kitty laughed.

"No, young ladies," she said, "I am obliged to wound your vanity by declaring that he never mentioned either of your particularly. He was going away 'for good,' as people say, and he asked me to make his fare-wells to all the family, and express his thanks for the kindness he had received."

"Probably," drawled Andrew, "he had too short a time to do justice to his emotions in presence of us all."

"Probably," assented Kitty with a mysterious half smile still hovering about her mouth.

"That's not my idea of making one's self agreeab'e, anyhow," cried Bertha, indignantly. "I would have taken the trouble to speak to people that had shown me as much attention as we have him, even if I staid over a train to do it."

"But, you see, he has done with us," said Jenny; "he is not coming back, and it makes no difference any longer what we think about him."

"That is very likely to be so," said Kitty.

"The young girl looked up at her aunt in amazement. If she had done as wiser people than herself occasionally do, made an accusation for the sake of hearing it confuted, she had no reward for her pains.

Andrew glanced from her troubled face to his wife's, which wore a look of open satisfaction, and frowned. It was certain he would not forget either expression.

"I suppose," cried Bertha, "you mean to imply that now Helen has gone he doesn't care to speak to any of us?"

"I have never said anything of the kind," answered Kitty laughing; "if you choose to infer it, you may do as you please. But," she added, "I will tell you this: you will all remember these things that you have been saying now, and they will sound very odd to you some day."

"Why?"

"O, Andrew, there you are again! Girls," she cried still laughing, "do all your talking now, for when you have husbands that are forever following you up with a 'why?' there'll be no chance for it. You are as full of investigations as to the reasons of this and that, Andrew,

as if I were some natural phenomenon. But, poor me !
I'm powerless to answer. Shakespeare was never greater
than when he made somebody say, 'A woman's reason,
I think it so, because—I think it so.'"

"There !" exclaimed Bertha, "how careless it was
in me !"

"I've not a doubt of that. What was it ?" asked
Kitty still greatly amused by some secret cause.

"I borrowed some white floss of Helen to put in
a few stitches with, and here it is still in my basket.
But there are only two or three needlefuls, so it's no
matter," and she proceeded to verify her statement by
unwinding the silk. "There is something written on
this scrap," she said, taking up the folded paper that had
served for a spool. "Poetry, as I live. Listen, friends,
to a voice from the departed."

"For shame, Bertha !"   .

"Well, grandmamma, isn't she departed ? This is
the voice, anyway."

> "'Nor grateful sunshine nor patient rain
>   Can bring dead love to life again.'"

"That's true enough," said Kitty. "I wonder where
she found it."

"Made it, perhaps," suggested Mrs. Edgerly.

"Oh, no, she is not given to sentiment, except—I

mean, she told me she never wrote poetry. That is excellent. Read it again, Bertha."

> "'Nor grateful sunshine nor patient rain
> Can bring dead love to life again,'"

repeated the girl obediently. "She writes a very stylish hand," she added by way of comment.

"Is that her own writing?" asked Jack.

"Certainly. I've seen it dozens of times."

"No doubt of that. May I look at it, if you please?"

Bertha glanced at him in surprise, but he offered no explanation as he reached out his hand for the paper.

He held it a moment, studying it silently, and then gave it back with a simple "Thank you."

He took his leave soon after.

Nearly an hour from this time Kitty went upstairs. She said she had left her scissors in her room; and this was true. But she would have borrowed Bertha's for the nonce had she not been secretly wondering what had become of Jenny, and had not a little tardy fear mingled with her surprise.

In the upper hall she called, "Jenny." But no one answered. She knocked at the door of her niece's room, but not receiving any reply even here, went in.

Jenny was crouched upon the floor, her face and one arm upon the seat of a large easy-chair she was leaning against. She was sobbing with all her might, as her aunt had thought on opening the door.

"My child, what is breaking your dear little heart like this?"

She seated herself on the floor beside her niece, and drew down the girl's head caressingly upon her shoulder. Jenny allowed it to remain there, but she did not cease her sobbing for some time, nor offer a word of explanation.

Meanwhile, Kitty sat silent, recalling with annoyance and some degree of compunction, the warnings she had slighted. After all, Bertha understood better than she had done, for her own thoughts had been so entirely upon another object.

She perceived it would never do for a society woman to be a person of one idea; her wits must be ubiquitous, else her mistakes would be too many to be tolerated. Yet how could she have been prepared for this, when she knew so well what would make it quite out of the question?

"Jenny," she said at last, stroking the soft hair lightly, "who has been distressing you?"

"You," answered the girl looking up at her half-defiantly. Yet in another moment she clung to her again, and added, "No, it was only a little your doing, all the rest was—mine, perhaps. Do you think I have been silly and vain, Aunt Kitty? Have I imagined—things, I wonder, or have they really been said to me? Tell me, do I compare so very badly with Helen? Tell me the truth."

Again she drew back, and faced her aunt with a trembling determination to learn the worst at once.

"You compare well with anybody, my dear, and you know I very much prefer your style to Helen Bell's."

" Others don't, though," sighed the girl; "and at any rate, he does not."

The persons whom Kitty had made to suffer were partially avenged at that moment. As she saw the color in Jenny's averted face, her pride received a severe wound.

"Insolent fellow!" she said to herself, and bent over her niece with a keen dislike of the task before her; for although she had so little scruple in giving pain to some people, she had no fancy for bringing sadness into Jenny's heart.

She recollected that this had come about because Helen was the kind of person that no one but she herself knew her to be.

"You mean Mr. Knight, Jenny?"

"Yes."

"He has no right to pay attention to you, dear."

"Why not? Is he married?"

"I don't know that he is, but—"

The color came back a little into the girl's face, grown white with her last question.

"I didn't know what you meant," she said. "If he is, Helen ought to be told."

"He has no interest in Helen Bell, in that way," cried Kitty quickly.

"I knew it must be impossible," said Jenny softly, her face beaming.

"Nor in you, nor Bertha either, dear; you may assure yourself of that. Whatever nonsense he has spoken, was only in that despicable way of flirtation, and I am very much annoyed that he has been insolent enough to say anything."

"'Insolent!'"

"Yes, Jenny, insolent; because—I must tell you something which you are to keep secret for a time. Will you do it?"

"Yes. What is it?"

She was very pale again, and her fingers locked and unlocked themselves nervously as she waited.

"Mr. Knight is not in a position to aspire to one of you, even if he were the kind of man I should want to see—"

Kitty hesitated.

"Me marry," finished Jenny boldly. "That's what we both mean, so we may as well say it."

"You marry!" echoed Kitty horrified. "Indeed, I couldn't even imagine such a thing, far less mean it. Why, Jenny, I would rather see you—I was going to say in your grave."

"But that is putting it strongly."

"Jenny, take care. Mr. Knight is only a—"

"A what?" the other asked in a voice full of eagerness.

"I cannot say for a few days; I am bound not to do it. But you certainly must put all thoughts of him out of your head instantly. Don't you see, if he had really cared about you, he would have made an opportunity to say good-by?"

Jenny's face fell.

"Let pride keep you from dwelling for a moment upon any silly flirtation which, as you see for your self, Mr. Knight very properly wishes to forget," her aunt went on; "he was only a transient acquaintance, now he has passed out of your knowledge forever. That sort of thing very often happens in society."

Jenny made no answer, unless the look that came over her face at the assertion that the young man had passed out of her knowledge forever were an answer. Mrs. Mason did not see this, for the girl had risen and moved away.

"Kitty!" called Mason's voice in the hall; and Kitty left her niece, to meet, she knew, an ordeal much more severe than this interview had been She came forward, however, with a smiling face.

But though her husband's manner was very grave, and he was evidently displeased, he only inquired about something he could not find in his room, and when she had brought to him what he wanted, left her with a cold "Thank you," unlike his usual genial manner.

Kitty felt that it was very hard. But time would help her—time and patience. She already possessed the latter; as to time, that came of itself. She perceived that, at least, she had been of great use to Jenny, and that the girl's own pride would now do all the rest.

But if, after Jenny had quietly closed the door behind this adviser when Andrew called her away, Kitty had seen the girl's face, she would not have been so confident as to the amount of aid she had given.

"Aunt Kitty is sure he doesn't care for Helen," thought Jenny, "and this is all that really troubles me. As to his going away without a word to me, I'll trust him, as he said so particularly I must do if anything seemed very strange. It may be Aunt Kitty doesn't know the whole of the matter, nor any more important a part of it than I do. I shouldn't wonder if he came back."

So Kitty rejoiced in the excellent results of Jenny's pride, and Jenny, for her part, rejoiced that not pride, but faith, kept the bloom on her cheeks, and the happy tones in her voice.

Before his morning at Mrs. Edgerly's Jack Holden had resolved upon his course. But that same night he stood looking out upon the stars hopeless. He had been meaning to seek Helen, to atone for his wrong, and, did he woo her never so humbly, never so earnestly, never so persistently, to win her at last.

But what was there left for him to do? This interest in himself which he was bold enough to believe had at first sprung up in her thoughts, he had killed, and to-night as he stood beside the window, he saw his own purpose slain by the same weapon. What could devotion or patience do for him now?

> "Nor grateful sunshine nor patient rain
> Can bring dead love to life again."

CHAPTER XII.

"MAMMA, the homeless author of 'Home, Sweet Home' must have realized perfectly the truth of that saying that there is always rest at the centre. I feel as if for the past few days I had come into that centre."

Helen Bell leaned back on the lounge in her mother's room as she said this, and clasped her arms behind her head in a luxury of repose. She had been painting for hours, and came out of her studio in that state of healthful satisfaction which follows earnest work with good result; and sweetens the hours of leisure with the sense of their being well earned.

She watched her mother's gentle face, and met the love in her beautiful eyes. What a blessed change from Kitty's unquiet ways was all this! She ought to have had a thoroughly pleasant winter, since Mrs. Edgerly had been so very kind to her; but, in truth, she felt great relief in freedom from daily annoyances, each one too petty to be remembered, yet vexatious enough while she had to endure it. In the gladness of her home-coming she was sure, she had learned only one thing thoroughly at Lowton—the advantage of keeping away from it in future. There, too, she had received a wound to her pride, or her vanity, as she called it, in her determination to be just.

The whole week since her return she had worked more steadily than ever.

"It is my life, mamma," she answered this afternoon when her mother told her she looked very tired. "Do you remember," she added, "who it is that says, 'Blessed is the man who has found his work; let him seek no other blessedness'?"

Mrs. Bell looked at her a moment with tender gravity, but made no reply.

"Carrie Claude handed in a letter she took from the office for you, Helen," she said after a pause.

"Did she?" cried Helen. "Where is it? On the mantel-piece?" and she was opening it before her mother could speak. "When did it come?" she added unfolding it.

"Half an hour ago. But I knew you would be here in time to answer by to-night's mail, if necessary; so I obeyed orders, and let you alone; since that is all you ever want."

"That was right, mamma. I see it is something about that picture; it has sold, no doubt, for an immense sum," and she laughed incredulously, not without a touch of bitterness.

But after a smothered exclamation as she began to read, she uttered no other sound, only stood looking at the words before her as if she could not fully comprehend them, pale, her eyes dark.

Slowly a light came over her face, and a smile. Then, with trembling lips she bent down and kissed her mother.

"Thank God, mamma, it is over now, all this sickness of hope deferred! What I spoke so scornfully is true; the picture has sold, and brought a great deal more than I dared to expect; and, too, the buyer has given me an order for a companion picture, and I am to choose the subject myself. How could she have understood I should make it so much better with this freedom?"

"'She'? Then it was a lady?"

"Yes; and do you know I am glad of that? It will always be pleasant to me to remember that my first upward step to fame was taken by the aid of a woman's hand. We ought to help one another."

Mrs. Bell laughed.

"That is a touch of sentiment, Helen, which may be pardoned you in consideration of the excitement of the moment. But, depend upon it, had it been a man who bought the picture, you would have found an equally good reason for satisfaction in it, and you would have had cause."

"Mamma, you are the only thoroughly sensible person I know. who is never hard-hearted. No, there is one other."

"Who is it? That Mr. Holden who, you used to write me, was so much at Mrs. Edgerly's early in the winter?"

"No, indeed!"

A look of annoyance and scorn came into Helen's face.

"It was Mr. Mason," she added. "Why do you speak of the other just now, when I am so happy?"

"You have not mentioned him for so long, that for the last two or three months I did not even know he was in Lowton. Has he power to make you unhappy?"

"Certainly not. But he annoys me, as he would you, if you knew him—" she stopped; "if you knew all that I do. about him," she corrected—"and I am Sybarite enough just now to be unwilling my pleasure should receive even a jar."

Mrs. Bell noticed the face momentarily turned away, and the constrained tones. She saw that she was not wholly in. her daughter's confidence. Helen was always much more ready to report pleasant things of people than disagreeable ones. ' Or, if there were. still deeper cause for trouble, the mother had even less reason to expect any sign from this woman who. from her childhood had been slow to speak of what she felt most deeply.. The elder woman's eyes grew full of trust and wistful love as she. watched .the other face struggling. back to its smile, and again turning toward her.

"Have you any subject ready for a companion picture?" she asked.

"I was thinking to-day of something that I could easily make of the same size, but I have not decided yet. It must be a better painting than this one."

"That is why you stand there looking as care-weighted as Atlas !"

"You are a saucy mamma," Helen answered smiling.

Her troubled expression did not return that evening, although several times she grew abstracted in considering what the other picture was to be.;

The next day Mr. Knight called. She was at work, and. excused herself. He went. away, promising to give himself the pleasure of seeing her before long; and he kept his word, for he came the following afternoon, just as she was preparing to go out. He staid until it was too late for her walk, but made himself so entertaining that Mrs. Bell's invitation to him to. come again was very cordial.

"I shall certainly do so," he answered with a bow, and a smiling glance at Helen which suggested to the mother a secret understanding between the two.

But the girl gave no response, she was only coldly polite.

"Is that the way you freeze your admirers?" asked Mrs. Bell when the door had closed upon him.

"If they are people like him, always; but he is not an admirer. I don't think he even likes me very well. I don't know why he should follow up the acquaintance. There is an undertone of assurance in his manner at times that makes me angry with him, for it is a covert insolence."

"I saw nothing of it."

"Of course not. It's more like lifting a mask for an instant than anything. I don't understand Mr. Knight; and, mamma, I don't like him. I hope he will not come here often."

"Unjustifiable prejudice, I think, Helen. In anything serious one can't be too careful—but a mere chance acquaintance like this. You are over-critical. You shall not be compelled to endure his company, though, because I find him entertaining."

"I should like him well enough if he amused you, but I have no faith in him. He is not genuine."

Mr. Knight, however, declined to be disposed of so

easily. Not only did he repeat his visit, and after that come again, but he seemed ubiquitous.   If Helen walked down to the post-office, she was sure to meet him; if she turned the corner at the foot of her street where, as in a fairy-tale three roads met, he seemed invariably to be turning some opposite corner; if she even looked out of her studio window, she so often caught sight of his sauntering or his hurrying figure, though he never glanced up toward her, that she almost resolved to look only skyward in future. She wondered what he was doing here, and what he had been doing in Lowton. Until now she had never troubled herself to wonder about it, but she was so tired of seeing him.

Then he disappeared as suddenly as he had come; and she breathed more freely as she went about the place, hoping he would not return.

Helen's days of indecision were over. She had found the subject for her companion picture, and had been hard at work all the morning outlining it. But the beauty of her conception seemed perpetually to mock the efforts of her skillful pencil.

After a while she grew very weary, and laying down her brush, rose and moved about the room.   Then she stood before her work, scanning it critically a long time; but her eyes kindled, and her breath came more quickly as she studied the grouping and pose of the figures. She saw a fault in arrangement which she came forward to correct, yet the picture promised well. She made the alteration, and laying down her brush again, leaned her hand upon the easel, and stood thinking.

She herself had known from childhood that this was her life-work, but now others were beginning to recognize it, which meant some little fame for her—a thing she did not pretend to scoff at—and probably before very long a modest competence, at least. So far as vantage-ground for her work was concerned, she would have the world before her where to choose. In fancy she had already collected about her all the comforts of life; and by degrees many luxuries would come, since, nowadays, some of them are so cheap. She was to be a woman of independent fortune, a lady of leisure when upon occasions she should choose it. Yet, she sighed.

Again she moved back and stood studying her work. She had been daring in her choice of a subject, and the knowledge of this stimulated her. As she thought of it now, her eyes wandered from her canvas, and rested upon the wall, where her imagination painted in life-size and glowing with color, the lights and deep shadows of life itself, the scene her hand was to imitate.

It was "Cordelia's Farewell to her Sisters." Goneril and Regan stand flushed with elation. The very sweep of their ermined robes is an expression of haughtiness.

Their lofty eyelids look down upon the disinherited sister. They silence her plea for tenderness toward their father by a reminder that she is but a beggar received "at fortune's alms." France stands at Cordelia's side the most chivalrous and most perfect lover in all Shakespeare. Petty souls abhor those buffeted by fortune. But never was a woman more nobly wooed than Cordelia. To France she was "most choice forsaken." "'Tis strange," he said, "that from their cold'st neglect my love should kindle to enflam'd respect." Her matchless betrothal is the one relief to the blackness of her fate.

As she turns to bid farewell to her sisters, one hand rests upon that of her betrothed. He has just said to her, "Thou losest here, a better where to find," and she knows the speaker well. She had been silent when a kingdom was at stake, and silent before her father's calumnies until France declared his faith in her; then love conquered her pride, and she told that her only offence was "the want of a still-soliciting eye," and a tongue she was the richer not to have. The light of triumphant love is upon her face. Yet, she remembers her father left at the mercy of Goneril and Regan, and fear for him tones her joy. Her other hand is lifted toward the open door, through which he has just passed out, and her eyes turned upon these sisters with the eloquent pleading forbidden to her lips.

Helen's delight in her art rose to a white heat as she stood before these glowing figures of imagination, more real to her than pencil could ever make them. She seized her brush again, and fell to work with renewed energy.

As she went on, seeing, instead of the ideal, more and more the canvas under her hand, and the thousand details necessary to produce the desired results, her thoughts turned from the enthusiasm of her vivid fancy to a no less eager imagining of the effect her work would have upon others. She seemed to hear it acknowledged, admired, treasured, and she delighted in her power to create beauty. She saw that she would still do this in poverty or in wealth, in joy or in sorrow; that the artist must live and grow, whatever might fall to the lot of the woman. The inevitableness of this made her fearful while it thrilled her. She accepted it as her portion in life; but was it all?

Her motions became gradually slower, until at last she sat idle while this question held her thoughts, and she searched the lessons of her past life and the possibilities of her future, so far as she could read them, for an answer. Fame loomed before her like a planet still on the horizon; but while she valued what it would bring her, she had little faith in its shedding any light of joy. Once a foretaste of the kind of nature its brilliancy would attract had come to her, and she had learned when the promise of her talent failed of swift performance how quickly her magnetic influence over such a nature ceased.

It seemed long ago since it had been learned. Yet this morning as she touched reverently the figure of noble France, by whom Cordelia despised was loved most, the lesson came back to her freshly again, and she felt deeply that realities could not be won by a name. She remembered that fame would not prevent false and cruel words being said against her, as they had been, and with this recollection the present and the older past faded out in more vivid memories. She sat a long time with her face in her hands.

"What aimless malice!" she said at last half aloud; and after a pause, "It will never be the same." Then, there was another pause. "It was love of truth," she added, so firmly that the tones roused her, and she went on again with her painting.

She would always have her work, and beyond a doubt she loved it. But she felt no more enthusiasm that day.

In the afternoon she went out for a long walk. She needed the fresh air, and wanted to think out and straighten a few things that the morning's meditation had shown her to be a good deal awry.

But as she opened the door, there on the sidewalk, not two rods off, was Mr. Knight again.

"Ah! Miss Bell," he said as he met her at the gate, "I was just coming to your house."

He certainly was a most cheerfully unconscious bad penny.

He refused the invitation to call upon her mother, and, instead, joined Helen in her walk.

CHAPTER XIII.

ANDREW MASON called at Holden's about two weeks after Jack's unsatisfactory trip to Boston, and settling himself in an easy-chair seemed inclined to make an evening of it. He talked little, and often by abruptly changing the subject showed that he was not listening to what was being said. Jack who had been unsuccessfully trying to entertain him, thought him unaccountably dull; and Mrs. Barney stole quietly out of the room at last— to go to bed, her nephew suspected.

Andrew's eyes were watching the door as it closed upon her, and when Holden met them again, he saw at once that now Mason was ready to speak.

"You've not looked in upon us very lately," he began.

Jack was busier than usual, and had been out of town two days.

"I wish you would come," persisted Andrew; "perhaps you could help me. There's a screw loose somewhere down at our house."

"A screw loose?" repeated Jack.

"Ye-es," said the other, and paused. "Kitty is sick," he went on, "and it is not a case for a physician; the poor child is suffering acutely from an hallucination. You may have heard something of it?" he added abruptly.

"No—well, yes—I don't know, it is possible. What is the hallucination?"

"It is an idea about Helen Bell that has taken hold of her."

"Yes; I have heard her speak strangely of Miss Bell."

"Um!" said Andrew, and meditated a few moments. "Depend upon it, Holden, she suffers from her belief; the poor thing is as really sick as if she had a fever, indeed it is a fevered fancy."

Jack said nothing, although he felt as if Mason were waiting for his acquiescence. He could not tell Kitty's husband his opinion of her state of mind, for he did not judge her with the same leniency.

"She has what she calls 'her proofs,'" continued the other, "and I am really afraid she will get herself into some trouble. You, as a lawyer, can warn her of the danger."

"I'm adrift now, Mason; I have never heard a word from your wife that the law could take hold of in any possible way. What do you mean?"

"She is possessed with the idea that Helen—but I would rather have her tell you herself. I shall trust your knowledge to convince her of her mistake; and then, you know, the opinion of an outsider has often more weight than the same opinion given in one's own family."

"I know that. But my legal knowledge is rather rusty, I'm afraid, from want of use. I ought to be ashamed of myself not to have practiced."

"Yes," said Mason deliberately, "it would have been a good thing; you might have given your work to people that needed it."

"I see," returned Jack gravely; "when I find what others do, I feel myself a very good-for-nothing fellow."

"Very," drawled Andrew. "Well, then, you will begin to improve by doing something for Kitty."

"I will try, certainly."

"Or," said Andrew rising, "it may be possible that it will prove to be Helen Bell whom you must help. Are you ready for that, too?"

"I will come to-morrow."

The next day Holden saw all the family when he called upon Mrs. Mason, for she asked him into the morning room and showed a desire for general conversation. Andrew was in excellent spirits, and Jack began to think he must have been playing some joke upon him the night before.

"Holden," said the subject of his meditations, "I must ask you to excuse us this morning, for I promised to drive these young ladies of mine to the 'Oaks,' and our friends will be expecting us. I want to start within ten minutes. Come, Bertha, don't take those 'two more stitches' you're so fond of."

"We'll be ready," answered Jenny, giving Bertha's shoulder a gentle tattoo as she walked past her out of the room.

"It will do just as well by and by," responded Bertha sullenly; "and Mr. Holden came to see you."

"No, I did not," laughed Jack; "I inquired for 'nary a gintleman at all.' I insist upon your not losing your drive, and disappointing your friends on my account, Miss Edgerly," he added, "if you even propose it, I shall go away immediately."

"Where is Mrs. Edgerly?" asked Jenny coming back bonneted and cloaked.

"She has been summoned," drawled Mason, "to see a visitor of distinction. She wants a new cook, and an Irish lady, a professor of the culinary art, has just called to look her over and see how she will suit."

Andrew and the two ladies drove off, Mrs. Edgerly did not return, and Jack was left alone with Mrs. Mason.

He remembered that other morning, early in the win-ter, when such disappointment had come to him through a little confidential conversation with this woman of charming manners. Now, it was the last of April, the snow had gone, and on a day so brilliant as this the earth seemed growing more beautifully green every hour. The fire on the hearth had been allowed to die down to a few scattered coals, and the sun-warmed air came softly in at an open south window.

But there was a change, too, in Kitty; she was not so alert, so smiling, so irresistible as she had been then. To-day her hands lay listless in her lap; she looked thin-ner than a few months ago, and there was certainly a shadow upon her face. Holden could not tell how much of this he should have noticed had nothing been said to him, but now he saw it all plainly enough.

"Bertha has really improved wonderfully within the last year," she said taking up the girl's work and ex-amining it critically. "She is so much more careful and thoughtful than she used to be."

"I am glad she pleases you better as you live to-gether longer," Jack answered. "As to improvement, why of course, there's room for that in almost every-body."

"'Almost everybody?' Do you know anybody per-fect?"

"Not absolutely, but so nearly perfect that I can't see what change ought to be made."

"Then, one of three things is true, Mr. Holden—you know the persons, or person, very slightly; you have no power of criticism; or you are in love."

She looked into his face with sudden penetration as she spoke.

"Whichever you please, Mrs. Mason; the most nearly perfect human being I ever knew was a man; others may be growing to the same moral height, but he had rounded his threescore years, and possibilities had matured into deeds in him."

"Oh!" said Kitty. "Yes, I understand."

She spoke of something else; and after this the subject of conversation changed again in a desultory way; but it never seemed to come any nearer to the matter Holden was waiting to hear about. He grew impatient, and wondered if she were waiting for him to introduce it, or if Andrew had not told her of his last evening's errand. "He may have left me," Jack thought, "to use my own discretion." They were speaking of something that had happened during the winter, and it was easy to ask if any of the family had heard from Miss Bell lately.

"Not directly for nearly a fortnight," she answered, "but I have had news from her through a friend, a gentleman much interested in her movements."

"Indeed !" cried Holden with more emphasis than he meant to use. He added quietly, "May I ask if it is Mr. Knight?"

"Yes."

He did not like her smile.

"The young man paid her a good deal of attention here," he said coolly. "It is not surprising that she interests people."

"Certainly not that she interests people of that kind."

"I thought Knight was a friend of yours, Mrs. Mason?"

"Friendly to me, Mr. Holden !"

"I do not pretend to understand you, but I know you would not introduce a gentleman into your home unless he were a person it was advisable to have there."

There was a troubled expression in his face.

Kitty laughed derisively.

"He was the very safest kind of person to have about one—under the circumstances."

"'Under the circumstances,' Mrs. Mason? You are sphinx-like this morning."

"Am I?"

"You certainly are. But you won't be sphinx-like enough to tear me to pieces, I know," he added smiling, "if I don't guess your riddle."

"No, I will not. It is a much more difficult riddle than the one about the creature that went on four legs in the morning, two at noon, and three at night, for that turned out to be human, and this is of something quite inhuman, something monstrous, which you could never believe, unless you had the proofs of it, as I have."

Holden was silent, waiting to hear more. But Kitty was silent, too. At last she said,

"Speech would be a relief to me, Mr. Holden, if ·I felt it were wise. Yet, why shouldn't I venture to tell you something that everybody will know very soon ? I don't see why I can't, though Mr. Knight cautioned me to give no warning. But you already know what her nature really is."

"Whose nature ?"

"Helen Bell's."

"I know she is one of the noblest women it has ever been my lot to meet. Of this I have become convinced, Mrs. Mason."

Kitty's listlessness had gone, her face quivered with eagerness, and there was the same fierce look in her eyes that Jenny had once seen there. She made a sharp gesture of denial.

"If this 'noble woman' had had her way, I should now be in my grave."

Jack sat staring at her. This was her hallucination? Poor Mason!

Kitty's face grew to a tragic solemnity as she added,

"My life has been in danger for weeks, Mr. Holden. But for a special Providence she would have succeeded, and I should not be living to-day."

"I am very sorry for you, Mrs. Mason."

"Thank you. No doubt you must be. The danger is over now; but I have suffered very acutely. I have been compelled to keep constant watch and ward, for I would almost rather have died than have had any such thing come out against a guest staying in our house at the time—it would have been such a disgrace. Now, the sooner it comes, the better. Yet Mr. Mason has no sympathy with me; he laughs at me, or begs me to be 'sensible,' or turns away looking so distressed I have to give up talking about it."

"He sees the matter as every one must, I suppose, and pities you for the dreadful error you have fallen into."

Kitty threw herself back in despair.

"You, too!" she cried. "But you must believe, both of you, when you have the clear proofs before you. You shall have them to-day. Listen!"

Jack was impressed by the difference between her manner now and in that last conversation about Helen

Bell. Then, as he saw in looking back to it, she had been at ease, smiling, wary, skillful in putting her statements in the best light, and chaining them to trivial facts to make the latter weigh heavily against the accused. But to-day she was pale and grave, and almost tearfully earnest. It seemed to him that her overwhelming belief in the truth of what she was saying swept away all thought of how she was saying it, and that she was more natural than he had ever seen her.

He followed her words carefully while these thoughts were going through his mind. She was speaking of the severe cold she had taken in February during her husband's absence, of her refusal to have the doctor sent for, and of Helen's bringing her some medicine in the night while she was coughing badly. She related her refusal to swallow it on account of its bitter taste, and Helen's anger, and attempt to persuade her.

"And if I had swallowed it," she finished, "I should have been a dead woman, for that bitterness was strychnine."

Her listener smiled.

"Don't you know," he said, "that physicians sometimes prescribe this prepared with other things? I believe in proper amount it is a tonic."

"I do know it. But I saw that prescription afterward—I sent for it—and there was no such thing mentioned in it. And, besides, I have found since there was enough strychnine in the phial to have killed a dozen men."

"Good Heavens!" cried Jack. "She will not take any? You told her about it?"

Kitty laughed in scorn.

"I have not told her one word of it; but you need have no uneasiness as to her making any such mistake."

"But she may have a cough at any time, and go to this; she may be about to use it to-day. Mrs. Mason, you must write—now—this moment—and warn her."

"Oh, no," she answered.

"But for your own safety you must write. When you know of such danger and do nothing to prevent accident, it is guilt."

"Guilt!" cried Kitty. "*I* guilty? This is too much! For my own safety, then, Mr. Holden, since you condescend to have any thought for that, which I must say did not appear at first, the phial is not now in Miss Bell's possession."

"Ah!"

The deep sigh of relief showed how intense his anxiety had been.

"I knew of an apothecary," he added, "or rather an apothecary's clerk, who gave oxalic acid in place of Epsom salts, and the patient took it. Her life was saved, but the culpable carelessness cost the man a good round sum, as it should."

"Things like that happen once in a while, no doubt; not so often as people imagine," was the answer; "but this was no apothecary's blunder."

Holden sat upright, and met Kitty Mason's significant look with what calmness he could summon, for he remembered this was her hallucination, and he must reason with her, and convince her, thus overthrowing her horrible fancies. To do this he must hear her out.

"This was no apothecary's blunder," she repeated, "it was Helen Bell's deliberate intention. She was not pleased with my frank speech to you about her, and this is the way she took to wreak her displeasure."

Jack could no longer sit still; he began to walk up and down the room hastily, and the great vein in his forehead was swollen and throbbing.

"Do you know, Mrs. Mason," he said stopping before her, "that the law can take hold of such an accusation as this, and punish you for it?"

"Certainly—if it is false. But this is true."

"I know that is impossible. But why do you believe it?"

"Am I so used to living with criminals—" Holden's face flushed and his hands shut involuntarily—"that I should suspect such a thing, unless the fact stared me in the face?" pursued Kitty. "She was too ready to give me this medicine, and too angry because I refused to take it, not to have had some purpose. I was sure of that when I came to think it over. And will you tell me, Mr. Holden, if you suppose guests are usually so thoughtful as to carry a tea-spoon upstairs with them at night, lest some member of the household should chance to have a cough? They must have something they are very anxious to administer, to do that."

"That proves no guilt, Mrs. Mason."

"And she had been sitting up," Kitty resumed—"for what? She could not have been at her interminable painting at that hour, midnight. She was waiting for some sign from me to give her the opportunity she had planned for. She came in, oh, so promptly, and you should have seen the look in her face when I refused to swallow her stuff. She was perfectly furious. She must have an angelic temper. I have thought a good deal about her excellent management. Everybody else in the house was asleep. Who would ever know she had given me anything, or spoken to me that night? Do you see?"

Jack walked back and forth a few times without answering. At length he said, looking toward her with a smile,

"So you imagine Miss Bell to have the gift of prescience? She knew before coming here that you would disparage her, and so provided herself in advance with a dose of strychnine?"

"You forget yourself, Mr. Holden," cried Kitty, her eyes flashing at his raillery and the obnoxious word "disparage." "What did I ever say against Helen which time has not shown to have been too lenient?"

"Everything. She is not what you try to persuade yourself."

Kitty was about to reply at length, when suddenly her look of anger vanished, and she broke into a light laugh.

"You don't believe in that French proverb, *Les absens ont toujours tort?* Very well, I honor your defense of the absent. Continue to be Miss Bell's advocate—" Jack started slightly at the word, and a look of resolution swept over his face—"and let me tell you," Kitty went on, "that I am not so stupid a woman as to have made the blunder you generously attribute to me. I never once imagined Helen brought the strychnine here with her, though she undoubtedly did bring the phial of medicine it was in. She added the poison afterward, and I have proof she got it in town."

"What!" cried Holden. Then his lips framed a repetition of the word, but no sound came as he opened them; he could only catch his breath gaspingly, and stand with his eyes fixed upon her, and his face deadly pale.

"Yes," said his companion, "she went out that very afternoon, in the beginning of the storm, and bought this strychnine. . If you want to be very sure, go and ask that apothecary on Willard Street.   I have asked him."

"You have accused Helen in this way?"

Kitty looked at him with her old smile.

"Not quite so fast, Mr. Holden.   The young lady was our guest at the time, and I believe in the old codes that would not let a man lay hands on his deadliest foe so long as that foe is his guest.   You may be very sure I gave Waters not the least suspicion of what I was really trying to learn.   But I found out, all the same."

Holden was silent.   He was beginning to recover his equanimity.   Mrs. Mason's first attack upon Helen had not been the result of hallucination, that had been pure malice, and he thought it not unlikely that now, in this, the same malice was an ingredient large enough to poison the innocuous medicine.

"He remembered Helen perfectly," Kitty said.   "There was another person in the shop at the same time, buying glycerine.   He had seen her before more than once, but could not think of her name.   He was struck by the contrast between the two purchases. . Helen told him she had a little pet dog very sick, and she was afraid of its going mad. She must have given him a long description of the creature pictured in her imagination, for he was quite interested, and asked me whether the lady found it necessary to put an end to her pet. I got out of the affair nicely by telling him I did not know any lady with a dog in that state. He said this lady was probably a stranger who looked like the person I had described. Then I came away, and he forgot all about it."

"Is it like Miss Bell to go into a minute description of her experience and her feelings about anything to a stranger?"

"Exactly what I noticed. The consciousness of guilt gives a person a new manner at once. She must explain why she wanted the strychnine."

"You strain probabilities to make them fit together, Mrs. Mason."

"Is a thing that has actually been attempted a probability?"

"You are not sure of Miss Bell's identity with the lady who bought the strychnine."

"I am. Only I would not say so to Mr. Waters. He described her perfectly to me, even to that very becoming black velvet hat she wears down over her forehead."

Holden sat thinking.

"What are you going to do to clear Miss Bell in your own mind as she ought to be cleared?" he asked finally.

"To clear her?" echoed his listener with a wrathful astonishment in her eyes. "I should think you would ask how I am to save myself from any further attempts on her part."

"It is impossible she ever made any, Mrs. Mason."

Kitty's eyes were colorless with anger.

"You do not believe me, Mr. Holden?"

"I see you are convinced of it yourself, but I certainly believe you mistaken."

"You will discover *you* are the one mistaken."

Her look of anger and threatening gave such force to her words that a dreadful fear seized upon Holden.

He stood watching her in silence, until seeing no change in her resolute expression, he said again,

"Do you realize how grave an offense it is to make a charge like this falsely against a person? If you dare to do this," he went on vehemently, "you shall feel the weight of your act, I promise, and I will keep the promise."

Kitty listened quietly. Then she leaned back in her chair, and smiled in a security that made a thrill of horror run through him.

"You have a somewhat threatening manner, Mr. Holden; but I can find it in my heart to excuse you. No wonder you are thrown off your balance."

"What do you mean to do?" he asked.

"In this matter? Nothing."

She saw Jack's intense anxiety give place to a half smile of relief.

"The thing must be sifted to the very bottom," he went on. "I will undertake to do it. None of us ought to rest until it is done."

"Some of us assuredly will not. But, with thanks for your kind offer, a person, who understands the business much better than either you or I, has undertaken to do that, Mr. Holden."

"You have thrown it into other hands? You have told your cruel suspicions to a stranger?"

"Mr. Knight can scarcely be called a stranger to Miss Bell now, whatever he was a few weeks ago; he has an intimate acquaintance, not only with her movements, but with her motives."

"Who is Mr. Knight?" asked Holden with the eager abruptness that a startling suspicion arouses.

"Mr. Knight," said Kitty, "is a detective."

A strange thrill of joy, like a gold thread in a web of black, shot through the terror that seized upon him at these words.

But it disappeared directly, for the situation was very grave. If there was enough to warrant a detective in dogging Helen's steps for weeks, circumstantial evidence must be strong against her.

"How could you !" he cried. "And do it, too, without having given her any chance to explain, or to justify herself!"

"She will have chance enough for that in good time."

"The shock of the accusation will kill her. At least allow her to speak for herself before you make your suspicion public."

"That is to say, 'Invite her to take a bee-line for the North Pole or the Amazon forests.' I told you the matter had passed out of my hands."

"Don't imagine that I fear for her, except for the horror it will bring upon her. She is as innocent of any such act as you are."

Kitty looked into his face, pale with an agony written upon it.

"Mr. Holden, you are under an hallucination respecting Helen Bell."

In spite of the situation, a grim smile quivered along Jack Holden's lips.

After a pause he said,

"I don't see how a Boston detective could stay in Lowton so long, and go about so much, without being recognized by somebody."

Mrs. Mason smiled.

"That was thought of," she answered. "Mr. Knight is a Connecticut man; he has lived only a few months in

Boston, and the very small risk there was we had to run. Probably no casual acquaintance would have recognized him, detectives have so many ways of disguising themselves. And you must remember," she added haughtily, "he was in different society from any his associates would be apt to frequent, and I don't believe he went about everywhere quite so freely as he appeared to do."

Holden left Kitty before Mason's return.

"If I had been an industrious man with a brain in' splendid trim now, from healthful work," he said to himself as he walked home, "I should reap the reward of it to-day. My indolent self-indulgence recoils on my own head, and that is a small part of the retribution."

"Aunt Delia," he said entering the house hurriedly, "I must take the next train to town; and I may have to be away a few days, I cannot tell now."

"O Jack, must you go? How lonely I shall be!"

"Send for Alice to come and stay with you."

"But you may be back to-morrow, after all."

"What matter if I am? A change will do Alice good, and she will amuse you."

Holden thought, as he said this, that it would be very convenient for him if Mrs. Barney had some occupation now.

"But I thought you always laughed at Alice, though she is a distant cousin, you know, Jack?"

"Don't tell her I ever laughed at her, and I'm sure I shall not do it this time."

Mrs. Barney noticed nothing peculiar in her nephew's tone as he made this promise, nor did he hear the asseverations that she should never mention his fault, and her complaint of his haste. He was already in his room, throwing a few things into his valise.

His horse and man were waiting at the door as he came down, and, with a word of farewell to his aunt, he was off before she could gather breath for a single question.

She consoled herself, however, by reflecting that this did not make so much difference as it might seem to do, for Jack never would answer questions when he was in a hurry. He was "downright obstinate," she said to herself, "a real Mede and Persian" about the thing.

She remembered, though, that with all his haste he had found time to give her practical advice, and she determined to take it, and to send for Alice.

CHAPTER XIV.

IF one could move with the speed of electricity! And this, unless it should outstrip thought, would at times seem too slow for us.

So Holden found the speed of steam. Only his watch could convince him that the train was running at its usual rate. For any of these precious moments might be the last in which he could do any thing to save Helen. If he could see Knight immediately, it seemed to him that something might be done. This was the first step.

On reaching town, he drove at once to the address Mrs. Mason had given him. He did not inquire for Mr. Knight, however, but for Detective Day.

That gentleman would not return until late in the evening, the inquirer had still several hours on his hands. They crawled by at last.

When next he asked for him, the detective was at home.

He was sitting wrapped in a gayly flowered dressing-gown, his feet in a pair of brilliant wrought slippers, and was busily reading the papers as Holden was shown into the room. The latter looked at him scrutinizingly, amazed at seeing how much of his style had been hung up in his dress coat. There was a certain jauntiness about him, but it required self-control and adventitious aids to make it gentility. Holden had not left his name in the afternoon, and to-night was shown in unannounced, so that he had time to observe before the other looked up from the paragraph which interested him, how very much Detective Day off duty differed from the gentlemanly, even if somewhat too elaborate Mr. Knight. Kitty was right, a casual acquaintance might easily have passed him by unrecognized.

There was a difference, too, in his greeting. He did not say, "Ah! Holden, how are you?" in the off-hand, Lowton way which, although Jack could find nothing in it to resent, had always annoyed him. He was equally unembarrassed to-night, but his ease was that of business relations, not of social intercourse. If he felt surprise in recognizing Holden, his expression of it was too slight for the other to perceive.

Jack told his errand with the directness it demanded, ending with an assurance that the character of the lady in question made it impossible she should have ever held the purpose Mrs. Mason was trying to fasten upon her, and a reference to the deceptive nature of circumstantial evidence.

"Yes, it is strange," returned the quondam Mr. Knight twisting the ends of his mustache meditatively, "how many of our aggravated cases are just where one would naturally suppose the thing impossible."

He had passed over the last remark.

"Have you informed Miss Bell of our reasons—my reasons—for being interested in her?" he added.

"It is the very thing I am so anxious she should not know," cried Jack. "I have not seen her since the day she left Lowton."

Mr. Knight smiled.

"I am perfectly aware of that. All the young lady's visitors, as well as her movements are known to us." Holden winced. "But I thought it possible you might correspond with her."

"I have told her nothing about it," he answered, ignoring the impertinence of putting the question in this way.

"You have been wise," said the detective. "It would only have alarmed the lady before the time, and she could not have escaped us."

"That would be the last thing she would ever try to do, if you left her free as air."

Knight bowed and smiled with the manner of humoring a man in his mistake.

"If you think my object is to try to buy off justice," pursued Holden eagerly, "you were never more mistaken. I shall never rest until the truth comes out clearly. But I am certain, absolutely certain, of Miss Bell's innocence, and I want her to be spared the consciousness of having ever been suspected of a crime."

"I see."

"The utmost I desire is a little time to investigate the facts before you speak. Watch all her goings and comings as carefully as you like, and mine too, if you choose —" here Knight shook his head in silent protest—"but give me this. Do nothing in haste. There is some great error here; I want a few days—say a week—to solve it. You will wait that time?"

"Impossible, sir."

"You have waited several, now."

"All the more reason for no further delay. I agreed with Mrs. Mason in the first place to say nothing while the young lady was in her house."

"Mrs. Edgerly's house."

"Indeed? All one to me. And, besides I was not ready myself. I had to get possession of that phial. She kept it locked in her trunk, and I had no chance until the night of the masquerade party. I managed to do it then with a key Mrs. Mason had kindly enabled me to have made by furnishing me with a wax impression of the lock.   I told her how it should be done.   Mrs. Mason is very apt; though she showed no wisdom, Mr. Holden, when she troubled you with all this."

"Did you take advantage of such a time as that?"

"By all means.   One of the best chances in the world. I should have shown myself unfit for my business if I had let it slip.   Then, there were a few other things to be looked after.   I have taken my time about these, and have quite enjoyed visiting Miss Bell in a social, friendly way.   But I am all ready now, have a very fair case made up, and may spring the trap at any moment."

Holden made an instinctive movement of dread, and repulsion.

"I have no fear as to the result of your attempt," he cried, "but the publicity of the thing will be terrible; it will kill her; you have seen so much of her, you must have noticed her pride."

An evil look came into the detective's eyes.   He had, indeed, been very sensible of it in his consciousness that he had not acted his part so perfectly that Helen Bell had not felt him to be less than he appeared, and had resented by silent dignity those occasional slight oversteppings of respectful distance which would never have occurred if his manners had not been an assumption.   Mr. Knight was therefore, not unwilling to break her pride.

"She will come out of it with honor—you say," he

answered. "I must perform my duty, that is all my lookout, and it is a part of it to be prompt in whatever I have to do. At any rate," he went on, "you may be perfectly sure the blow will fall the hour you attempt to communicate with Miss Bell."

Holden sat silent with his eyes on the ground for so long a time that Knight wished he would go, and leave him free to finish reading his newspapers.

"Will you let me look at the phial of Miss Bell's in your possession?" he asked finally. "I only want to examine it in your hands," he added in answer to the other's defiant glance, "to see the number of the prescription."

"Oh, I understand," said the detective. "With great pleasure, sir, by and by, at the proper time; at the examination if you wish. Not to-night."

Holden rose, and for the space of a full minute stood looking down at the self-satisfied little man in contemptuous silence.

Then he went away without having been able to compel himself even to bid him good-night.

But in the street his anger gave place to something still more importunate. The detective's conduct was important only in its consequences, and Holden's mind turned upon these.

He saw that he must have the number of that prescription immediately and learn where it was put up. He ought to have done this in Lowton. But he had not been prepared for Knight's behavior. How could he get the needed information now?

Telegraph to Mrs. Mason. He knew she had given the detective this number, and the name of the apothecary before he got possession of the medicine itself.

But in the office, with the pen in his hand to write the telegram, he hesitated.

There was no predicting what Kitty would do, he thought, further than that it would probably be something disagreeable.

He sent the telegram to Andrew.

"I believe when Mason speaks, she obeys him," he reflected, "though, Heaven knows, she does a good many things without leave or license from him."

He waited in the office for the answer which, through his insistence perhaps, came promptly. Then it was too late to do anything more that night, and the next day the opportunity might have gone by.

The morning sky was as clear as if it were overhanging a world without a cloud of care upon it. But it was one of those atmospheres in which lurk hidden vapors that often gather into heavy clouds and rain before sunset.

Holden went first to the apothecary. His store was

in the same town with Helen. He was a tall, pleasant-faced young man with close-cropped auburn curls and the reddish brown eyes that often accompany this color. He was decided in movement, vivacious in expression. Holden had a heart-sinking as he looked at him; he did not appear at all the kind of man to make blunders.

Yet Jack was sure the accident must have happened here, in some way, if not stupidly.

He asked for a list of the ingredients in the prescription he named.

This was given him with evident wonderment.

He then bought a certain amount of each drug in the list, and slipping the different bottles into his pocket, went directly into town again and left them with an eminent chemist to be examined for strychnine.

He had not caught a glimpse of Helen.

He wandered about the city to pass away the hours until it should be time to return to the chemist. It was impossible to read, he was too anxious to try to amuse himself in any way; luncheon helped him through a little of the time. He hoped much from the search, yet he could not help feeling that Knight must have done this same thing.

He kept his appointment to the minute, and was obliged to wait half an hour.

Then the chemist told him that there was no trace of

strychnine in any of the medicines.   He had, of course, not had time for any careful analysis, but they seemed to nim unusually pure.   He should recommend the apothecary.

Holden had scarcely strength to stand as he listened to this statement.

He walked the streets, seeing and hearing nothing that was going on about him, trying to think out what ought to be done next.   He had no more idea than before that Helen was guilty, but she was in terrible danger.

The sky had darkened, and the heavy clouds seemed overburdened with rain, for every now and then a great drop fell to the earth with a splash, warning the foot-passengers on the thronged pavements to seek shelter.

Holden did not notice the coming storm, he had almost reached his hotel, and was going in there for want of anything better to do, when something made him look up; he had been walking with his eyes cast down, paying no more attention to the passers-by than was necessary not to jostle against them.   The street was not so crowded just here, and he saw Helen Bell coming toward him.   The umbrella held over her head showed that the rain had begun, but he still did not think of it; he felt a sharp spasm of pain as he looked at the grave serenity of her face, for the hand that held the umbrella so carefully over her head and accommodated itself so readily to her motions, was the hand of Mr. Knight. His steps were keeping pace with hers, and his watchful courtesy of manner was horrible to Jack. Helen seemed to him under some dreadful spell and this ever-present detective a monster who circled around and around her, coming closer and closer, until in his grasp not even her thoughts would be free, but must turn constantly upon the agony of the poisoned thrust he was to give.

It was not given yet.

But even this consolation was cut short, for Knight was looking at him with a triumphant leer which made the other clench his hands to prevent himself from spring ing upon him. Perhaps she would not even get home free.

Holden was looking straight into her face with his thoughts so fixed upon the horror of her position that it was not until he stood almost on a line with them in passing that he remembered to return her bow.

As soon as they had gone by he turned and looked after them, perceiving then how coldly she had greeted him.

In another moment the two were lost to sight in the endless procession on the sidewalk.

Jack kept on to his hotel, picked up his traps, and went home. He decided that Andrew must do something here. At all events, he would consult him.

Andrew was out of town, however, not expected back until very late at night.

Every moment he would buy up with gold-dust, if he could, and he must wait another weary night without even an attempt at work. In his restlessness he even thought of going back to Boston again, but he saw that in this way he might lose time. He must stay and do nothing, and look over his newspaper, when he did not even know whether he were doing the wisest thing or the most foolish.

Alice had come, and she and Mrs. Barney alternated between gossipping busily together and turning their combined artillery of questions upon him. He did not surrender the fortress of his own counsel, however.

"Oh, it's of no use, Alice," said Mrs. Barney, with a spirited twitch of her knitting ball, "there is an obduracy about Jack which I'm very sorry to see;" she ignored the presence of her nephew sitting opposite with a Review in his hand as completely as if he had been a lay figure.

"Why," responded Alice, accepting her hypothesis and speaking with weighty deliberation of tone, "I suppose it's none of our business if he does not want to say why he went away in such a hurry, and why he looks so sick to-night. He told you something he had undertaken to do was going wrong."

"But everything that is his business is mine, too, when I am so interested in him," pursued Aunt Delia. "You haven't sufficient imagination to teach you what my feelings must be, Alice."

Alice, thus dubbed the unimaginative, acquiesced in silence. She had not a high opinion of herself, and she knew that nobody else had. The best of the matter was, she had so much to do always that she never found time to give this more than a passing thought once in a great while. Yet her dead brother's children, if they had been old enough to speak in the matter, would have borne witness that she understood very well how an aunt should feel.

Jack had never known her when they both were children, she somewhat the elder, and living a few miles from Lowton. It was only within the last few years that he had perceived how small pleasure her lot afforded her and how little it promised. Since this time her affairs had taken a turn for the better. She could not see exactly how it came about, but this took nothing from her enjoyment of the new comforts. She told Holden one day that she believed she should always have them now; he thought so too.

"He is not always wise by any means," continued Aunt Delia, taking fortune at the flood, for a patient listener and an inexhaustible subject formed the climax of her satisfaction. "For instance, now, the last time I went to Boston I saw a very fine picture painted by an artist we know, a Miss Bell, whom Jack and I helped on the way to Lowton through that dreadful storm the night I came here."

"I don't see how," interposed Holden.

"Ah! you're listening. You know what is said about listeners."

"Are you going to prove it to me?"

"Oh, no; I was only going to say I praised Miss Helen's painting very much to you—by the by, Alice, you must have seen her at our party—and of course I thought you would buy it. But you didn't take the hint. It is too late now; the thing is sold, as it deserved to be. I saw it in the paper. Some lady who knows how to adorn her house purchased it."

Jack made no answer. He began another paragraph.

"I remember Miss Bell," said Alice with her usual deliberation, "and I have seen her somewhere since then, but I can't think where it was. No, I can't think," she repeated sitting with her needle poised in her hand, and her slow-moving brown eyes fixed on the shadowed corner of the room which represented vacancy. Her mouth was large, but it closed well, her nose was undeniably clumsy, and her complexion decidedly the worse for her dyspeptic tendency and too careless exposure to the weather. But her plain face was cheerful and reliable. Jack Holden, glancing at her as she sat trying to recall where she had seen Helen, felt a respect for her goodness. Yet he was sure he could never help being amused at her precise speech and her droll ways. He had been obliged to restrain a smile several times this evening, though never mortal felt less like mirth than he did now.

"I wonder where it was I did see her last!" she reiterated. "No matter though," in an undertone as Mrs. Barney spoke to her on another subject. In answering she forgot all about Helen.

But her question gave fresh keenness to the recollection that had never been absent from Jack's mind. He could not bear the thought of where and how companioned he had seen Helen Bell last. The security of his own position, the serene undercurrent of these women's lives, made too sharp a contrast for him. Their trivial talk and his aunt's petty, half good-humored complaints jarred upon him too much. Alone, he could at least show his restlessness. He went to his own room.

The next morning, directly after breakfast, which at his request was earlier than usual, Holden started out upon the errand he could not accomplish the night before. He might have to wait for Mason, who was a late riser, but even that was doing something for his object.

At his own gate he met Alice ready for walking.

Both looked surprised, and she laughed.

"Are you going down town so early?" he asked.

"Yes; I have a great many errands to do, and I like to take my time about them; and the sun is very hot in the middle of the day with one's winter things on."

Jack forbore to ask her if it was the sun that had "one's winter things on." He held the gate for her to pass out, and as he followed, she walked on beside him.

"You are going my way?" she asked after taking a few steps.

"That depends. I am going to see Mr. Mason on urgent business. I shall be happy to have you take the Cedar Street way, if you will pardon my leaving you when we come to Mrs. Edgerly's."

"Oh, la! yes. That won't make any difference."

She spoke with such evident sincerity that Holden did not know whether to say "Thank you," or not.

They walked on amiably together until he reached his destination.

"Very likely I shall meet you down street, yet," she said as he left her with an apology. "I feel as if I should."

Jack thought it unlikely.

But he had forgotten Alice as he laid his hand on Mrs. Edgerly's door-bell.

Andrew had not returned yet, he would probably come by the next train; Mrs. Mason was going to send to the station for him.

The next train from the direction in which he had gone was not due for two hours. Holden said he would call again.

He went to the post-office, resolved to stroll along at his leisure toward the station, and meet Andrew as he came in.

But he found strolling a difficult pace this morning, and had more than once to remind himself that the train would be no swifter for his haste.

He met several acquaintances, and stood talking to one and another. But his inward fever prevented him from remaining long anywhere. He began to question with himself whether it would not have been better if he had not waited for Mason.

"There, I told you so!" said the voice of one hurrying on behind him, and Alice touched his arm.

The eighth wonder of the world is the man or woman too magnanimous ever to say "I told you so."

She asked him to go with her into a store near by, and he did it.

Then she said she had a few other errands to do. Would he not go to those other places too with her, if he was not busy?

Holden glanced at his watch. Alas! there was nothing he could do for an hour.

At any other time he would have enjoyed Alice's shopping. She held the goods up to the light to see they were not flimsy, she examined a specimen pin from the papers to find out if they had points as well as heads, a precaution she assured Jack her experience made necessary. She peered into, and over, and around everything that she even talked of buying, and then frequently decided she would not take it until to-morrow. Sometimes, on the other hand, she made queer purchases on the mere possibility of wanting the things.

"Only one more store," she said encouragingly as she heard her companion's impatient sigh. "I've only one more thing to get, and that is for Aunt Delia. Over here."

So saying, she led the way into the shop of Waters, the apothecary.

CHAPTER XV.

HOLDEN followed reluctantly. He wanted to have nothing to do with this man at present, for he did not believe he could question him with Mrs. Mason's skill, and elicit information of Helen's having been there and her purchase, without at the same time arousing any suspicion in him, especially, since the ground had already been gone over. If the matter must become public, then, he thought, would be time enough to question him. Or, in any event, the other part of the matter came first, as this was only negative evidence.

Alice executed her commission for Mrs. Barney, and then she lingered here. She took up the cologne bottles, and admired their pretty shapes without ever thinking that Jack would immediately make her a present of one of them.

Still she lingered, looking at this thing and that, asking questions and talking a little in a desultory way. Secretly, she felt very much inclined to a little chat, for she had that kind of acquaintance with the apothecary which arose from her having made small purchases of him at different times; but she stood somewhat in awe of her cousin's opinion of such a proceeding. She remembered, also, that he was to meet some one later, and she must not keep him too long. Mr. Waters however, was a smiling, talkative little man, and although the clerk, a half-grown boy, held out no hope of brilliancy, he had the most good-natured face in the world. These things, and the comfortable coolness of the store after the hot sunshine, were strong temptations when combined with a recollection which made her twice open her lips to address the apothecary. But she closed them again as she glanced at Holden; he stood apart with an air of abstraction that she feared might express annoyance.

At last he started, and looked at his watch.

"You will excuse my leaving you at once?" he said coming up to her; "I shall not have more than time to reach the station before Mason gets in."

"Oh, yes, indeed," she answered; adding, "you'll be home to dinner?"

"I suppose so."

"Good morning, then."

And she turned back immediately to the counter, laid one arm upon the frame-work of the glass-case, and looked eagerly at Mr. Waters.

"My little dog didn't die after all," she said; "he got better as soon as I showed him the bottle, knowing little Tyke !"

"Ah ! indeed ?" said the apothecary smiling blandly to hide the blankness of his recollection. "So you didn't have to give him any medicines to cure him ?"

"Cure him !" echoed the lady. "My goodness, sir, what do you call curing him, I'd like to know, if that would do it ?"

"We sell so much, and to so many different people," apologized the man, "we can't keep track of everything. What was it I gave you ? I can't think this minute of anything good for a dog. Was it a little one ?" he added with great depth of interest in his tones.

"A little darling, and a beauty, too—though I believe everybody's dog is a beauty to the one that owns it. But Nelson is downright handsome, such curly—"

Here she turned her head with the sudden consciousness that she had not heard the door close behind Holden.

He stood like a statue, his hand withdrawn from the latch, his eyes fixed upon her, his ears drinking in her words.

She stopped speaking, and looked at him in amazement.

"Why, John, I didn't know you were so fond of dogs.

But you needn't be troubled about Nelson—you remember him, I see, dear little fellow!—for I didn't have to give him the strychnine; there was no danger of his going mad, after all; it was only Harriet Ann Bonner that scared me so about it, and—no, you don't remember what a storm I came for it in?" and she turned to Mr. Waters. "I was determined, you see, John," looking at Holden again, "that nobody but I should have anything to do with the little thing, if it was really necessary to put an end to him, and I had heard that was the way the agent of the 'Prevention of Cruelty to Animals Society does it—by poison, you know; a neighbor told me he did so to their dog when they lived in town and sent for him. He uses Prussic acid, but I'm afraid of that, so I got the other."

"When was this?" asked Holden.

"It was just before Valentine's Day. I can remember the date, because I know I kept Mr. Bolton waiting in the snow while I got something for the children. He drove me into Lowton. But won't you miss your friend, John?"

"No—yes—no matter. I am interested in hearing about your dog."

But before Alice could begin any account of her pet's present good health and amusing ways, he said to the apothecary,

"Don't you recollect, Mr. Waters, who the people are to whom you sell poison?"

The man grew red and then pale. He saw confidence and custom slipping away from him in Holden's stern look, a mirror of public opinion, if that were roused. He exchanged a significant glance with his clerk.

"There were two of 'em here at the same time," explained that functionary coming to the rescue—"two ladies, I would say," he corrected—"and I suppose we must have got 'em just a little mixed. One was buying gum Arabic, or somethin' or other of that kind; it's easy, you know, when there's lots of people in."

"I told you, you know, at that time the lady was asking," he added in an aside to his employer, "I wasn't quite certain 'twas the one you said bought it; but you was so sure, and she'd be likely to think you had the right of it."

"Pshaw! That's of no consequence," answered Waters confidentially. "I know all about her. I only wish your wits were as good as your memory, Tim. She was just asking things for the sake of talking; she'd never think of it again. No trouble about that."

Holden listened with an impassive face. It would not have been prudent to utter his thoughts at that moment.

Suddenly, he turned to the boy.

"Have you been serving in this store all winter?" he asked.

"No, sir, only off 'n' on."

"Considerably off, for that matter," said Waters with alacrity.

Holden stood a moment in thought. Perhaps, then, Knight had never seen him.

"Did I understand you to say that you told a lady some other person bought strychnine of you last winter, when it was my cousin, here?"

"It was only Mrs. Mason that came in one day—I remember all about it now—and I'm sure I don't know how we got talking of such things. She had been admiring some of my cut-glass cologne bottles, just as that lady did now, and took one of them. We were speaking of the weather and what storms we had had; she spoke of the one we'd just been having. I remember, as your cousin says, it was about the middle of the month, and Mrs. Mason shivered and said, wasn't it dreadful, she hadn't got over the cold it gave her; it was just the weather for suicides, she said, if people were disposed to it. That set us talking about such things, and she asked me if I had ever had the misfortune to sell anything dangerous to anybody that made a wrong use of it? I told her 'no.' Then I laughed, and said a lady came in the other day, after the storm had begun, and wanted some strychnine to give her dog. She was quite interested for the moment, and wondered if she knew anybody who had a sick dog, and asked me how the lady looked. My boy says I got her mixed up with somebody else that was in at the same time; but, you see, Mrs. Mason didn't really care at all. I know she forgot all about it the next minute, for she branched off into something quite different, and went away without another word about it."

"Are you quite sure it was Mrs. Mason?"

"Sure. Wasn't it, Tim?"

"Oh, you want my memory this time, do you?" responded the boy with a grin. "Yes, 'twas Mrs. Mason," he added to Holden.

"There's one thing sure, anyway," interrupted Alice— "you'll miss your friend."

Holden made no answer; he stood a moment in thought, looked at his watch again, asked the apothecary for paper and envelope, penciled a line hastily, addressed it, and going to the door with it in his hand, turned to say to Alice,

"Tell Mrs. Barney, please, not to wait dinner for me. I am quite sure I cannot be there; and don't be anxious if you shouldn't see me to-night."

"Why—" she began, but he had gone.

"Quite his share of curiosity, for a man, hasn't he?" remarked the apothecary with a sigh of relief as the door closed. He was not as grateful for having got off so easily as he was annoyed at having been found in the wrong.

"For a man!" echoed Alice indignantly. "I never saw a man yet that wasn't twice as anxious to find out every living thing that ever went on as any woman could be. Talk of women's gossip, indeed; it isn't a circumstance compared with men's! Good morning, sir."

Before the astonished little apothecary had recovered his breath, she was half way across the street, making for home at a speed increased by her wrath at this masculine slight to her sex, and her amazement at Holden's behavior. She was about to talk everything over with Aunt Delia.

Jack, meanwhile, was on his way to the train, not to meet Andrew now, but to go himself to town.

He wondered why he had not thought before of his present plan in regard to Mason. He felt that he could not stay here another hour when he did not know what might be happening to Helen. He asked himself, as he started, why he was so relieved and at ease? There was no reason for it so far as Helen's danger of arrest was concerned. This evidence he had just gained was purely negative. She had not bought the strychnine where Mrs. Mason said; it did not legally follow that she had not bought it at all.

One thing was proved conclusively, however, by the story he had heard this morning—that there was a spice of willfulness in Kitty Mason's hallucination; for she had not been willing to accept the clerk's suggestion of a mistake as to the purchaser. She had not even mentioned the possibility to Holden. Perhaps it was this which made him feel as if all the rest of the evidence were equally easy to break down.

Yet he knew he was wrong here; the matter had been already tested.

But interrupting all his thoughts and plans, more clear to his mind and persistent than any of these, was the picture of what he had seen the day before: of Helen with her noble face and look of grave unconsciousness, and at her side the evil genius of her circumstances who could cloud all her days. He meant to do it. Holden had read this determination in the grin of triumphant malice turned upon him as the two passed by.

Was it done already?

He moved restlessly in his seat. How slow this express train seemed.

"There he is now," cried a voice from the opposite aisle. "'Talk of an angel,' etc."

"Or the other way, if you ladies like to put it so," reached him in tones that could be no other than Dewey's.

There came a subdued giggle.

He looked in its direction. He was in the same car with Bertha, Miss Grierson, and Dewey. Worse than this, they recognized him; still worse, they saw that he recognized them.

Bertha beckoned vigorously, but he had already turned away with a bow.

In another moment Mr. Dewey was at his elbow.

"They want you over there," he said. "I can offer you a seat."

Holden could find no excuse for refusing.

But it was Bertha who offered him a place. She had slipped from Jenny's side into the seat Dewey had been occupying, facing them, and now looking up said,

"Sit here, Mr. Holden."

She paid no heed to Dewey's blank look, nor the angry glare that followed it as he subsided into the vacant place beside Jenny. Holden saw no way of escape until the train stopped. He resolved to bolt then.

"Are you going to the matinée?" asked Bertha.

"I did not know there was one."

"Come now, Holden," grunted Dewey, "that's just a little steep. There are as many as twenty persons from

Lowton in this very car going to town for the express purpose, and I don't know how many in the train. Don't you think you will change your mind about it when you get to town? Such things have happened to people."

Bertha laughed teasingly, and Jack would have been angry if he had considered the young man of sufficient consequence to regard his insolence.

"Won't you change your mind?" echoed Bertha.

"Impossible, Miss Edgerly. I have a pressing engagement. Has Mason come home?"

"Yes, we passed him on the driveway as we were starting."

"He likes that answer," thought Jenny.

Dewey began to talk about the matinée, German and Italian music, the ideal and realistic schools, and some of their disciples, liberally sandwiching in his own opinions and spicing highly with criticism. Holden listened to him' only when directly addressed, and, notwithstanding Dewey's vigorous efforts, would not be drawn into an argument. In vain the other grew eloquent, Holden had only monosyllables, when he answered him at all.

"Why don't you compose an opera yourself, Mr. Dewey?" asked Jenny at last with her most demure expression. "Then we all shall see at once everything you mean, and the result of your methods."

"To tell the truth, Miss Grierson, I have indulged

myself in publishing a song or two, but you will never get the other thing from me. . It is too laborious, and I'm not fond enough of work. I leave that for the 'digs' who have the divine industry popularly called 'afflatus.' The real difference between man and man is ambition, rather than ability. For example, now no doubt you or Miss Bertha could paint quite as skillfully as that friend of yours, Miss Bell, if you had as much ambition, and found it necessary to work."

Holden's hand took a sudden, firm grasp upon the arm of the seat. But when a moment after he perceived Jenny smiling broadly at this statement, he smiled, too.

"Thank you for your good opinion, Mr. Dewey," she answered when Holden's sympathy had turned her smile into a laugh. "Mr. Knight is a very fair draughtsman, perhaps you include him also?"

"Certainly; although he would have the masculine stamp of work."

"The 'stamp out' you mean?"

"Be quiet, Jenny. What nonsense you always talk when you get—"

"'On the rampage,'" Bertha. "I wouldn't be too elegant to say it, for that is exactly what you mean. It's true I feel so already, and when the inspiration of the music comes, I don't know what will happen."

"Has Mr. Knight been down this week?" asked Dewey with evident disapprobation of her mirth.

"No—yes—I believe so. Didn't Aunt Kitty say he called the other day, Bertha?" and she turned a guileless countenance, flushed with her laughter, upon her companion.

"I saw him last week when I was in Boston," he went on after Bertha's answer. "He was walking with Miss Helen, and seemed to be in high feather. They both had a very lover-like air."

"Kit says she is sure something will come of that," remarked Bertha.

Holden happened to be looking at her opposite neighbor as she said this. He saw that the color had faded entirely from her face, and that her eyes were dilated.

In an instant she had recovered her self-control.

"I don't think that," she said lightly; "it is not like either of them, certainly Helen."

"At least, no one here knows yet," he thought. "But can Miss Grierson care for a rumor like this?"

So the conversation rambled on. Holden did not try to follow it, and after a time the others, finding him in so unsocial a mood, left him to himself.

In imagination he was holding conversations with Knight, or skillfully cross-questioning that apothecary, out of whom it did not seem possible any satisfaction could be had, and here it was that he hoped so much from the aid of Mason's keenness.

Occasionally, a few words of the talk around him found lodgment in his brain, generally a brief one, for his own fancies, taking up their swift march again, soon displaced them.

But at last one sentence came to him in this way, a remark of Dewey's, in itself trivial, and having not the slightest apparent connection with anything but the proposition of Bertha's which it was meant to answer. Yet the truth in it flashed an illumination to Holden, and showed him the possible cause of his failure.

He started up.

"What's the matter?" cried Jenny.

He looked at her a moment, as if not comprehending what she had said. Then, instead of reseating himself, as he seemed at first about to do, he answered,

"We are there! We have arrived, Miss Grierson," he added deliberately, smiling as the train began to slacken its speed and cross the many tracks on its way into the station.

"Oh, we did not notice," said Jenny; "it's only the abstracted people who see and hear everything."

Holden laughed, for he had really started up from the impetus of his sudden thought, and fortune had been kind enough to favor him with an excellent reason for not sitting down again in some confusion.

He helped Bertha from the train; and then, with a word of apology for his haste, raised his hat and disappeared directly.

In two hours, however, he was again at the station, eagerly watching the passengers that alighted from the Lowton train. He had almost satisfied himself that the blow had not fallen yet; but it must come very soon, unless he could ward it off.

Business men walked by with hurried tread, ladies richly clad, attended by gentlemen, or looking out for carriage or horse-car sailed past; there were women with bundles and shabbily dressed, a long procession in all. But it was not long enough for Holden, since it ended without bringing to him the man he was hoping to see.

He watched and waited, until he was sure they were not merely being separated by the jostle of the crowd.

"No, he has not come," he said. "Could she have hindered him? I am sure not, unless—"

You are quite right, Jack Holden, to turn away impatiently, angrily—you are quite right, to go at once, alone, to your self-appointed task, since you are not to have the help you counted upon, and there is not, indeed, a moment to be lost; but, for once at least, you are doing

Kitty Mason injustice in supposing she has kept back your note to her husband until too late. She really knows no more about it at this moment than he does. Andrew's non-appearance where he is so earnestly wanted has a much simpler explanation than this.

If you could have followed the course of that little, bright-eyed boy to whom you intrusted your precious note as you came out of the apothecary's shop this morning and hailed a passing hack, you would have seen it to be much more eel-like than arrowy. You saw him start off in the right direction, to be sure, for he was a child of good intentions; but he had fallen into a habit of using them as paving stones for certain underground quarters. When he promised to deliver the letter immediately, he meant to do it; but he met a companion, he stopped to tell him of his good luck, and your quarter found its way out of the boy's pocket a long time before your letter did; for it was not until after nine o'clock that evening that he laid an imperative hand on Mrs. Edgerly's front door bell.

Andrew, who was crossing the hall at the moment, opened the door.

A little, panting urchin thrust a crumpled paper into his hand with the brief statement that it belonged here, and dodging back, scampered down the steps, and was out of sight in an instant.

Andrew held the note under the hall gas, and read with some difficulty, for the never too legible penciling was not made plainer by its many creases:

"Meet me in the station in Boston by the noon train from Lowton. Don't fail to come. I have no time to explain until I see you. Your wife knows what it is about.

"Yours,

"J. R. HOLDEN."

"Kitty!" he called as Mrs. Mason sat listening to Bertha's account of the afternoon.

She came to him with a smile, and eyes that watched furtively to learn what his mood might be.

He put the paper into her hand.

She read it, and looked up at him questioningly.

"Explain what it is that he says you know," Andrew demanded.

"But how did you get it at this time of night? Why didn't it come in season?"

"A small boy brought it, which probably answers both questions."

"I am very sorry you could not go to Mr. Holden when he wanted you."

"What is it about, Kitty?"

"Why—I suppose it must be something about Helen. I confided to him what she attempted to do to me."

"What you willfully fancy she attempted to do, Kitty."

"What I firmly believe—yes, know, she did attempt; and so would you if you would listen."

"I don't think it is best for you to dwell upon it; this only makes you more obstinate."

Kitty was silent.

"But why is Holden in such a hurry now? What is the special need for it? Is there anything new about Helen?"

She hesitated.

"I have heard nothing new," she said at last. "I have not seen Mr. Holden since the day before yesterday morning when you went to the 'Oaks' with the girls. He was terribly anxious then to clear up the matter instantly. He finds it more serious than he supposed."

"There is no telling what harm this boy's behavior about the note may have done," said Mason, "though I can't see anything imminent. But Holden is not the man to write in this way for nothing."

"He is very much excited," suggested Kitty. "And so was I at first. Only think of what I have endured, Andrew."

"I grant it is a dreadful nightmare."

"'Nightmare!' O Andrew, why won't you see?"

"Then you cannot explain why Holden has written in this way?"

There was a long pause. Twice Kitty from under her downcast lids glanced stealthily at her husband, to see if it would be safe to attempt a diversion. His eyes never wavered from their stern fixedness upon her face.

"I suppose," she answered looking at him firmly, "he is afraid the thing will come out, as, of course, it must do sometime."

"Did you tell him it was your intention to bring it out?"

"I told him—I had nothing to do with it."

"Who has, then?"

Kitty's head drooped; she leaned her hands heavily upon her husband's arm.

"You do not care for· me," she sighed; "you will not believe that I have been really in danger. Did I not know you would not if I told you then? You have not one thought for what I have endured. This is not like what you used to be. Take me away again to the old, quiet home where you were always so kind, and sorry for me if only my head ached."

"I really think it would be better for you if I did, Kitty."

She was breathless a moment, weighing the quality

of his tone. Did it express conviction only, or determination with it?

"You would not like that now; you would find it dull
with only me."

"You recollect we had a few neighbors. For myself,
I should like it better than here. I dread to see you
grow into a society woman. Don't mistake me; the
more persons there are who love you and enjoy your
bright ways, the better it pleases me, since you are
pleased; but I think you are coming to build a little upon
people's admiration—to be disappointed if you do not
get quite as much as you expect, and to put forth
efforts to win it. Now, Kitty, that's an investment that
won't pay; you will always put into it more than you
will get out. It swallows up self-respect in the first
place, and goes on crying, 'Give, give!'"

"Do you think all that of me?" asked his wife. But
her sigh was one of relief. She preferred a homily to
some questions.

The relief was premature; for Andrew turning up toward his the face that had fallen upon his shoulder, asked,

"Was it for this—belief of yours about Helen that
Knight has been here? Is it he whom you have made
your confidant in the matter?"

"I was compelled to have some one. I was in danger
of my life."

"No; I will not admit that."

"You will admit that I firmly believe so, then?"

Mason was silent. Many things hitherto unexplained were growing clear to him.

He withdrew his support, and stood facing her.

"So you brought a spy into—our aunt's house?" he said.

CHAPTER XVI.

WHEN Holden reached the apothecary's, he was nerved to the coolness of desperation. His faith in Helen helped him, too; he felt that he was at work upon a problem capable of a satisfactory solution; he had only to find it. Only! How he wished that Mason were there, to put, at need, one of those keen queries of his which always threw so much light upon anything they touched.

The apothecary at once recognized him as the man who had bought medicine in that strange way a day or two before. Having secretly resented this, he met him with a suspicion which would require careful management, else it would turn into antagonism.

He was alone in the shop.

Holden said good afternoon, cordially, remarked that he had heard the quality of his medicines highly recommended by Mr. ——, the famous chemist, and begged permission to ask him a few questions.

The compliment greatly pleased the apothecary. But he looked at Holden with suspicious curiosity as the latter made his request.

"Is it a new dodge in advertising?" he thought. "He hasn't just the cut of an agent, but you can't spot those fellows, after all; they are a gentlemanly set, some of them. He'll tell me fast enough though, if I let him have a chance."

"Certainly, sir. Won't you sit down?"

"Thank you," said Holden complying. He fitted his arms comfortably on the arms of his chair, looked the expectant apothecary full in the face, and asked,

"How fresh were those medicines you gave me the other day? They were of excellent quality," he hastened to add as the other's brows contracted; "it is not for that I ask."

He was following out the hint Dewey had unconsciously given him that same morning when Bertha proposed going for more of some stuff she had bought the week previous. "In those large stores they never have the same piece two days running," he said; "and one lot is never like another, if you come to the matter of matching it."

But the apothecary not perceiving this excellent reason for the question, stood eying Holden with severity

"May I know for what, then?" he asked.

After a slight hesitation, Jack answered,

"A foreign ingredient has been found in something that was bought here some time ago, which was not in any of the drugs I got of you the day before yesterday, although the parts are the same."

"Did you buy it?"

"No."

"Who did?"

"It was probably bought here early in the winter, either then or before that time, not later."

"There has been no foreign ingredient put by me into anything ordered at this store, sir."

"Not you, but the clerk probably."

"I have no clerk."

"I mean quite by accident, you understand."

"Accidents are culpable in medicines, sir."

"But not in the same way as if the thing were done with intention."

Holden threw off the careless manner he had assumed, and rising, came up to the apothecary with the earnestness of his purpose in his face.

"This thing was done by you accidentally," he went on, "or by the purchaser with deliberate intention. To-day it is a private question, to-morrow it will very likely be a public one."

The other returned his steady gaze haughtily.

"That will not injure me," he said. "I am not to be threatened. Are you a detective?" he added.

"Oh, no, I have no official capacity. I am here only as an individual. I don't want to threaten you, or anybody else, but the case is very serious indeed."

"Sorry, sir," he answered coolly.

Some one came in at this moment, and Holden was obliged to wait while a prescription was being put up. It seemed to him the apothecary did not hurry himself at all.

But the man, too, had been thinking the matter over, perceiving that his questioner must have a great deal at stake, and feeling a little self-reproach at this way of treating him. When the customer had gone, therefore, he leaned over the counter and asked Holden,

"What was the 'foreign ingredient'?"

Jack looked up surprised at the interest in the tones, and answered,

"Strychnine."

He would not have told this five minutes before.

A smile of contemptuous pity curled the hearer's lips.

"Quite impossible that should be a mistake made here," he commented.

"It seems so; yet it must have been, for the bottle containing the strychnine was certainly got here."

"Strychnine and all?" asked the other.

"Yes," answered Holden firmly. His face was so white as he spoke that in looking at him the scorn went out of the apothecary's expression.

"Such things are very hard to believe," he said with a real compassion.

Holden straightened himself suddenly. He was about to speak, but closed his lips again.

"You say you have no clerk?" he asked finally.

"No, sir. I have a boy who comes in for a time every morning to keep things in order about the store and do my errands. But he never touches the drugs."

Holden sighed.

He looked at a paper he held in his hand.

"Have you any objection to my asking you a few questions?" he repeated.

"None at all. As many as you like. Be assured, I sympathize with you, sir."

"Thank you."

He was going on to question when another customer came. But the apothecary was not long in serving him.

"Will you tell me if all the medicines on this list have been bought lately?" began Holden.

"The list I gave you the other day? Certainly. Name the first one."

He took up an account-book as he spoke, and as Holden began the list, looked down its pages with a rapid glance.

Presently, he checked off the first. He had bought a supply of this medicine in February. Holden noted it down. The next date came in December, but it was after Christmas, again too late. The third ingredient was a January purchase, and another date was a fortnight ago. The last one on the list he had had in the shop for some time.

"It must be that," said Holden.

A light came into his eyes as he spoke.

"You forget," said the other. "I gave you that, too, and it was examined with the rest. Did you find anything wrong there?"

Holden had forgotten this.

"True," he said.

He fell thinking, his head bowed, while the apothecary watched him, himself thinking also. But the cogitations of both were apparently without result.

"Who bought the medicine?" asked the latter a second time.

"One who could not by any possibility have mixed poison with it," Jack answered.

"You prefer not to give the name? That is natural."

As Jack made no reply, the apothecary took up a

large note-book, and stood with it open in his hand, considering.

"I can't remember anybody lately whom I put up this prescription for," he said at last, "except Miss Bell. She can't be in any trouble about this, can she? I remember she came and got it herself one day. She is quite a near neighbor of ours. We went to the Grammar School together when we were children, and we've always kept up a pleasant speaking acquaintance. Do you know her?"

He put the last question incisively.

"I understood you that this prescription was not a very uncommon remedy for a cough," returned Holden. "You trust to your memory a good deal when you say you have put it up for only one person; but I shall certainly not try to shake your belief. What I want to learn," he went on laying his hand firmly on the counter, and looking at his questioner, "is whether you have not any duplicates of these medicines, in bottles nearly empty, perhaps, and forgotten, from which this prescription might have been taken. Will you have the kindness to look?"

"I shall not find anything."

He made a thorough search, however, and at last came back to Holden with a rather small bottle in his hand.

"This is the only duplicate I have of anything in the

prescription.   I remember about it now.   The last time
I bought this syrup, I had a little more than would fill
my other bottle, and what was left over went into this
one.   But it disappeared, and I forgot about it.   I found
it just now in an out-of-the-way corner.   But I'm sure it
has never been used.   Look at the dust on it."

He set it down on the counter, feeling that he had
now done his whole duty by the stranger, who would be
wiser to cease questioning him and take his leave.   The
day was warm, and he was heated by his search along
the upper shelves of his shop, and annoyed at the refusal to trust him with the name of the purchaser whom
he still half suspected to be Miss Bell.   An injudicious
move on the part of the other would rouse the threatened antagonism.

Holden took up the bottle and examined it leisurely,
waiting for the other to grow cool again.   After the
apothecary had shown by some pleasant remark that he
had recovered his equanimity, Holden asked,

"How large a proportion of this syrup is in the prescription ? "

"I will tell you exactly.   It is quite large."

He looked it out, and told him.

Holden took up the bottle again.

"More than that quantity has been taken from here,"
he said.

"I tell you it was never fuller than that," answered the other.

"And you have no clerk, you say?"

Everything is done by myself, and under my own eye. When I have a fresh supply of drugs, my shop-boy washes the empty bottles and brings them to me to be filled. He puts away things not needed, too, which, I suppose, accounts for the disappearance of this bottle, and I didn't miss it, having plenty more of the syrup."

Holden set it down.

"You may have used a little of it, however, before it was put away," he said, "and I must not let—" he interrupted himself. "I will take a little of this," he added.

The man looked at him, this time in undeniable anger. "Won't you take a sample of everything in the store?" he cried. "No; I will test this for you myself, sir. Here is the answer to your insulting questions about my bungling, my putting strychnine into the medicine I sell. Your conduct has passed the bounds of endurance. I fare like the people I sell to. I'm ready to drink the whole of this harmless stuff. Look here."

"For Heaven's sake, don't!" cried Holden springing forward to catch the arm of the speaker.

But the counter was between them, he could not reach him, and his eager cry of warning only served to make the apothecary's smile the more contemptuous as he raised the bottle to his lips, and took a swallow from it.

But instead of setting it down on the counter again, he held it still before him, and re-examined the label carefully.

"This has a strange taste," he said, "it is very bitter. It ought not to be so."

"Try the bottle from which you gave it to me," said Holden.

The apothecary brought it to him.

"Taste this for me, please," he said; "you have had it examined, remember, and the bitterness in my mouth would overpower anything else."

"This is sweet," said Holden complying.

"Only that? Not at all bitter?"

"Not at all."

"It should be sweetish merely," said the apothecary. "I'm afraid there *is* some mistake; but it can't possibly be strychnine, though it tastes a good deal as I have supposed that did."

"It *is* strychnine," cried Holden pale with dread. "Tell me where to find a doctor."

"Nonsense," said the other. But his face was ashen, and his eyes had a strained look. He brought a small phial, and pouring some of the bitter medicine into it, gave it to Holden.

"Have that examined," he said, "it will not help you, but you will be satisfied."

"I must call the doctor," was Jack's only answer moving hastily toward the door. "Where shall I go?"

"You are very foolish, but if you insist, I—"

Suddenly he stopped. His arm twitched convulsively, and such a look of horror and deadly illness came into his face that Holden sprang toward him. He pointed and tried to speak, but, either through the intensity or the violence of his seizure, the words refused to come. His finger still pointed persistently across the street, however, and at last he articulated,

"There! Call him."

Holden, following the direction with his eyes, saw a man coming down a flight of steps. Throwing open the shop door, he obeyed. The stranger answered the hasty summons directly, and a sense of relief, a feeling of strength, seemed to enter the place with him.

Yet, he wore a very grave expression as his keen, professional eye fell upon the apothecary.

"What is the meaning of this?" he asked Holden with authoritative brevity.

In as few words as possible Holden explained what must have been done.

The doctor took up the bottle, and touched the moistened stopper lightly, with his tongue.

"Put that on the shelf, and come and help me," he cried; "there is not a moment to be lost."

They did not lose one; they worked over the apothecary untiringly; the physician called for this thing and that, sent his companion now to the end of the shop, now to a house close at hand, to bring what he needed; and Holden did everything with a deftness and dispatch which plainly won the doctor's approbation.

In the intervals of his service, while the physician waited to see the effect of his efforts, he, too, stood beside him and watched the agonized man with an overwhelming sense of horror and remorse. For, if he had managed better, this would not have happened. It was true, nothing had been further from his thought than that such a result could be possible, and he had really been obliged to put the questions. Yet, here lay a man dying, who, if Holden had never entered his shop, would be in full health.

He recollected that probably it had been only a choice between this victim and some other one, innocent even of having made a mistake in the matter. But he could not help remembering that he would not have been in the remotest way connected with any other accident, or even have known about it.

"Is there no hope?" he asked at length, seeing that the convulsive movements had ceased and the apothecary lay cold and apparently insensible.

But, as he spoke, a shuddering gasp from the prostrate man 'proved that life was still there, although his rigidity, and his dilated pupils that the full light could not make contract, seemed to Holden like death itself.

"Don't give up yet," cried the doctor. "It will not be pleasant for you, at least, if we don't keep the breath in him."

Astonishment rendered Holden motionless for the moment.

Then, he saw that it was really so, and a strange thrill went through him. Did he stand so close beside Helen as to snatch her away from danger only by taking her place himself?

People anxious to be assistants if necessary, and spectators in any event, had not been wanting. The physician had turned them all out with the autocratic authority of his profession and the two were alone when he said this to Holden.

"I understand how it was," he added, watching the other's expression keenly.

Jack made no answer, his eyes were fixed upon the apothecary.

It was two hours from this time that he walked rapidly to Helen Bell's home.

He wondered if, after all, he were too late.

As he reached the gate he saw far up the street, on a

little open space in which were a few trees, a man leaning against the largest of these, reading a newspaper, but not so much occupied with it as to prevent him from eying Holden with scrutiny as the latter went up the few steps that led to the porch, and keeping a sharp lookout upon the door as it opened and closed again.

This sight changed Jack's purpose. It had seemed a very simple thing to assure himself of Helen's safety when he was so near her, to look at her and say a few words before he went into town again and put a stop to all intended proceedings against her. But now, believing himself watched, he recalled Knight's warning, and saw that the detective might learn of his presence here, and already be on his way to Helen, as he had threatened, before it was possible to intercept him.

Then it occurred to him that this might be the very hour the detective had chosen for her arrest. Consequently, when the door opened in answer to his ring, he inquired not for Miss Bell, but if Mr. Knight were there.

He was there.

Jack asked to speak with him at the door.

The detective came forward with a smile of satisfaction upon his face.

"Mr. Holden?" he said, "ah, indeed. I am not surprised to see you here. Pray come in. I am sure

Miss Bell will be pleased to meet you; and I am quite sure you and I have nothing to talk about which will not be interesting to her."

As he spoke he moved back close to the door from which he had come, the door of the room in which Holden knew Helen must bè. Full of this thought he reached forward to grasp the other and compel him to listen outside, but to do it he had to cross the threshold, and the detective was too quick for him. In a moment he was within the room again, signing to Holden to follow.

Holden was so intent upon having his explanation out of Helen's presence that he would have risked an apparent rudeness which he should never be able to explain to her rather than that she should know what had threatened her. There suggested itself to him the idea of making an appeal to her and requesting a moment alone with Knight in the room, since the young man refused it at the door.

But a second thought satisfied him that this would only precipitate matters, and turn an imminent danger into a certainty, for the detective was not a man who could be driven in this way.

But Jack had only a moment then to spare for him. In another instant his eyes were dwelling on the face of Helen Bell, and he was holding the hand she slowly extended to meet his own.

CHAPTER XVII.

IT was hard to take Helen's hand in his, to feel the
touch of her fingers, to know that she was in danger,
to see the power that was threatening her close at hand
and intrenched in security, to be ready to spend his life
to save her, and yet be compelled to do nothing. He
must conform to the apparent tranquillity about him,
and seem as unconscious of impending calamity as the
quiet room he was in, which, according as the fever tide
of impatience within him ebbed and flowed, alternately
soothed him with its restfulness and chafed him by its
inappropriateness to the present situation.

While this undercurrent of thought was going on, he
perceived that Helen was pale, that she looked wearied.
But he saw also that her manner to Knight was perfectly
calm. This, and the smiling face of the detective, like
that of a person whose purpose is not yet declared, gave
him a happy assurance. He had not gained his information too late to save this noble woman from a shock
which would have prostrated her like the spring of a

tiger. Now, he had only to hint the truth to the detective, and she was saved. Life seemed of great value to him at the moment.

"Did you leave our friends in Lowton well?" Helen was asking him.

"Yes," he answered; but after a moment's hesitation added: "every one, except Mrs. Mason. She seems greatly out of health. She does not keep her room, but her husband is much troubled about her. It is some slight mental derangement, I fear."

"Indeed!" said Helen. "I am very sorry. It must be a sudden thing. Yet, I—"

She stopped. A look of regret came over her face. She was thinking that if this were the case, she had not been lenient enough in her judgment of Kitty.

"Her 'derangement' then is clearer than most persons' arrangement," said Knight with a low laugh of exultation which reached Holden like the touch of cold steel and roused him to defense.

Helen stood between. He could not thrust at Knight now without wounding her, too.

She perceived the tone of Knight's reply without comprehending his reason for it.

"This has been since I left?" she asked Holden.

"Further back than that," he said. "I have reason to believe as early as February."

She was silent. The secret eagerness with which she had asked this question left a flush on her face. Holden saw the detective's eyes fixed upon it triumphantly. It was another pass at him, but he recollected that the man's hour would come.

Helen changed the subject.

The minutes went by slowly to Holden, and still Knight sat there and talked on and on, taking the lead in the conversation, and following his own lead well.

"Why won't the man go," thought Jack, "and give me a chance to tell him that this little game of his is up? Does he mean to outstay me?"

He forgot that it was Knight whom he had inquired for as he came in.

But he remembered the man beside the tree in the distance, and he believed the detective had really come to arrest her—to arrest *her* for attempted murder!

"Yet, how can he be planning to do this to-day?" he asked himself, watching the talker's smiling assurance of manner in describing an amusing scene he had witnessed. The face gave him a momentary relief, until, suddenly, he caught sight of the eyes. There was a dangerous glitter in them.

Then he saw that it would not do to wait for the man to go away. He must by some means inform him here of the discovery just made, and do it, too, before it was too late to save Helen from the knowledge of what had threatened her.

Yes, unquestionably he must warn the detective, but how?

He had been too much engrossed by his perplexities to hear the story Knight was telling, but this closing sentence caught his attention—"I told Knowles," he said, "it recalled the old proverb, 'All that glitters is not gold.'"

"Very true," assented Jack quickly; "and, oddly enough, that is just what I was going to say to you, Mr. Knight, in regard to that business affair you and I were talking over the other day. I was quite sure then you had made a wrong estimate, and I have proved it to-day by finding the right one."

"Really?" said the other incredulously.

"Yes, beyond a doubt," cried Jack, his repressed eagerness betraying itself through his quiet tones.

"Mr. Holden, then, does sometimes care to be successful?" inquired Helen with a mischievous smile.

"Indeed, I do; and one ought."

"He has not proved himself successful," sneered Knight, "he has only shown us he imagines he is so. Suppose you give us the whole story, Holden, and let us judge of your success. Or, Miss Bell shall be umpire. She will infallibly perceive which of us is right."

Jack looked at him in utter dismay. The words he had been about to speak would not come. His first involuntary comparison had been just; the danger that threatened was the spring of a tiger. Thank Heaven, he held the creature in leash. But he feared he should not be able to prevent a vicious blow at Helen.

This fear gave to his face a pallor and constraint which she noticed with surprise. It looked to her as if there were something in his business relations that could not bear investigation. But she remembered that this suggestion was out of keeping with what she knew about him.

"I have never heard what your business is, Mr. Knight," she said, "though I remember your talking with Mr. Mason one evening in a way that gave me the impression you were a lawyer."

"Now I shall know what he means to do," thought Jack quivering in every nerve as he listened for the answer he could not prevent.

"You are very shrewd, Miss Bell," said the detective with a smile of subtle meaning. "I certainly am in some way often connected with the law, but it is not in the way of laying it down to others," and he made a deliberate little pause sufficient to point his remark. "You can get an idea," he added, "from what Mr. Holden was saying just now in answer to my quotation that 'all that glitters is not gold.'"

"I was saying nothing that could enlighten Miss Bell," interposed Jack hurriedly.

"Pardon me," returned the other in his blandest tones, "but your answer did exactly explain it. You said the proverb referred to a little matter of business we were talking over the other day. That's quite right. It *is* my business to distinguish between what glitters and what is gold. I am what is called an expert, Miss Bell, when I find it worth my while to do anything at all."

Helen caught sight of a quick expression of relief in Holden's face.

So did Knight.

"And you judge of precious metals? You are an assayer?" she asked.

"Of a certain kind, yes. My metals are always valuable in a certain point of view. And so when a novice, like our friend here, presumes to tell me I am mistaken, I venture to doubt it."

"You may 'venture to doubt it,' if you like," returned Jack in a low, stern voice, "but if you venture to act upon any such incredulity, you will find the conse-quences very serious for yourself."

Knight shrugged his shoulders with an exasperating insolence. "Indeed, my dear fellow," he said, "I'm used to threats; they don't affect me at.all."

Holden made no answer, and for a moment the two men eyed each other in silence.

Then he took out from his pocket-book a scrap of paper that looked like an old envelope, and with a word of apology to Helen went to the table, and taking up a book to lay the paper against, wrote a few words and passed the envelope to Knight.

"If you will go to that address," he said coldly, "you will find I have not spoken without knowing what I was saying."

An expression of satisfaction came over Holden's face as he handed the paper to the other. All that duty now required of the detective was to read it, and take his leave, in order to satisfy himself of the accuracy of its information. He would never return, and Helen would never know what disaster she had escaped.

The long silence that followed the other's reading of the few words written on the paper surprised Holden. He grew impatient, but would not break the pause to give him any excuse for staying another moment. Detective Day receiving a gentle hint in Miss Bell's presence, might, with a malice Jack was not wholly at a loss to account for, refuse to understand it. But with this plain statement before him, no other course than quiet withdrawal was open to him, at least for the time.

Detective Day, however, was of a different opinion.

He had a still deeper reason than Holden guessed at for wanting success in this affair, at least so far as to the publicity of an arrest, and the suffering it would bring Helen. He would like to gratify Jenny Grierson's aunt. Some day he might be glad of her influence in his behalf.

He made no move to go. On the contrary, he sat down again after having twice carefully read the paper which Jack had called him to the table to receive.

"Unprecedented conduct, Mr. Holden," he began very deliberately, "for gentlemen to be writing and reading secret messages in the presence of a lady. And this one has a very mysterious sound. I wonder if you can help me decipher it, Miss Bell?"

"No, no," cried Jack hastily. "Impertinent—"

"No, no!" interposed Miss Bell also. "Mr. Holden does not wish it."

"'Henry Clayton, 58 Ashland St.,'" began Knight imperturbably, "'he has found the strychnine and almost died tasting from the bottle it was in. Dr. Stephens with him. Inquire before you dare to act.'"

As he finished, he glanced quickly into Helen's face. She was looking very much puzzled.

"How little she dreams, my poor darling!" thought Holden.

"If this is business," she said, "I confess that I have no head for it; I don't comprehend. But I hope the poor man did not really die," and she looked at Jack. "Or perhaps this is a kind of cipher writing, and means something quite different?"

"No," said Jack. He was smiling now. The worst was over; why should he have even feared it could have conveyed any meaning to her, or that she would have asked an explanation? Only the good remained, the detective had been told.

"Go and see for yourself," he said to Knight in an authoritative tone which made Helen glance at him wonderingly.

"I need not take all that trouble," was the answer with a bow that to Jack had infinite mockery in it. "Mr. Holden's assurance is quite enough to satisfy us both. But, Miss Bell," he continued, "since Mr. Holden is not disposed to do it, politeness requires me to explain something of the meaning of these enigmatical words; they have some reference to you, as you may have guessed."

Helen looked at him in astonishment.

A hand was laid roughly on his collar, and Holden's voice said,

"If you dare to attempt that, I will shake you into the street like a dog, and shut the door upon you."

"Oh, very well. You'll have to open it to me again in the name of the law, which, to say the least of it, would make it unpleasant for this young lady. She would then be called upon to answer questions, instead of asking them, which, you know, is much the easier of the two."

Jack released his hold.

"Jove's thunder without Jove behind it," sneered the other.

"Never mind me," cried Jack, "but have you no feeling?"

"A good deal, on my honor," answered the detective re-adjusting his crumpled collar; "a good deal, in spite of your having endeavored to shake it all out of me?"

"What do you mean by asking admittance here 'in the name of the law'?" said Helen. "Mr. Holden," she added, "you must see that it is no longer possible to keep back any danger that hangs over us."

"No," he answered, "but the danger has passed, be assured; and you might have been spared all knowledge of it."

"Not quite so fast, please," interposed Knight, "*I* have not said that all danger was over. Miss Bell, let me inform you, since I will have the courtesy to suppose you unaware of the fact, that there was a large quantity of strychnine in the medicine you wished to give Mrs. Mason last winter—more than enough to have caused her death."

A long silence followed this statement. Helen's eyes were fastened upon the speaker's face in a wonder that deepened into horror. She sat without moving; but though her face was very white, it was not with faintness, all her faculties were keenly alive.

At length she turned to Holden. There was an unconscious appeal in her look which he could not endure in silence a moment.

"It is all made clear," he cried. "I have seen the whole explanation myself to-day, as I always knew I must. Do not be troubled. There was no reason why you should ever have known this," he repeated.

She said nothing. Slowly, her natural color came back, and a faint flush followed it, which before it could deepen, lost itself in a flitting smile.

After a few moments more of silence, she said to Knight,

"Was this the reason why I lost the phial of medicine I brought with me to Lowton?"

"Yes."

"Did you take it?"

"That is a hard question, Miss Bell. Excuse me from answering it, but remember I am under orders, and compelled to do many things which are very much against the grain."

"Mr. Holden—" Jack noticed how much gentler her

tones were—"will you please tell me what you have learned to-day about this thing?"

"I have learned how the strychnine came into the bottle," he answered, and he gave a full account of the scene in which he had just played a part, prefacing it for Knight's benefit by his interview with the Lowton apothecary.

The detective listened with close attention, taking notes here and there.

"How did this man attempt to account for the presence of strychnine in the syrup?" he asked.

"He was able to speak very little when I left, but he thought it must have happened when his errand-boy washed bottles for him. He probably mixed them up a little, and supposed this one had been cleaned, and the colorless fluid which he shook out of it lightly was only a little of the water left from rinsing, instead of the strongest solution of strychnine. The apothecary remembered afterward using that bottle once before it was pushed back out of sight."

"Um! Did he tell you that?"

"He told it to Dr. Stephens and me; the doctor has taken the syrup in charge. You will find the matter all out from him."

"Um!" repeated the detective; and considered a few moments.

Then he rose.

"I shall be back in a short time," he said to Helen, "and I must request you not to leave the house in my absence; indeed, it would be of no use to attempt it. But I shall hope to return with the brightest of news for you, Miss Bell. At all events, I hope you will pardon the unpleasant part I have been obliged to play, and that when we next meet it will be under more agreeable auspices."

With quite his old manner he bowed himself out of the room.

"I shall never speak to him again," said Helen when he had gone, "not because he has watched me, for that may have been in his duty. He must really have something to do with the police?" she asked.

"Yes," said Holden.

"But because he has pretended friendliness and interest," she continued. "I never liked him. I have often wondered how he could find encouragement enough to come so often. Yet he quite amused my mother. If she had only known! Will you see him when he comes back? Ashland Street is very near, he will not be gone long."

"Certainly, if he come. But he will never return. He is keen enough to know when his occupation has gone."

Helen made no answer. Reaction from the terrible excitement of the last half hour, in which she had heard her own accusation, and listened to Holden's refutation of it, was coming on. Relieved from the tension of the detective's presence, she yielded to the exhaustion the interview had brought her. After these few words to Holden, which she uttered standing as she had been when Knight left them, she sank down upon the sofa, and folding both hands over its arm, laid her face upon them, and remained for some time motionless.

Holden had never seen her unnerved before. She had been quiet and grave sometimes, as if oppressed by weariness or a hidden anxiety, but this even momentary abandonment of herself to suffering was something quite new in his experience of her. It seemed to make her infinitely tender and beautiful.

He checked his desire to speak words of consolation. He saw that she must understand his sympathy in this silence, else she could not treat him like a friend as she was doing now.

Contrary to his intention she had learned how much he had had to do with this speedy discovery of the truth in regard to the poison. But this very fact, of which she was showing her appreciation, restrained him.

She would like best to have him say nothing. But as he stood by the window, waiting until she should recover herself, and watching to see if Knight did by any possibility come back, he looked at her with silent admiration and tenderness.

The heavy coil of her dark hair left the shape of her perfect head revealed, the bend of her neck and her shoulders was grace itself, and in her attitude there was an evidence of silent suffering which touched him almost more than he could bear.

He recalled how cruelly she had been treated, traduced, persecuted, dogged by a spy, accused, only because she was too beautiful and too good. He was in no condition to give credence to any suggestion of honesty on Kitty's part. He saw, as he watched Helen, that she was going over all her experience again.

He did not believe there were tears in her eyes, he could not imagine her overcome in this way; but he knew that her face when she raised it must be very sad and full of pain.

And yet there surely ought to be something besides pain in it. She had just cause for anger. He knew she must be feeling it, for she was not a person too weak to be capable of righteous indignation.

Surely, when he saw her eyes again they would flash with a sense of the wrongs and indignities to which she had been subjected. She would have some word of keen condemnation for the way in which she had been treated, like those he had heard from her in view of lighter offenses.

When was she going to look up again? She was so perfectly still, was it possible she had fainted? To see if this were so, he moved slightly. She looked up at the sound. The pallor of her face, and the feeling in it were even greater than he had expected. A horror was written there. She passed one hand over the other, as if to assure herself of her own reality.

"If she had taken it, it would have killed her," she said, "and I urged her to do it. Think!"

And as she spoke a grayness crept over her face.

This was the way in which she had been dwelling upon her wrongs.

The man made a hasty step forward, then stood spellbound. The storm-tide in his heart beat against his lips.

> "Nor grateful sunshine nor patient rain
> Can bring dead love to life again,"

spoke the voice within him. And was he to beg her to be grateful to him for saving her from public examination and newspaper reports? The spirit of sarcasm whispered that this was a fine opportunity; he had had a striking example of the high place which the rights of others held in her mind; in such a moment as this she had forgotten what had been maliciously done against herself to recall what she might in perfect unconsciousness have done to another. It was the most opportune time to urge his own dues; no doubt she would be very grateful to him, especially as he had been obliged to tell of his efforts himself.

When next he moved, it was to take a seat further away from Helen.

"Only a childish hate of bitter tastes fenced her off from death," she added, "and this safeguard seemed to me so puerile. How can we ever judge anything at its real value?"

"I suppose we seldom can," answered Jack. "But I have thought a great deal more of the insult you have received, and the trouble you might be exposed to, than of this momentary danger."

"That is natural, I think. One was over before you knew of it, the other was in the future, and—you have been very kind, Mr. Holden."

Helen remembered that he had said Kitty's mental derangement began in February, and that he still believed her earlier representations.

"I do not think," he answered, his self-repression producing a slight embarrassment, "that it is being 'kind' to right what one sees going very wrong, to prevent a dreadful injustice that the sufferer would feel through life. You must not consider it so, or indeed think of it at all; it is quite a natural thing to do."

Stupid Jack! He saw in a moment what he had said. He had been so anxious to remove any sense of obligation from her and not to take unfair advantage of the situation, that he had ended by declaring in effect that he would have been equally ready to do the same thing for anybody.

"And with you," he added hastily, "of course, you must see it was very different."

"Yes," said Helen simply, "when you know a person, I can understand that even you would be a little more quick to realize the case."

"And one like you who would feel the thing so deeply," he said, wondering if she had meant her last words as a hint of repulse.

"Yes," she answered, "it would very possibly have affected my career as an artist, or at least it would have clung to me like a shadow, and dogged any reputation I may perhaps win. You certainly have been very kind, Mr. Holden, although you will not allow me to say it."

Her smile as she spoke was like a faint ray of sunshine that breaks through the clouds and at once disappears again. It seemed only to make the sadness of her face more noticeable.

Holden sat lost in his sympathy for her. How could he suppose it possible she did not understand that what he had just done would, he hoped, help in some way to atone for the false ideas he had once held concerning her, beliefs that were now inconceivable, and that had humiliated him.

"Do you see him coming?" Helen asked shrinking back upon the sofa again as Holden looked into the street.

"I am sure he will not come. Do not be troubled about him. The man in the Park—" he stopped abruptly. "There is no danger of Knight coming back," he said.

"There were two of them?"

"I fancied so this afternoon," he admitted reluctantly. There was a silence.

"My mother is spending the day in town," Helen said. "She will be—"

She stopped, and the tears stood in her eyes, a sob rose in her throat. It was plain that she was overwrought. The strain of previous hard work and of this fearful accusation now had been terrible. She was awakening more and more to a realization of her situation, and this last shock produced by her vivid picturing of the two men who had come to arrest her for the most frightful of crimes, the shock and the rebound of relief that she was saved from it all, broke down her self-control completely.

With the remnants of it she rose, and held out both her hands to Holden.

"Thank you," she said in a voice that thrilled him—"and good-by."

It was long after this that Mrs. Bell came home.

"What! Are you sitting here alone in the dark, Helen?"

"Do you want a light, mamma? This is so much pleasanter when we have nothing to do."

"Certainly much pleasanter for castle-building," laughed the elder lady.

"Very true," answered her daughter sadly. "There are a great many things one can imagine real when only the twilight stars are looking on, that the lamplight, or the daylight, show us are quite impossible, absurd even."

"And you want to go on with your dreams?"

"No, mamma; but I have something to tell you, and I can talk better in the dark."

"Is it a dark thing, Helen?"

"Yes, indeed," answered the girl, so earnestly that her mother became grave at once, and seated herself near her daughter in silence.

"There is one thing I must correct," began Helen

at last. "Very likely you have forgotten what I said, but it was too unjust to be passed over. The day the news came about my picture, we were talking and you happened to mention Mr. Holden. I spoke slightingly of him, and said you would not like him. It seemed so to me then—or perhaps I said more than I ought from some unreasonable feeling. But I was wrong, mamma. He has been here to-day with—another man, and when I tell you what he has done, you will see how ashamed I am of that petulance."

Then Mrs. Bell learned all that Helen knew of Kitty's suspicion and Kitty's conduct, and of Holden's successful efforts to save her from a public accusation of plotting murder. Helen brought out these efforts much more fully than Jack had done, she had perceived them through the silence behind which he had screened himself as much as possible.

"I suppose he will come to see us some time when he is in town," said Mrs. Bell. "I should like to be able to thank him myself."

"I think not, mamma. He will not continue the acquaintance, I am sure. Friendliness is not friendship, remember, and he only helped me as the knights of old times aided any poor distressed damsel they encountered in their travels."

Mrs. Bell, who had not been enlightened upon the

subject of Jack's attentions and Kitty's machinations early in the winter, was naturally somewhat puzzled to understand how a person who could take so much trouble for another should not care even to call upon her.

But when Helen quietly reiterated this assurance, she made no further comment.

She did not, however, shut her eyes to the fact that there was something peculiar in all this, something which her daughter's reserve would not permit her to speak of, even to her, and Mrs. Bell knew that she was more in Helen's confidence than any one else was.

CHAPTER XVIII

MAY passed, June, and July. It was early in August. The summer had been upon the whole unusually hot and dry, the intervals of coolness and refreshing rains were brief and comparatively few.

Alterations were going on in Mrs. Edgerly's house. The work ought to have been finished in June, but carpenters and plasterers still went and came after midsummer, and the family flitted to the seashore only one or two at a time, and for a few days together.

Kitty, who had been most earnest in advocating the changes now making, was heartily sick of all this delay. She had not that power of entertaining herself which her acquaintances would universally have accorded to her. She was a brilliant woman, but what was the use of being brilliant in empty rooms? If fire is to come from flint, the flint must be struck against steel.

She had a great deal to do this summer in winning back Andrew, who was seriously displeased with her, and she was as good as could be all the day long, and every day, but under these circumstances it was very hard not to have a little gayety as an encouragement. Reading was excellent, no doubt, and later, when she went away, she would need to be "up" in the current topics; but it was very stupid not to have somebody to discuss the books with as they came along. There was Andrew, always glad to have her come to him to talk about anything, but Andrew was too clever; he laughed at her—in the kindliest way, to be sure, but still laughed at her—if she grew very enthusiastic over any popular subject, and cautioned her not to go ahead of the fashion. Then he never said anything about the books which was of any special use to her. He was wisdom itself sometimes, but his speeches were always so characteristic, so exactly like Andrew and so wholly unlike Kitty, that they could not be amplified and retailed with impromptu grace when occasion required.

She had, too, another cause of disturbance much more serious than the absence of suitable critics for books she had read or ought to have read. More than once rumors of Knight's presence in Lowton had reached her. It was true that he might have come on business, just as he had done at her summons. Yet it was unlikely that he would take the same character again so soon; also, to offset the supposition, here was Jenny, who had grown fond of solitary walks this summer. It was not always Bertha's fault that she left the house alone; she often slipped out quietly, and on returning in the twilight would glide up to her room if no one saw her, and frequently say nothing about having left it. If she met any of the family she would come into the drawing-room flushed and happy with her pleasant exercise, and full of praise of the Lowton air which suited her so well. Kitty was very uneasy, but she had had enough of espial for a time, at least. She had promised her husband that there should be no more of it, and she meant to keep her word.

One morning, the latter part of July, Mrs. Bell came into her daughter's room with two letters in her hand. The first was from Mrs. Edgerly, begging herself and Helen to go with them to the mountains as her guests, and to remain as long as they did.

"Your rooms are engaged," she wrote, "and we start the twelfth of next month. I am depending upon having you both with me, so don't write me of any other arrangements; give them up, if you have made them."

' In the same envelope was a little note from Kitty to Helen, slipped in as Mrs. Edgerly was closing her letter.

"Dear Helen," it ran, "I shall not feel that you have really forgiven my sad mistake unless you and your mother consent to go with us, as Aunt Bertha and all of us desire so much."

"What do you say?" questioned Mrs. Bell.

"No, mamma, I cannot go. Leave me here. I shall do nicely. Or let me go with Margaret Heath into the country for a few weeks, as we talked of doing. You must accept the invitation for Mrs. Edgerly's sake. She knows no special reason why I should not go, and after the first generous disappointment she will forget all about it in the feeling that I am doing what is best for my work and for myself."

"I shall not go unless you do, Helen."

"O, mamma!"

The girl's tone was hurt. This determination placed her in a very unpleasant position. Her mother's health required a change; Helen could give her nothing like this which was here offered her—a month of invigorating mountain air with pleasant company, and every considerate attention. She knew that when her mother spoke in this way she had made up her mind irrevocably. There was nothing left, therefore, but to sacrifice either herself or her mother. She knew that finally it must be herself; but she hesitated, for pride is so difficult a thing to conquer.

"Very well, mamma, I will go with you," she said at last; "since you are not willing to arrange it in any other way."

Mrs. Edgerly's invitation and Kitty's note were not

the only letters received by that morning's mail.   There was another one also bearing the Lowton postmark.

The writer of this other letter begged Mrs. Bell to induce her daughter to accompany them this summer. The letter said that Kitty was truly sorry for her mistake and would do all in her power to make amends.   It added further, that although impossible to speak more definitely at present, the conviction that the expedition would be of great benefit to Helen was borne in upon the writer.

Mrs. Bell said nothing of this epistle, as it had been plainly intended she should not.   She herself, too, understood the danger of speech.   But the consciousness of the note lying in her pocket enabled her to meet with equanimity her daughter's disturbed and reproachful look.

It was a few days after this that Holden was seated on a rustic bench in his garden, his elbows on his knees as they had been for the last half hour, his eyes on the ground where, heedless of the grass and flowers, he was seeing before him only the history of his own mistakes and their punishment.   He had given up the attempt to read his newspaper which was lying beside him, for the only lines perfectly clear to him this morning were those which so often stood between him and everything he tried to enjoy or think about—

> "Nor grateful sunshine nor patient rain
> Can bring dead love to life again."

Suddenly he heard footsteps on the path, and looked up.

His first glance at the somewhat short and stout figure approaching him with easy indolence was far from being one of welcome.

But in another moment he rose and went forward to meet his visitor. If he were to be interrupted at all, he would have chosen Mason as the intruder. For there was a certain unspoken sympathy in him, as if, though he himself took the world so easily, he was not above caring for other people's troubles. Yet Holden could not possibly have spoken to him upon the matter he had so much at heart.

With a cordial grasp of the hand, and a simple "How do you do," Mason seated himself on the bench, and taking off his Panama hat, began to fan himself slowly with it.

"Delightful place here," he said after a time, looking about him with an expression of satisfaction.

He seldom came into this garden without some word of appreciation. For it was no agglomeration of flower-beds shaped and arranged in a vain endeavor to modify the garish effect of brilliancy in undue proportion to space. Here was abundant space; many smaller areas held a greater number and variety of flowers, but in this garden each of these gems of the sunshine and the dew seemed to have its proper setting. The pansies, royal in purple and gold, were enthroned upon a bank with the rich green of the myrtle vines on one side, while on the other the blades of the fine grass stood up like tiny bayonets of defense.

A woodbine about the trunk of a great elm standing against the garden wall, had once in some storm swung up a spray into the lower boughs, which caught there and hung in a fantastic loop, while the vine climbed every year higher into the tree. As Andrew looked at it that morning, scarlet leaves were already appearing here and there, hinting of the fire that in the early autumn would quiver through the sunlit air, and send its harmless flames far up into the heart of the elm.

On all sides the soft brilliancy of the velvet grass delighted the eye. It was so deep and rich in tone, that it rivaled the beauty of the flowering vines that hung against it, trailing from basket or stump. Here and there upon the grounds were arbors covered with clematis, with honeysuckle, or climbing roses, each blooming abundantly in its season. On the walls grew the woodbine, the ivy, and other creepers. The later lilies stood in their gorgeousness, striving, perhaps, to eclipse the sweet memory of their exquisite white sisters.

For a few moments Andrew admired in silence the beauty about him. Holden, too, said nothing.

"I saw that apothecary of yours the last time I was in town, Holden," he began. "He looks in perfect health again, and I don't doubt you could explain a certain well-to-do air about both himself and the shop, which a neighbor of his commented upon as a recent thing."

"Of course," answered Jack, "one has to do something for nearly killing a man, though it was quite contrary to intention."

"That was last June," pursued Andrew. "I have scarcely seen you since. Did it occur to you that I might be waiting to have some of my visits returned?"

"Really," said Jack looking disturbed; "why will you do that, when I am so often busy, and always glad to see you?"

"Busy contemplating the growth of your trees and your vines! It is astonishing how your taste for horticulture has developed this summer."

Jack's only answer was a short laugh.

"Have you seen Somerton's new shrubbery?" he asked presently.

"Ye-es."

Then Andrew spoke of the changes in Mrs. Edgerley's house, and how it had kept the family at home.

"But we mean this month to make up for our quiet," he added, "for we have a delightful party engaged to meet us at the mountains."

"Indeed!" said Holden, without feeling sufficient interest in this statement to ask who were to make it so. And taking up, the morning's paper, which lay at his feet, he began to talk of some political question.

Andrew followed his lead, and it was some time before he asked abruptly,

"Holden, where do you summer this year?"

"I think it very probable I shall stay at home, and be quiet. There is an everlasting amount of claptrap in all these places, and no satisfaction to be got out of them."

"Satiety?" drawled Andrew giving him a keen glance as he spoke. "Hosts of people are sighing for your opportunity to spin over the world, while you sit here in a pensive desire for quiet. It seems to me this aspiration of yours to vegetate away the summer is a new wrinkle?"

"A crow's foot, I suppose," retorted Holden quickly, with an evident wish for no further questioning.

Mason looked at his friend, handsome and vigorous in the prime of his manhood, and gave a short, unsatisfied laugh.

"You had better come with us this summer, Holden, it will do you good."

"Thank you very much, but I don't see how I can."

"The Morrises will be there," continued Andrew, "Mrs. Bell, and Miss Helen, and several others."

Jack looked up eagerly a moment, but his face clouded again, and he said nothing.

"Wonderful opportunity!" persisted the other. "I'm advertising clerk of the affair, you see—fine society, excellent accommodations, superb scenery, magnificent weather thrown in, at least a part of the time."

"Where did you say you were going? To the seaside?"

"No, to the mountains," and Andrew repeated the exact destination, even to the hotel, perceiving that this time Holden was listening to him.

"You'll call and see us before we go?" he added, giving the date of their expected departure.

Holden said he should be happy to do so, and again the conversation turned to other subjects.

But when Mason had taken leave with the remark that Holden had better think it over, instead of deciding too hastily not to join them, he came back, and laying his hand upon Jack's arm, said,

"You have this advantage over a family man, Holden; you may go to the north pole, or the equator, and nobody but the man who sells you your ticket will be the wiser for your intentions when you choose to say nothing about them beforehand. That's a most useful privilege sometimes. Good morning. Very hot, to-day."

And the two walked leisurely toward the piazza, and thence to the front gate, where they parted.

That evening Bertha remarked that Cousin Andrew's eyes had crinkled worse than usual all day.

The morning was beautiful. A general air of bustle and expectancy pervaded the house. Andrew alone, who felt himself responsible for everything, walked about with the easy gait of one who has nothing to do. Half an hour before starting he came into the morning-room.

Kitty was there, cutting the leaves of a book that was to beguile the weary hours of the journey. She glanced up at her husband, and smiled at him with a look more of pleading than mirthfulness, a look that said, "Have I not yet proved my right to be taken back to the old place of trust?"

"What have you there, Kitty?" he asked, nodding and smiling as he passed her too quickly for her to perceive the expression of sadness that came into his face.

In a few moments he came into the room again.

Bertha was carefully rearranging her traveling hat before the glass.

He beckoned to her mysteriously.

"What is it?" she asked, following him into the hall with the lively curiosity he had foreseen.

"That is yours?" he asked, pointing to a mammoth trunk.

"Yes."

"And this?" indicating one of moderate dimensions.

"Why yes. You don't expect me to go without any baggage?"

"No, not by any means. But look here—what's this?"

"My shawl-strap."

"And this?"

"My bag, of course. Every lady wants a traveling-bag."

"And this?"

"Why, Andrew, that is a package of books from the 'Franklin Square Library.' I couldn't tell which one I might want to read on the way."

"Ye-es. You'll not open any. And what's in that paper box?"

"Only a few little things I forgot to have packed last night."

"And, as I live, a brown paper parcel. I can see it peeping out from under your sun-umbrella. No, two little parcels. What are they, cookies, or candy?"

"Cookies? How perfectly absurd! Is this what you called me out for?"

Andrew came up to her with a supremely grave face.

"Bertha," he said, "I assure you, my dear, this will

never do. So much baggage! Why, everybody would set you down as an old maid beyond a question."

Bertha's countenance fell. The very feather on her becoming hat seemed to droop suddenly.

"What shall I do?" she inquired piteously.

"Are your trunks very full?"

"I suppose so. Perhaps not."

"Give me your keys."

"She will do very well now," he said aside to his wife soon after, "if she has no time to exercise her passion for accumulation."

When the carriage was at the door everybody wondered what had become of Jenny. She was not in her room; she was nowhere to be found.

At last, one of the house-maids delivered a message which she had forgotten in the general haste. Miss Grierson went out not long ago she said, and at the door stopped to say that Mrs. Mason was to be told she had thought of something she could not possibly go to the mountains without, and that if she did not return in season, they were not to wait a moment for her, she would come by the next train; she was used to traveling, and could find her way perfectly well.

Kitty turned a pale, frightened face upon Bertha.

"There is something wrong," she cried. "What shall we do?"

"Nonsense. What is the use of always imagining horrors?" answered the other settling herself comfortably in the carriage. "Andrew will be waiting for us at the station with the checks and the tickets. What can you do but be sensible, and know that Jenny is old enough to take care of herself?"

Kitty yielded to her fate, but she did so with many misgivings. It seemed to her as she looked back that Jenny had been fitful in mood lately, not quite the sunny-faced girl she used to be. And if everything had been quite right she would have told her, instead of a servant, of the errand that took her away at the last moment.

The day was not, upon the whole, a happy one to Kitty.

It was late in the afternoon when the stage that had brought the travelers from the railway terminus drew up at their hotel. Helen looked out from it, interested in the crowd upon the piazza and the owners of missing baggage who came forward eager to find their lost traveling companions.

"My trunk is marked 'B. H.,'" said one, "it looks like that."

"But that is mine," cried a voice from the stage as the first speaker approached.

"Are they never going to let us out of this ark?"

exclaimed Kitty impatiently. "Why don't they attend to their passengers first?"

"You're rather mixed up on trunks there," laughed Andrew opening the door for himself, and helping the others to follow.

"Has mine come yet, it was marked 'D. N. B.' on one side?" cried a familiar voice, and Helen, looking in its direction as she stepped upon the piazza, saw the plump, pretty figure of Mrs. Barney.

"My dear," cried the latter rushing forward, "we are fated to meet in summer and winter alike. Such a pleasure! So many pleasures," she added shaking hands cordially with all the party. "Jack ought to know."

"He does know," said the person in question, looking over her shoulder, "and he appreciates the kindness that is desirous to make him a sharer in every favor of fortune."

So Jack is again holding Miss Bell's hand, and looking into her face, though his expression, and his words, all the world about them may see and hear.

"You are well?" he asks, and that he does not release her hand until she has answered the question, is, she understands, because he has so much sympathy with the mental suffering he knows she has endured.

Mrs. Barney quite forgot her missing trunk, and

moved from one to the other in a flutter of enjoyment.

"Now, this is what I should call jolly, if I used slang," she cried.

"You will hear plenty of it for the next few weeks, I'll engage," said Kitty as she passed into the house.

She had taken in the whole thing at a glance, and had flashed at her husband, unobserved, a swift look of angry suspicion. All summer she had been doing her level best. Was this the way he repaid her? He had taken down the flag of truce. This revelation, and her anxiety about Jenny, too, had fallen upon her in one day in the place to which she had come for rest and pleasure. She went upstairs to her room with a sense of injury in her heart, and an access of dignity in her bearing.

Holden looked after Mason as the latter stood at the desk in the office entering the names of his party in the visitor's book.

"He has never hinted that he looked for me there," he thought. "Mason is a clever fellow, I'll follow his cue—'Silence is golden.' It could not have been managed so well if Aunt Delia had been in Lowton. How delighted she was when I swooped down upon her in her 'rural retreat' as she calls it, and brought her up here."

Then his thoughts went back to Helen.

"How kindly her mother greeted me!" he mused. "I suppose she has told her. But *she* is very pale, although the surprise of seeing me brought a flush to her face for a moment. I know that I can gain nothing by this, except the delight of seeing her and being with her. I will have all of that I can. And, perhaps—"

But what was to have followed the "perhaps" never transpired, for Andrew came up, and Holden said to him,

"I thought Miss Grierson was to accompany you?"

"Ye-es," answered Mason, "she's coming. Something detained her, and she will be here by the next train. But if she should not come to-night, don't notice her absence to my wife; she is very anxious about her already."

"Certainly not. I think it would be pleasanter for her to take the early train to-morrow; this next one is so often detained."

"Ye-es. I shouldn't wonder if it were pleasanter," said Andrew. "And Aunt Bertha's house is still open."

CHAPTER XIX.

JENNY GRIERSON had no intention of spending that night in Lowton. She proposed to join her friends by the next train, as she had sent word to her aunt. The only thing about which Kitty had any reason to feel anxious was the way in which she intended to do it.

When she left Mrs. Edgerly's house her errand took her directly to the station of a different road from that on which her friends were so soon to travel.

The train was to leave in a few moments. She bought her ticket, and stepped on board.

Two stations beyond Lowton she was joined by a gentleman. He was handsomely dressed, and carried himself jauntily. He was quite the same Mr. Knight of the previous winter, except that now there was a joyousness in his face.

"How did you manage it?" he asked, seating himself beside her.

"Very easily," answered Jenny. "I only wish I were as certain of being wise as I was skillful."

"Can you doubt that?" he whispered with a tender glance. "In two hours, little one, you will have settled the question to the life-long satisfaction of us both."

The girl colored, and turned her face toward the window.

"Everything is all ready?"

"Quite ready, and waiting for you. If one could ever love waiting, it would be for you."

"I'm afraid somebody will hear you," she said, glancing about her shyly.

"I was going to say 'I don't care.' But if it troubles you, we will talk only prosaic common sense for the present."

"Do you know," she said, "I like my own name so much better, I had a cry last night at the thought of giving it up?"

"'Day' is not bad, darling. Very many great and good things have been due to the days."

"I shall teach you to stop punning."

An ominous flash shot from the young man's eyes, and then with a face all smiles he turned to his companion.

"You were angry," she began, "because I said 'I

shall teach you.' But people always must teach each other, if they are to live happily together."

"Of course," he answered, adding hastily, "I am no longer 'Detective Day,' love. I have gone into business, as you insisted, and am now one of the firm of 'Wesley and Day.' That sounds well."

"Yes."

After this answer she was silent a few moments, evidently absorbed in her thoughts, though the young man was talking to her.

"You know you will meet Helen Bell there?" she asked abruptly breaking in upon what he was saying.

"Disagreeable. But we shall get over that. She will say nothing about it; nor your Aunt Kitty, you may be sure. Does Bertha know?"

Jenny would have found it difficult to say why it struck her as presumption in this man, whom she was soon to make her husband, to speak of her aunt and friend in this familiar way.

Kitty was right in finding her niece moody at times. Latterly, Jenny had faintly perceived in her lover what Holden found in him when off duty, what Helen had always recognized. Probably, he did not realize the necessity of keeping up all the manner and surface instincts of Mr. Knight with a girl who was enough in love with him to promise to marry him clandestinely because she knew that her friends would not consent to their union. Probably, too, the closer intimacy of an engagement made the thing much more difficult, if not impossible. He had proposed the elopement only in the previous interview, and had urged, hurried, and over-persuaded Jenny, who was here now in accordance with her hasty promise; yet, who, as she said, more than doubted the wisdom of the step. She certainly intended to marry him, but there was no reason why she should do it immediately.

"Rufus," she said softly after another pause, "let me go on to Aunt Kitty just as I am, and come with me if you like, or leave me at the branch road. Let us wait a while to marry, we are both young. The more I think of it, the less I like to do this secretly. Perhaps papa would be willing after a time, when you get well established in business."

Day had his own reasons for knowing that it would be some time before he was well established in business. His face darkened in an instant.

He drew away from Jenny, and looking at her defiantly, said,

"If you are tired of me, Miss Grierson, say so; but I am not to be played with. If you refuse me so insultingly now, I shall understand it will be forever."

"Played with!" echoed the girl tremblingly. "How

can you speak of such a thing? Haven't I consented that it shall be as you say? Only, I think—"

But Knight bent over, and whispered caressing words into her ear, and Jenny's doubts were at least silenced.

Meanwhile, the train was bringing them nearer to their Rubicon.

"I wish it had been somebody else, not you, who had had to do with Helen," she said after a time.

"Then I should never have met you."

"I don't mean that part of it," she answered with a bright smile; "but I don't like to think of your having had anything to do with bringing pain to a person like her."

Jenny had heard from him the account of his dealings with Miss Bell, no doubt somewhat modified. It was open to question whether he would have tried to marry Miss Grierson in an assumed character, but Kitty had left him no choice in the matter.

"Business is business, love," he said, "and I've seen better persons."

"Never mind about saying things now. Aren't you sorry yourself?"

"Very sorry—that I couldn't bring the business to a successful termination. I should like to have made out my case."

"What!"

"Yes," he answered smiling with the superiority of wisdom at her consternation. "It would have helped me very much to have had my name brought forward in a case in high life, and Miss Bell is well connected. It would have made quite a stir, if that officious Holden had not broken it up."

"Did you see through it before?"

"No, indeed; it must have been a kind of magic that made him ferret out the truth. But I wish he'd been in Jericho first."

"Would you have liked Helen convicted of an attempt to poison?"

"She would not have been. The truth always leaks out after a while."

"But the notoriety of it would have clung to her all her life," said Jenny; "it would have been dreadful!"

"Not so very; and I couldn't help that if it would. You and I live in a work-a-day world, my love, and you will find that if a woman has time in it to sentimentalize, a man must look out for himself. So, though I shall be as deferential as you like to Miss Bell, I shall secretly wish all the same that I could have made more out of her. For instance, supposing she had really tried that little game on your aunt. It did not succeed, you see, so Mrs. Mason would have been safe; as to Miss Bell, it would be the old proverb, *Suave qui peut;* and as to me, pet, I should have done something worth while, and have been able to make life pleasanter to my little girl. Do you realize that we're almost there? Only three stations more."

He looked at her with unfeigned admiration and satisfaction. She was very pale, and he saw that he had said too much in regard to Helen. But he was to all intents at the goal of his hopes now, and it did not make so much difference. He would be more careful next time.

He talked on, trying to banish from her mind the recollection of his too plain speaking.

She was silent for some time, when suddenly she interrupted him to ask for a pencil and a scrap of paper.

"What for?" he said handing her the pencil, and diving into different pockets in search of the paper.

"I want it," she answered simply.

He watched her as she wrote. She did not seem quite like the dimpled, blushing little Jenny whom he had joined two hours before. There was a resolute look in her face now, and her color had quite gone.

"Plenty of grit there," he mused, leaning back in a satisfied survey of his prize. "She is nerving herself for the *coup d' état.*"

When she had finished writing he held out his hand for the paper, in a half-playful, half-masterful way, which grew stern for a moment as she slipped the note into her pocket, and quietly returned the pencil to him.

"Oh," he said breathlessly. Then, with a laugh, "What, Jenny, beginning with your secrets already? I shan't allow that."

But she did not smile back. They were coming into the station, and as the train slackened she occupied herself in preparing to leave the car.

"The minister's house is a very short distance from here," he said, putting her into the hack hastily, "and we have a full half hour before the train starts—plenty of time to make you into my charming Day lily."

The girl faltered, and drew back an instant, but the driver stood at the door of his hack, and behind was her lover helping her into the vehicle, and waiting to spring in after her.

"How frightened she is, poor little thing!" said the young man to himself, watching Jenny, who during the drive did not speak one word.

Arrived at the minister's, Day ordered the hack to wait for them, and went into the house with his companion.

Mr. Dunton had been expecting them. He was in his garden. His wife offered to find him.

"Let me go with you," cried the young man, "then I can say what is necessary to him as we are walking in together, and we shall not lose time."

He got up as he spoke and moved across the room restlessly, following the lady into the garden.

Miss Dunton, a pretty girl of fifteen, remained in the room.

A look of relief came into Jenny's face as she watched the young man's retreating figure.

As soon as he was out of sight she rose hastily, and came close up to the young lady.

In a very few moments Mrs. Dunton re-entered.

"Why," she began, and stopped abruptly, reading bewilderment and anxiety in her daughter's countenance.

· Day followed with the minister. He, too, glanced about the room in astonishment, then, catching an expression which passed between the two women, he crossed the room with hurried steps and looked out of the window, a sudden strange sinking at his heart.

"Where is the hack?" he cried, turning sharply upon the girl.

"She went off in it, sir, directly you went into the garden, and she begged me to give this to you."

It was the paper she held in her hand. He recognized the note Jenny had been writing in the train.

"Forgive me," it ran, "I dare not do this so hastily, and you have just told me there is no other way. I am afraid of a man that must look out so carefully for himself in the teeth of other people's well-being—especially, women's; I think some day he might run athwart mine. I shall always remember you, but I dare not marry you.

"Jenny."

"There will be no wedding to-day," he announced with a hard, dry laugh; "the bride is missing, you see. I did not intend to trouble you so unnecessarily. Good morning."

He bowed himself out with another low, unnatural laugh, and took his way to the station.

But he did not find Jenny there.

She had asked the hackman how soon the next train in the direction she was to take left the place. "In three or four minutes," he told her.

"Double fare if I catch it," she answered.

She did catch it, and when the young man reached the station she was already on her way, finding that by waiting at a different place she could still make the right connections, and reach her friends that night.

The next morning she did not appear at breakfast, and later sent a message requesting Helen to come to her room.

Her eyes were swollen with weeping, and she looked feverish and miserable.

"I am afraid you have taken cold," said Helen anxiously.

"No, but that is as good an excuse as any. I sent for you to tell you what is really the matter with me. It is mental suffering. I have been thinking them all over, and I decided upon you. Will you be a good, patient father-confessor?"

"I know enough about pain to have learned something of patience, and to be very sorry for you," said Helen tenderly. "I will give the best advice I can."

"I don't think there is any room for advice, the thing is all over. But I want you to tell me if you don't think I was right."

And Jenny gave the history of the previous day.

"Aunt Kitty suspects me I think," she finished, "for last night she came running out of the house the moment the stage stopped, and asked so anxiously at the window if I were there. Then, when she found me, she explained her eagerness by saying how afraid she was lest I should lose my way in the darkness; you know, it really was very late. But I am sure she will say nothing unless to Uncle Andrew, and nobody else dreams of it. Tell me, Helen, do you think they do? Did you?" she added suddenly.

"Yes, I felt uneasy. But it never entered Bertha's mind, or we should certainly have heard of it."

"I remembered yesterday what a very wise lady told me once," continued Jenny. "'My dear,' she said, 'when you marry, you may be sure, after the novelty has worn off, that your husband will treat you in exactly the same way that he treats other people.'"

"He may have a little more affection," said Helen, "but so far as the instincts of chivalry are concerned, he will feel the same toward you as toward other people—no more, or less."

In speaking, she seemed to forget her hearer in some recollection or suggestion her own words called up; for she sat meditating, while a wistful look came into her eyes, and a smile that was almost sadness was on her lips.

Jenny watched her in silence for a time.

"Don't you think I was right?" she asked at length.

"Perfectly right—not to marry him, feeling as you did—but wrong ever to have consented to this."

"But, you see, the leaving him is forever."

"I am glad of that, dear child, and so will you be before long."

By this time Jenny's face was buried in her pillows.

"I suppose it's only a fascination," she sobbed; "but I know I never shall be glad, and you don't have one thought of pity for him. It sounds egotistical, but he did care about me. He will take it hard, I know."

"I am sorry for him, Jenny, but I should have been much more sorry for you in the other event."

"It's all Aunt Kitty's doing," cried the girl, lifting her tear-stained face in sudden anger. "I should never have seen him if she had not behaved so badly to you."

Again the little face went down among the pillows.

"Comfort me, Helen!" she said between her sobs. "Can't you comfort me?"

Helen soothed her as well as she could, being all the while inwardly too thankful for the turn the affair had taken, not to remember that Jenny's grief would probably be short, and her cause of congratulation life-long. She forebore to speak too plainly of the young man's character. This was not merely to avoid rousing the girl's loyalty to him; but, also, because she herself was unwilling to speak ill of one who was already suffering.

She hoped, and believed, that judicious help in self-restraint, and plenty of diversion would work a complete cure in the girl.

When Jenny grew quieter, her friend reminded her that no one must know all this, and that she ought to come forward as soon as possible. She must certainly make her appearance at dinner. Jenny readily promised this.

As Helen came down-stairs, she met Mr. Holden in the hall.

"Have you been sight-seeing this morning?" he asked.

"No. I have been no further than the piazza. Do you call that going out of the house?"

"Hardly. There is a magnificent view a very short distance from here that I am sure you would enjoy."

"I am very sure I should."

The two were moving toward the open door as they spoke.

"Mrs. Barney," said Helen stepping out upon the piazza, "will you come to see a magnificent view Mr. Holden kindly offers to show us? Mamma, I can count upon your readiness. Mrs. Edgerly is not here, I see. Miss Morris, and Bertha, and Mr. Van Huyden will you not come? And Mr. Mason?"

"Are you not going to invite me, too?" asked Kitty coming through the hall at the moment, and speaking over Helen's shoulder.

"Not until I see you," she answered lightly, adding courteously, "You will come?"

"Let me walk with you, my dear Miss Bell," cried Mrs. Barney, "unless you prefer some of the younger people."

Helen smiled, and in answer laid a hand upon her arm. Holden walked beside them.

Bertha followed with Miss Morris, and her cousin,

Mr. Van Huyden. Mason did not go, and for a time Mr. Dewey honored Mrs. Bell and Kitty with his society; but at last opportunity favored him with a place at Miss Morris's side, and he devoted himself to her assiduously.

"A more absurd man never lived," laughed Kitty to her companion. "There never was a creature so interpenetrated with the idea of woman's inferiority to the lords of creation. Yet there is not another silly mortal more quickly carried away by the sight of a pretty face than he is. Although he has a great regard for solid charms as well. He has been dancing attendance upon Bertha a long time, but he can never help chassé-ing off with every new face. Bertha does give him a snub once in a while, which I hope is the precursor of the final one. She has had, and will have, much better opportunities. She likes Mr. Holden very much as a friend," continued the speaker, "but he was seriously interested in her several months ago; and probably would be to-day if he found encouragement; although, with all my real regard for Mr. Holden, I have noticed he is inclined to fickleness. Perhaps this is not to be wondered at in a very wealthy man who knows that a wide range of choice is open to him."

There were many walks like this in the following days, and there were excursions to the surrounding places of interest. Nobody thought of anything but amusement, even Helen seemed much less busy than usual. Holden was a great deal in her society. He was always ready to join in the general conversation when she was present, and it frequently happened that after a while one and another of the party strolled away or began to talk to new acquaintances upon other subjects; so that the group of which they formed a part was small, or sometimes it fell out that they had the conversation quite to themselves.

Jenny was very brave. She took her share in everything, and if at times she was more talkative and gay than she used to be, she made up for this in her own room. The piano was a great solace to her, as well as a pleasure to others, and she played a good deal. Mr. Van Huyden would listen to her by the hour together; he professed himself very fond of classical music, and Jenny did her best to gratify him in this respect.

One evening she had been playing an *étude* of Chopin's to a circle of admiring listeners, when Andrew strolled in from the piazza.

"This is not your only audience, Jenny," he said in a voice subdued so as not to reach beyond the room; "there is a group of the natives standing under the window, drinking in the harmony. I kept very still, for I thought a little disinterested criticism might be an excellent thing for you."

"Well, and what did they say?" cried a chorus of eager half whispers.

"One man spoke in a mystified tone to a companion: 'That gal's been playin' ha-alf an hour,' he said, 'and she hasn't played a single toon yet.' 'Oh,' retorted the other sententiously, 'them's pieces without toons.'"

"We must seem a very strange set to the natives," said Mr. Dewey as the general laugh subsided.

"Ye-es," answered Mason; "you see, they have a power of just criticism."

"I wonder what the general effect of summer boarders will be upon country places," remarked Kitty. "We bring in so many new ideas and ways."

"As to the ways," said her husband, "the country people might adopt some of these with advantage, to be sure, and perhaps the influence of the mountains will keep them above the follies. But about our bringing new ideas up here, I'm not so clear of that, unless you mean ideas about frills and such things," and Andrew nodded his head toward the stream of richly dressed promenaders on the sidewalks.

"You seem to have no liking for grand toilets," laughed Mr. Van Huyden.

"Ye-es," said Andrew, "I admire them. But they

don't show off well by starlight; and then these purple shades of the mountains are very trying to them. We are so fond of art in America, and we spend so much breath on its culture, that it's a little discouraging to think we don't perceive the picturesque ought to come into play here, instead of the elaborate. We carry our city dress and city airs about with us everywhere, as the turtles do their houses. Now, if our souls were instinct with artistic perceptions, or quickened by artistic culture, we should be trying here to get ourselves up as picturesque accessories of mountain scenery."

Holden, coming into the house with Mason, had taken his place beside the window and behind Helen's chair.

"That is not all the preparation one needs for comprehending what the hills have to declare to us," he said, bending forward a little, and speaking in a tone that was meant for her alone.

"No," she said turning her face up to answer him, "but it would be more of a help to deeper perceptions than we realize. I believe that outward circumstances often lead to states of mind, as truly as it is the other way."

"You ought to know," he answered softly, "for you have always, everywhere, the effect of simplicity and picturesqueness."

"I have the reality of simplicity in attire," she said lightly; "but with me, this is not a fair test of choice, for I have not the money to do otherwise if I would. So, after all, you can tell nothing about me, Mr. Holden."

She glanced up at him smilingly as she spoke. But in a moment her eyes fell again, for the look that had met hers was like one she had seen months before during a swift gliding between snowy, moonlit fields.

"Mr. Holden," cried Kitty, "Andrew has been criticising those poor pedestrians so mercilessly, that I feel as if my duty in the matter were to go and join them, to try to make amends. Won't you come with me?"

Jack consented readily. He knew that Helen liked the moonlight. If she would come, too, he would cheerfully be at Mrs. Mason's service for as long a time as she desired.

But Miss Bell declined going out that evening, and throughout Mrs. Mason's brilliant talk Jack occupied himself with wondering if Helen were offended with him for his boldness.

The next morning, soon after breakfast, Helen walked off by herself into some very inviting woods that she had seen from her window. She was intending to sit down for a time under one of the great trees, where the stillness and beauty would refresh her.

But before she had gone far enough for this, she heard footsteps coming up a path that led into hers, and in another moment Mr. Holden was speaking to her.

After returning his greeting, she moved aside to let him pass. But he stood also as she waited, and when she moved on again, walked beside her.

"It is much pleasanter here than on the piazza," he began.

"I think the piazza is delightful," she answered.

"Yet you prefer this, or you would not come."

"I surely do on such a morning."

"The ladies seemed to be enjoying themselves in the parlor," he said; "I looked in as I came by." He did not add that he had done so to make sure it was really Helen whom he had seen in the distance.

His listener glanced at him with an amused expression.

"Were they talking very confidentially?" she asked.

"It strikes me they were," returned Holden, making a pretense of being interested in her answer to study her face attentively. But beyond this he was discretion itself, for he had resolved to be sure not to offend her to-day.

"Then they were probably discussing the subject of servants," she said, "and illustrating it by a series of remarkable examples of stupidity and total depravity. Only think what a misfortune perfect attendance would be. It would cause the loss of a theme upon which anybody can be eloquent."

"You are severe."

"I suppose I am; but one gets impatient with any subject that goes by a crank. I can sympathize with a burst of hearty indignation once in a while. I have felt that myself, especially one day when an orderly Biddy of ours laid together some paintings I had standing about to dry, and put them to press under my paint-box."

Holden laughed with her at the recollection.

"But afterwards," continued Helen, "we had to give up our Biddy for a while. It came hard times, and I found that occasional mistakes are much easier to put up with than having to do all one's own drudgery. I think people often make too much of things, and do not make enough allowance for the difference between education and ignorance."

"*You* ought not to have drudgery to do," he said half unconsciously with a look at her which she did not see as she stooped to pick a wildflower in her path.

"Oh, I have not now—in that way," she answered, adding after a moment, "but, Mr. Holden, I should be good for nothing if I were not willing to submit to drudgery in my own work. Nobody truly cares for a thing who is not willing to labor for it. Suddenly, her earnest tone changed, and she said lightly, "It is the only ladder to success; and, as I have told you before, I am fond of success."

"Yes," answered Holden, "it's safe to infer that one is fond of the things, or the people, one works very hard for."

Helen stood breathless an instant in the clutches of some startling thought.

"You need not lay such stress upon success," he went on, "for I know that the work itself is very dear to you."

She recovered her composure instantly. He had forgotten the service he had once rendered her. She smiled, and he saw that the eyes turned upon his face were full of her subject, not of himself.

"Work was an ordinance of Eden, you remember; it is only the thorns and briers that have come in afterward."

"Yes," he answered.

Helen bent her head over the purple asters in her hand. She was still remembering how her companion had labored for a cause in which she was concerned, and remembering how plainly he had told her that the interest which prompted his action was desire for justice. She believed this all the more firmly because his uncomplimentary words had been inadvertently spoken, and she had seen that he would gladly have recalled them instantly, could he have done so.

"You have a great love for realities, Mr. Holden," she said, after a silence.

"When did you find that out?" he asked earnestly.

She hesitated a moment, for she could not say, "When I heard your answer to Kitty Mason concerning me."

"One learns things in seeing a good deal of people," she answered at last.

"I think that depends upon circumstances. We may learn more of another's character in a moment under some stress of joy or pain, than ordinarily in years."

As he spoke, he again saw Helen lifting her head from the sofa, pale and horror-struck with the thought of what unconscious injury she might have done to another. But Helen remembered the words that had been said of her that winter morning in Lowton, and how haughtily she had passed through the room in reproving them. It was not that she regretted her act, or believed the man beside her unkind enough to be directly alluding to it now. But she recalled it, and that he had fixed the beginning of Kitty's mental trouble later than this first accusation.

They did not sit down under one of the trees, as,

when she came out, Helen had meant to do. But the pine woods were fragrant, the sky beautiful, the air. delicious, and they strolled on and on, one, at least, forgetful that they would have to walk the same distance home again. They talked of many things—of new inventions and discoveries, of the history that the nations are living to-day, when with science almost annihilating time and space, every year strikes off some fetter of race or caste and opens up to all countries common interests and aims. They found many things which they loved and hated together. Holden would have been supremely happy, but for the ghost of that dead love which he could never hope to bring back to life again; and never would Helen have enjoyed a walk more but for that harsh judgment which still hung over her. Her companion had indeed refused to think her guilty of contemplating murder, but he still believed in her calculating ambition, and she was too proud ever to try to change his opinion.

When they came to the hotel several of their party were seated on the piazza.

CHAPTER XX.

KITTY looked up from her embroidery—she was doing a beautiful pattern in the Kensington stitch—and watched the progress of these two down the street and up the steps to the hotel.

She saw upon their faces that look of mutual satisfaction in each other's presence and conversation which, although not reaching the summit of happiness, has already begun to climb the hill. Helen's face was grave under her broad-brimmed mountain hat, as if her thoughts had been dwelling upon some serious subject, but her eyes were full of the light which is kindled when high thoughts break into earnest words and are answered in the same ardor. Kitty saw the loveliness of her expression, and saw that Holden's eyes rested upon her, and that his face, too, was aglow with feeling.

All her ingenuity exerted, and this the result!

She could not bear it. She resumed her work, made a wrong stitch, and looked up again as the pair stepped upon the piazza.

Mrs. Barney was beside her, endeavoring to learn that mysterious performance with the needle and thread which produced these admirable results. Miss Morris and Bertha were near. Mr. Dewey was reading a novel to them, or rather he considered himself occupied in that way; but his paragraphs were so short, and his comments upon them so lengthy that it would have been nearer the truth to say that, instead of reading, he was filling the post of censor. Mrs. Edgerly with several acquaintances was seated on the other side of the broad front door at some little distance. She greeted Helen audibly.

"Oh, here you are," she said. "We were wondering what had become of you. Where have you been?"

"Over in those woods," answered Helen, "and it was so beautiful there, we kept walking on, and forgot how far we were making it to come back."

"Yes," said Kitty with soft distinctness and a smile in which an assumption of mirth struggled vainly with malice, "it was 'beautiful,' no doubt; monopolies are always charming, I believe, to the monopolist. We have wanted Mr. Holden all the morning, truant that he is," she went on to say hurriedly, "to show us that beautiful view he promised us to-day. We were talking of it last evening."

Every one about her had heard her words to Helen;

and her attempted explanation could not efface the recollection of them, as she would have been glad if it
could, when she saw Mason standing in the doorway,
his eyes upon her face.

In spite of herself, the hot color mounted there, and
for an instant her fingers were unsteady as she turned
back to her instruction of Mrs. Barney.

Helen did not seem to hear her, or in any way to
change her course; yet in the few steps she took from
where she had stood to the hall door, Holden saw a
haughtiness come into her face which had been wholly
absent from it.

"Mrs. Mason," he said with a distinct deliberation
equal to her own, "I do not feel it necessary to apolo-
gize for my monopoly; for if I had not seen Miss Bell
go off for a walk this morning, and followed her, she
would have enjoyed the beauty and coolness alone. I
have not been depriving you of the pleasure of her society."

With a bow, he passed along the piazza out of sight.

Andrew, who was still in the doorway, saw Helen
stop as the words reached her, and when they ceased,
go on again toward the stairs.

She was in her room until dinner. At table she
was cool and bright in manner. That mood in which
Holden had seemed to be getting nearer to her had
quite gone.

After dinner he stopped her in the hall.

"You are coming with—the others, to see that view this afternoon?" he asked.

"Thank you; but I have work to do."

"But we do not go until five; that will surely give you time enough."

"I am afraid not."

He perceived she did not want to be detained, and let her pass.

Kitty saw nothing of her husband, until with several others she returned from the little expedition Jack had spoken of the day before, and went to her room to make ready for the evening. While she was doing this, Andrew came in.

She began to speak volubly of the view she had just seen.

Her husband neither answered nor interrupted her. He went on for some time brushing his hair in the abstracted way of a person whose thoroughness and length of time in performing his task depend much upon the fact of its being the mechanical expression of mental intentness upon some far-away object.

Mrs. Mason talked as long as possible; but, although she struggled against Andrew's unresponsiveness, it conquered her at last. She completed her toilet almost in silence. At length she stood before the glass arranging the lace at her throat, noticing how well her dress became her, and thinking with a thrill of satisfaction that not even Andrew's displeasure could take away her good looks.

"Kitty," he said, "I always thought you had a horror of vulgarity."

She glanced at the pretty, delicate face, at the perfect color and fit of the dress, at the quiet elegance of the whole figure reflected before her, waiting for the stimulus of social intercourse to give it the irresistible charm of a vivacity never superabundant, kindling it into brilliancy, like the flash of jewels. Then she glanced at the speaker with a smile of conscious security rippling through the interrogation of her face.

"You did a vulgar thing this morning," he went on, ignoring the charming lady of fashion, and looking the petty-souled woman full in the eyes.

The woman shrank and cowered perceptibly.

"I, Andrew?" she said, her tone of wonder breaking into appeal.

"Yes," he answered. "Errors in speech, and failures in conventional rules are faults of education, and may mean only want of opportunity. But spitefulness is a coarse grain in the soul, it is inherently vulgar, no surface manner can ever polish it out of its nature, and this morning your spitefulness came up against the company with a rasp. Everybody saw it."

"O, Andrew, I did not mean it! I spoke before I thought; and, besides, I'm sure some people understood."

"Understood that your speech to Helen was deserved? Do you mean to say this?"

But Kitty did not answer this question. She knew the speech was not deserved, and that any plausible attempt to prove it would only make matters worse in Andrew's eyes.

"I spoke before I thought," she repeated softly. "It was very foolish."

"Yes, very foolish," echoed Andrew. "It will have one good result, however, which is more than can be said of most follies—it will no doubt, bring the two people at whom it was aimed to a better understanding of each other."

Kitty turned about suddenly, and with the movement gave her husband a quick look of consternation. He met it with a short laugh.

"Don't you see?" he asked. "You have forced Holden to defend her, and she has heard him. You couldn't have made a better move."

Kitty said nothing. She saw it all well enough now.

"But," he added, his tone changing to sternness, "another such attempt will make you and me take the next train back to Lowton."

She looked up at him. Yes, there was no doubt he meant it. Tears came into her eyes.

"You are harsh to me, Andrew. I own it was a mistake—whichever way it worked, I mean. An old mood came over me. But I am not all like this; all the 'grain of my soul,' as you call my temper, is not coarse. You know that."

She came close up to him with an appeal in her face he found it hard to resist; for now, at least, she was not a scheming woman; she was, he knew, what she seemed to be—a loving wife.

"It shall not happen again," she cried; "but don't speak so, and don't turn me out of your heart. Remember, I shall be homeless if you do."

No amount of nurture and watching will implant the nature of an oak in a flowering shrub. Andrew Mason understood this now more clearly than ever before; so clearly that he would not need to be reminded of it again, and this perception changed his tone to his wife.

"Kitty," he said, laying his hand gently on the fingers that were tightening over his arm, "listen to me, and try to be wise. Nature never meant you for a diplomat. You lose your head and let your feelings run away with you, as you did to-day. You have not the brains for large schemes, not the eagle glance, Kitty, and the swoop of a bird of prey. You flatter yourself when you attempt that *rôle*. Now, why can't you be content with being pretty, and attractive, and admired? Unless, as Heaven grant, your ambition one day take a nobler flight. Is your own happiness so light a thing to you, Kitty, that you are willing to destroy other people's?"

"But this was not a happiness that had been gained."

"I believe it would have been, but for you."

Had this suspicion come through Holden, or through Andrew's keenness of sight? In either case she had no wish to pursue the subject. She was silent.

Andrew waited a few moments, looking at her gravely.

"Think it over well, Kitty," he said at last. "The Lord made you small in some ways instead of great; and, considering the new disposition you have developed, this is a thing to be very grateful for. But give up trying what you have not skill enough to carry through, and turn your abundant energies to something good. In such a cause there is always a Goodness and Greatness to help out our small abilities to grand results. And, Kitty, perhaps I ought not to plead for myself, here, but I want to respect my wife."

He laid both hands upon his wife's shoulders as he finished, and his indolent blue eyes, open to their fullest extent, looked into hers with a depth of feeling few people had ever seen in them.

An expression almost of terror came into Kitty's eyes,

and a sense of helplessness, quite new, overpowered her. Had she lost Andrew? Her social triumphs could not console her then. He said he wanted to respect his wife; did he fail to do this now? Whatever disgrace had fallen upon her, Helen was the cause of it all. Yet she must see Helen go forward to her success, and not lift so much as a finger to bar her progress. In this game she had been playing, all power of motion had been taken from her by her husband as if he had been her foe. It was easy to see that she was an injured woman, that her husband, whom she loved so dearly, was cruel to her.

Tears gathered in her eyes and fell as Andrew watched her—tears of sorrow over her possible loss, not unmingled with those of chagrin at her defeat.

At length her face brightened. She had come to feel that her husband could of course never cease to love her, and his appeal had elevated her mind. She was willing to yield the point gracefully, this point which was already lost, and so win back his respect.

Her head sank softly until her cheek rested in a caress against one of his hands upon her shoulders.

"You may trust me now, dear Andrew," she said. "I will not offend you again. I will try to be as you like."

And she put up her lips pleadingly to be kissed.

firmly resolved that not even the sight of Helen triumphant should tempt her again, especially when yielding
would take her back to Lowton at once.

She would not offend him! She would be as he
liked! Was this what his appeal had meant to her?
Andrew asked himself; was her conscience no further
reaching than the horizon of *his* desires?

He gave her the kiss very gravely. Then he turned
away with a sigh and left her.

Jack Holden was standing on the hotel piazza. He
had withdrawn himself slightly from the others, and
stood with a gloomy face, thinking. The last week
had been full of disappointment and trial to him. Since
that walk with Helen, which Mrs. Mason commented
on, he had seen nothing of her. Of necessity he had
met her daily, sometimes hourly; but always with others,
always interested in somebody's conversation or somebody's plan for amusement; never even abstractedly moving off by herself, in which case he was desperate enough
to have intruded upon her reverie. He had fully resolved
to ask her to marry him; he feared infinitely more than
he hoped from such a question; in truth, he scarcely
hoped at all. But he was not the man to tempt Fortune's frowns by cowardice. And, at the worst, Helen
should have the proof of how entirely her truth and no-
bility had conquered him. He would draw out the sting

from Kitty Mason's slurs. But her refusal would send him away from her, and he dreaded this unspeakably. He determined to see more of her, to talk with her as he had done the other morning in the woods, and change her present mood.

He sometimes forgot, in his longings for even so much as this, that, could he have spoken, he must for a time have repressed the words he was always dreaming of saying to her, and have foregone the response that had become the only bright possibility of his life. The imperative thing seemed a word and tone from her which should be all his own, if the word were one of friendship only, and the tone breathed nothing but quiet trustfulness.

He had not supinely borne his hard fate; he had struggled against it, but vainly. As he looked into the sky, which had begun to soften and warm in that afternoon glow of space and cloud-tint that precedes the sunset glory, he was wondering whether it would be of any use to try again the next day what had proved unsuccessful twice before. For he had twice made up a party for an excursion, sure of finding in the ride, or making during the day, an opportunity to be with Helen and talk to her. But it had always been another hand that gave her whatever help the climb or the slippery path required, and if by the exercise of a rare skill he succeeded in securing a place beside her, somebody was always at the other hand, for if the rest failed them, there was Mrs. Barney, who had by no means forgiven her nephew for not having bought Helen's painting, and who still cherished the delusion that he was very far from appreciating the young lady.

Jack was at his wit's end. Having nothing else to do, he was even angry with Helen for considering Kitty Mason of so much consequence. But here he reminded himself that it cost her no effort to keep away from him. This thought did not have a tranquilizing effect.

Some movement about him made him suddenly conscious of his surroundings.

There sat Bertha Edgerly, not far off, with Jenny and Van Huyden. He recalled now that she had twice looked up at him within the last few moments. He was sure she would speak directly, and call him to her. He must move away before she should find her plea.

But at the first step a hand was laid upon his arm, and a face looked quizzically up into his.

It was that of the well-known and admired Mrs. Lorrimer. She and Holden were old friends; but she had arrived only that day, and had not spoken to him before, except across the dinner-table. Helen had watched her then with deep gratitude, for it was Mrs. Lorrimer's hand that had been stretched out to help her—it was she who had bought her picture and ordered its companion. As the lady accosted Holden now, Helen was not on the piazza; the mail had just come in and she had gone to carry a letter to her mother. Holden had been waiting for her to come back, perhaps with the vague hope of some inspiration seizing him upon her re-appearance, or perhaps waiting only that he might watch her again.

"Well, Mr. Jack," began Mrs. Lorrimer softly—she was a good deal over fifty and had been a schoolmate of his mother—"I have seen your artist friend, and I don't know that I wonder at your infatuation. Oh, you didn't tell me any such thing. Why should you? there was no need of it. Why, here you've been hanging about for the last hour waiting for her to esconce herself in a quiet corner where you might follow and have the field all to yourself." And the lady's rippling laugh drew Bertha's eyes upon her immediately.

But Bertha was too far off to hear her words.

"What did she say when you told her about it?" continued Mrs. Lorrimer still laughing.

"I tell her!" echoed Holden. "Not for the world."

"You want me to do it, then," persisted the other. "I will with pleasure."

"Heavens! No," cried Jack, with an expression that increased Mrs. Lorrimer's merriment.

"You have not done so much as intimate that you recommended the picture to me?" she exclaimed, unconsciously raising her voice a little in her surprise. "You have kept poor Amy and her ocean waves boxed up all this time, and not even asked the artist what she is going to give you for a mate, nor when it will be done? Patience, thy name is man!"

As Mrs. Lorrimer raised her head in speaking these last words, she gave a little involuntary start, followed by a slight inclination, and a smile so arch, so full of bright mischief, that Holden knew intuitively what had happened.

Helen had returned. Coming from the hall out upon the piazza, she had caught these last words which would have been an enigma to nearly all the others. To her they were plain enough.

As Holden turned, their eyes met: his were full of entreaty; in hers there was a flash that, he feared, argued badly for him.

He made a step forward.

She drew back, so that they were still the same distance apart.

At this instant when the attitude of these two figures, the intense look on both their faces, and Mrs. Lorrimer's significant smile illuminating the situation like an electric light would in another breathing space have aroused general attention, the tea-gong sounded deafeningly in the hall and brought that universal movement which precedes a general uprising. Sentences halted midway, books were closed, newspapers folded, fancy-work gathered up to be brought indoors, and Jenny Grierson sprang to her feet lightly, exclaiming, "Oh, I'm so hungry!" The march for the onslaught began, and in the general movement Helen had gone.

Mrs. Lorrimer still stood with her hand on Holden's arm.

"That's the way of it," she commented. "We pass a sleepless night with the weight of the nation on our shoulders; to-morrow may bring us sorrow, ruin, the death of our brightest hopes. But it is certain to bring us the breakfast-bell, and we must heed that. We are harassed by anxieties and borne down by defeats, nothing seems further from us than gayety, or more undesirable than a longer lease of life, and dinner is announced. We must go to dinner. Our fate trembles in the balance; with all our souls we are pleading for mercy, and for hope; and the tea-gong peals its horrid discords into the remotest corners of our helpless tympanums; and we must obey that, too. Come, my friend, I have not done you so bad a turn, though it was unintentional."

She leaned a little nearer to him, and her eyes looked up into his with their keenest glance. Then she drew back and moved away, a breath of soft laughter floating toward him as she passed.

After a moment Holden followed. He knew now what he would do, but his heart was far from echoing Mrs. Lorrimer's laughter.

The sunset was magnificent. The sky glowed with rose and violet, with gold and crimson, here vividly contrasted, there toned to every shade in the scale of color, until upon the border-land of the dun masses on a distant horizon they melted into soft, warm gray, and into pearly clouds.

"Hurry, good people, or you will lose all this gorgeous skyscape," cried Kitty Mason. She had left the dining-room a few moments before, and coming back now stood in the doorway, a fleecy, scarlet shawl about her shoulders while a corner of this vivid drapery was lying on her dark hair.

Mr. Van Huyden looked up at her, then whispered to Miss Grierson whom he had chosen to sit beside,

"Your aunt is very effective."

Jenny had it in her heart to answer,

"Quite too 'effective' sometimes." But she only looked at him with a smile, and said, "Yes." In a moment she added, "I am going to join her. I don't want to miss the beautiful sunset."

"Nor do I," cried Van Huyden. And they rose.

Several others, catching their enthusiasm kindled by the flaming splendors without, followed them into the open air. Helen was among the number. As she passed through the hall Jack was by her side.

"Miss Bell," he began at the door, "will you give me a few minutes? I want to explain something to you."

Could Helen have heard him? Her eyes were still fixed on the sunset.

"How magnificent it is!" she said to Mrs. Edgerly, into whose arm she had slipped her hand as they left the dining-room.

"Don't you want a walk, Helen?" cried Bertha, coming up with several others.

"Yes," she answered readily.

"And you, too, Mr. Holden?"

"Thank you, Miss Edgerly; but I have just pledged myself to explain to Miss Bell a little matter of business which I have reason to think has been misunderstood, something about an order for a picture she is painting. It is necessary to make it clear to her at once, if she will have the kindness to give me a few minutes now."

While Bertha stood in open-eyed surprise, Helen folding her white summer shawl about her, stole a glance at Holden.

She had never seen his face so full of nerve and resolution. He would surely give this explanation to her sometime, and she owed it to him to listen.

Excusing herself to Bertha by a word, she turned and moved beside him down the steps and through the crowd of promenaders.

They went on for some time in silence. It was Helen's part to listen, and Holden was in no haste to speak. Now she was near him, they were walking side by side. When he had spoken they would be separated. Yet she was here only on the plea of his speaking, he had something to say, and he must say it.

Still they went on silently a few steps further. The greater part of the crowd had fallen some distance behind, and now they were quite alone. They reached the end of the sidewalk, and he made a move to enter the road beyond it, whose grassy edges were broad and good enough to meet the wants of the country people. She hesitated an instant, then moved forward slowly, saying as she did so,

"You had something to explain to me?"

"Yes," he answered, "I want to explain to you that fact about your paintings which Mrs. Lorrimer's carelessness made you aware of this afternoon."

"And perhaps," said Helen, "Mrs. Lorrimer will not take the other."

He stopped abruptly, and turned upon her with something almost like fierceness.

"Yes, I will have it," he cried, "since I have lost

you, blind fool that I was! I *will* have something your hand has touched, something you have loved. I hold you to your compact, Helen."

This was not the way he had meant to begin, not what he had meant to say, but her voice had overthrown his well-built sentences.

"I know that I once insulted you," he said, as she was silent. "I am not likely ever to forget it; the thought eats into my life. Not that I do not understand your nobleness well enough now, to be sure you would forgive me. Perhaps, seeing how bitterly I repented, you have done that long ago." Helen made a slight movement, but said nothing. "But my punishment was that your own hand proved to me how I had thrown away the possibility of happiness. I don't mean you ever really cared about me," he went on hastily; "but it seems to me that at one time with patience, and my own love, I might have taught you this. You remember what you wrote?"

"No," tremulously.

"You don't remember?"

"No. What was it?"

Holden's face lighted. "No matter," he said eagerly. "It may have been all a mistake. It may—"

"What was it?" asked Helen. "I don't understand you. What did I write?"

"It was this," he answered handing her a scrap of paper that had been crumpled and smoothed out again. "Miss Edgerly threw it away after she had finished examining it." And he related Bertha's finding it one morning in her work-basket.

Helen held out the paper under the paling sky, and read,

> "'Nor grateful sunshine nor patient rain
> .Can bring dead love to life again.'"

"You wrote it?" he asked, watching her breathlessly, and trying to hope against hope.

"No."

"That is not your handwriting?" he cried in sudden joy, ready to believe the whole scene of that morning a concerted scheme to deceive him a second time.

"Yes," said Helen; "I wrote it down, if you mean that."

"But you don't believe it?"

"I do," she answered. "How can we restore the dead?"

Holden was gloomily silent.

They walked on further.

"Tell me this," he broke out at last. "Do you think that even at the very first you could have learned to care for me?"

" Yes."

Another long silence.

" Helen, can't you possibly come back to that mood again? Be my wife, and I will not despair, I will make you care for me."

He turned to her as he spoke with a quick gesture of entreaty.

She made no answer.

"Once I hoped," he went on; "once life—a higher life than I have ever lived—lay open to me; but my mistakes, yes, and sin—for it was a sin to doubt you— have blocked up my way. Once you might have cared something for me," he cried, "and now—"

His eyes were lowered dejectedly. The flutter of small white objects falling at his feet made him stop suddenly. She had been tearing to pieces the scrap with her writing on it.

As the last bit fell from her fingers, she looked up at him.

For a moment he was bewildered. Then his face flamed with joy.

He held out his arms to her.

"'And now,'" she said, taking up his words, "'now,' I love you."

THE END.

9 783337 000561